# Reflections of Love
## Novella Collection
### Books 1-4

# TAYA RUNE

# Reflections of Love
## Novella Collection
## Books 1–4

# TAYA RUNE

Purple Realm
PUBLISHING

# Romantic Women's Fiction

**Reflections of Love Collection**

Lacy (2022)

Grace (2022)

Priya (2022)

Giselle (2022)

For more information on all titles head to tayarune.com

# Newsletter

To receive up-to-date information, news and exclusive offers online
please sign up for the Taya Rune newsletter.

https://www.tayarune.com/subscribe

Content Warning

If you are concerned about content, please check Taya's website for a
list of warnings for all of her books.
It can be found under the **Books** tab.

tayarune.com

# HANNAH

Reflections of Love Novella Collection

Book One

## TAYA RUNE

# Hannah

### Chapter 1

THE HARSH, FLUORESCENT LIGHT of the restaurant bathroom reflected the betrayed face of Hannah as she attempted to stop herself from blubbering. She took in large gulps of air and splashed bracing, cold water on her face, not caring what would happen to her perfectly applied makeup. Nothing worked. She sobbed. Hannah's shoulders shook as she sank to the floor, not caring who walked in or if the floor was dirty. The scene played over in her head for the twentieth time.

Hannah had been sitting in the trendy Egyptian restaurant, in the heart of Sydney, waiting for her husband of six years. She had spent the afternoon in the salon getting her fiery-red hair blow-dried and it now sat perfectly, framing her oval face. Hopefully, he would notice the effort she had gone to, as he always complained she wasn't taking care of herself. She sipped on her cosmopolitan, feeling self-conscious, and attempting to look relaxed as she surreptitiously checked her phone every few minutes. The belt that cinched her pretty floral dress was becoming uncomfortable as she perched on the barstool.

Luke had finally arrived nearly an hour late. She watched his interaction at the door and felt embarrassed with the brusque manner he showed as he handed over his coat and briefcase to the head waiter, it wasn't only her he treated condescendingly. He sat next to her, at the bar, without any acknowledgment of her presence. Luke ordered a shot of single malt whiskey and a gin and tonic without enquiring if she would like another drink. Without a glance in her direction, he downed the shot. Finally, he spoke, "Hannah, you could have worn a more fashionable dress. What happens if we run into one of my colleagues? You look like you are going on a picnic."

Hannah was crestfallen that he hadn't noticed her hair, but was not surprised that he had found fault. It was typical Luke behavior. Once all he had given her were compliments, but that felt like a lifetime ago and now he only detailed the perceived flaws.

He looked at his expensive, Rolex watch that she had given him for Christmas as if preoccupied with something, and then took a long drink from his G&T. "I want a divorce."

Before she could register what he had said he plunged on. "It's a cutthroat world out there and you just aren't suitable for it. I need a go-getter. A woman who is as ambitious as I am, who wants to be by my side, hosting dinner parties, and after-five functions. Networking, not crafting and crocheting, like an old woman." His voice was derisive.

*When did being calm, reflective, and creating with your hands become bad things?* she thought absently. Though she hadn't made anything in years because he had made fun of her every time she had started a project. Her brain attempted to process what Luke was saying. Everything was happening too quickly, it was like the remote button was on fast forward.

"I don't want to end up like him, stuck in a job going nowhere." He waved his hand dismissively at the attractive bartender, who was cleaning glasses at the other end of the bar. She guessed he was in his mid-thirties, only a few years older than Luke.

God, she hoped he couldn't hear Luke's insult.

"I have to grasp my chances with both hands before they slip away. There is a big promotion coming up at the bank and I need a sophisticated wife with style, one who can engage people in conversation without putting them to sleep." Luke sounded so matter-of-fact as if discussing the next car he was thinking of purchasing.

Hannah looked at Luke, she had loved him deeply once. His five foot ten, muscular frame from hours in the gym had turned her on. His large grey eyes that had looked at her once with adoration and had won her heart. That love and desire had shattered years prior when the cruel jibes and confidence-destroying remarks began. Now she was a shell of her former, friendly, funny self, doubting every decision she made.

She had fled to the bathroom when he had ended his speech by telling her that he had never truly loved her and that their entire marriage had been a mistake.

Eventually, the tears subsided and she pulled herself up off the bathroom floor. Her head swam with what Luke had just done, but she was confounded that underneath the shock of the situation she wasn't surprised at how callous he had been or that he had chosen to do it in a public place. He had been growing nastier and more distant over the last few years of their marriage, but she had been too scared to leave and start again. He had told her for so long she was useless, that she knew it had to be true.

Her blue eyes were red-rimmed and itchy, and she had streaks of mascara upon her blotchy cheeks. The buttons of her floral dress and the neckline were askew from the dramatic slide down the tiled wall earlier and her pale neutral lipstick was completely chewed off. Hannah assessed the mess and decided that the best she could do was scrub her face clean with water and tissues and the only way her eyes were going to stop itching was to remove the contacts she wore and put her glasses back on. Thankfully she always carried tissues and her black-rimmed glasses in her bag.

Once she was barefaced, with only a hint of lip gloss the bespectacled Hannah texted her best friend, Amy, to ask if she could spend the night. She knew it might take a while for Amy to get back to her, she wasn't great at checking her phone once she got home and put on Netflix. Hannah stared at herself in the unforgiving light of the bathroom mirror for a few moments, trying to ignore the romantic song being piped through the stereo system. She decided to go out and face Luke.

He was gone.

## Chapter 2

Tears threatened to spill down her cheeks again as Hannah looked around the Egyptian restaurant. She was mortified she realized her husband of six years had not only dumped her but left her in the middle of the city, at night, with no care for her safety or how she would get home. Not that she would be returning to their family home that night. Hannah looked down at her iWatch, desperately willing a response from her best friend, to come through. The screen remained black. People were staring curiously at her, or at least that is what it felt like and she spun quickly and headed back into the bathroom.

This time she went into one of the two empty cubicles and closed the door. Hannah felt like she would drown in the wave of emotions that continued to wash over her. Conflicting thoughts filled her head as she took deep breaths and fought down the rising panic. The words asshole, bastard, and prick came to mind as she dabbed at her face with toilet paper to stop the flow of tears.

A random thought, that made her feel ill, popped into her head, and though she tried to ignore it rose and grew until it consumed her. Had she been one of those ignorant women that you read about who had no idea their husband had been cheating on them until they had left? Could it be true? Were there warning signs of an affair rather than him just being a neglectful, nitpicking man who didn't think she was capable of anything?

Hannah tried to quiet the crying and sniffling as the bathroom door opened and a patron used the facilities. Another two women used the bathroom before Hannah felt she was capable of leaving the sanctuary of the cubicle. Her watch vibrated and lit up while she washed her hands. Disappointingly it was only a reminder for her to put out the bins.

She took a large steadying breath and pulled open the bathroom door to find the restaurant empty of patrons, only the staff remained to begin the nightly clean up. *Ahhh, I can't possibly cry again,* she told herself as she felt the heat of her tears at the back of her eyes.

"Would you like a drink before you go?" the handsome bartender that Luke had insulted earlier asked her kindly.

"I don't want to hold you up, you're closing." Hannah always hated being an inconvenience.

"It really isn't a problem." His accent was intriguing. "Come, sit." He poured her a glass of champagne as she took a seat at the bar.

Hannah held up the drink. "What are we celebrating?"

"It seems to me that you are free of someone unworthy of you."

"You heard what happened?" Her face flushed with embarrassment.

"I didn't mean to, but he was rather forceful in the way he spoke to you."

She didn't know how to respond to that so she took a sip from the champagne flute and checked her watch again.

"I'm Baniti." He offered his hand to her.

She took his hand and he shook it firmly. "I'm Hannah. Thank you for letting me stay."

"That is no problem. How handy are you with a tea towel?" He smiled and dangled a drying towel at her.

"It is one of my many skills." She laughed and stood up, taking another sip of her champagne before taking the proffered towel. "I am waiting for my friend to text to tell me it is okay to stay at her place. I am not going back to mine."

"That is totally understandable."

She followed him into the kitchen, where there was a chef busy scrubbing an industrial stove. "Hannah is going to help me do dishes," Baniti told the chef.

"Whatever you say, Boss."

Hannah looked to the handsome man. "You own the place?"

"No, no. My family owns it. I am just the barman and dishwasher for them during the evenings they want time off."

Hannah was fascinated when Baniti pulled up the handle of what looked like a square, metal box to reveal a large plastic tray filled with clean but damp dishes. He slid the tray to the left and onto the countertop, before grabbing an already stacked plastic tray of dirty dishes on the right and sliding it into the washer. He pulled the handle down, bringing the metal box-like cover down, and pressed a button. "We have twelve minutes before that ends and we do this all over again."

Dishes were swiftly dried and placed either in another tray to be taken out to the bar area or Baniti put them away in the kitchen area. In no time, the kitchen was sparkling and the chef bid them goodnight. Hannah helped carry a tray out to the bar and settled back onto her barstool to finish her refilled glass of champagne. Her watch pinged and she looked down to see a message from Amy.

**You are always welcome. See you when you get here. Xox**

The final gulp of champagne hit her and Hannah felt slightly tipsy, only then realizing she had not eaten at all that evening. She fumbled with her purse. "I need to pay you for all of my drinks or did Luke...?" she let the sentence go unfinished.

"He paid for the drinks you had before he arrived. The champagne is on me. You earned it by doing the dishes."

"That's all I'm really good for. He asked me to stop working when we got married, now I am not qualified to do anything. Late twenties and already washed up." Hannah was feeling maudlin. "I don't know if I can start again," her voice wavered.

"Nonsense. I have traveled the world, experienced and lived in many countries and now, at the age of thirty-five, I go to University and sit in a classroom full of nineteen-year-olds to become a teacher." He took the glass from her. "If I can start again so can you."

Hannah straightened her shoulders and sat a little taller on the stool. "Thank you for the pep talk. I'll call an Uber and get out of your restaurant. You have been incredibly kind to let me stay so long."

"Where does your friend live?" Baniti asked.

Hannah told him.

"Only a few suburbs from me. I will take you if you want? You can let your friend know my car registration and name if it makes you feel safer."

She considered her options and the fact her head was still lightly spinning, Baniti to her was a much safer option than an Uber. "Thank you, a lift home would be appreciated."

"I just need to turn off the lights and lock the back door. I'll be right back, don't go anywhere."

*No, I won't run away as my coward husband did,* she thought as she sent Amy a text to tell her that she was leaving the city in a few minutes. Hannah pushed back the thoughts of Luke as they threatened to again make her cry and held her chin a little higher as she waited for Baniti.

**Chapter 3**

"Any preference in radio station?" Baniti asked as he started the car. *Sweet Caroline* began to play on the stereo.

"I didn't pick you for a Neil Diamond fan," remarked Hannah.

"I don't mind him, but that's Dad's radio station. It reverts back to it every time I start the car."

"Fair enough. I don't mind him either, but if I have a choice, I do enjoy today's music a little more."

"Great." He used the old-fashioned dial and found a radio station that had Taylor Swift's new song playing. "Will this do?"

"Fantastic. I love her."

As Hannah and Baniti drove across the Sydney Harbour Bridge, Hannah took a few moments to admire the view. The sparkling lights of the neighboring suburbs and the moonlight that reflected off the dark water below were beautiful. A few ferries and cruisers were still out on the bay and an enormous cruise ship sat docked, ready for the morning's passengers.

Hannah settled into the plush, leather seat of the vintage Mercedes and marveled at how dated, yet grand the dashboard looked. The car had clearly been well-loved over the years and was still cherished today. "Great car," she commented.

"It's my dad's pride and joy. I don't have a car of my own. Too many student loans and saving for an apartment comes first. Public transport in my area is pretty decent. I get the car when I help out in the restaurant in the city."

"Your family has more than one restaurant?" She guessed by the way he had worded his reply.

"Yes, my sister's family has a smaller version and do a great deal more take-away. It is very much the same dishes."

He changed the conversation. "What did you do for a job, Hannah?"

"I don't do anything now, but I once managed the jewelry and watch section in a large department store. It's how I met Luke; he came in to buy a watch for his dad." She looked out the window and tried to bury those memories as they surfaced. "Now I just take care of the house and Luke's needs. He wanted someone to be there for when he required things done and my job wasn't as important as his or as well paying, so I gave up work." A sick feeling welled up in Hannah as she understood clearly how much she had sacrificed for a man who told her tonight he didn't think he had ever truly loved her. Tears slowly slid down her face and she didn't have the strength to control them. Hannah dug into her bag to find a scrunched-up tissue at the bottom. It would have to do.

"Look at it as starting fresh," Baniti spoke quietly, as if not sure his words would be an intrusion or helpful distraction. "You now get to decide exactly what you want, and you are never too old to start again. This is a perfect time to decide who you are and who you want to become."

Hannah wiped her eyes and sniffed as she got her emotions under control. Luke would not get the better of her. "Thank you. You said you were back at school to get your teaching degree. What type of teacher?" Hannah began the conversation again.

"At the moment I teach immigrants English, but I would like to be a High School teacher and give them my experiences entwined with their book learning in History and Geography."

"That sounds wonderful. Can you tell me three places you have loved when you traveled?"

"Just three? That is a hard task. I will give you three, but on the condition I get to add or change when or if I think of other places."

"That is fair, I have put you on the spot," she conceded.

"Mmmm... let me think about it. Okay, the first one is easy. I am going with Spain as a whole. There are the starkly different types of architecture from the modern Guggenheim Museum to the incredible Gothic Cathedrals and the still incomplete, crazy creation that is Sagrada Familia. All of that coupled with the divine concept that is

Tapas. And as a caveat, I will admit, I fell in love in Spain, which I think added to the appeal of the place. It didn't work out, but I think it helps with the fond memories."

"It sounds wonderful."

"Next would be the lantern festivals at the old night market in Hoi Ann in Vietnam. It is magical. You can pay to float down the river and launch your own lantern, making a wish as you do. The people are friendly and on one side of the river is a grand, old market with no motor vehicles allowed and on the other side a row of restaurants, where you can sit and eat any cuisine you fancy and watch the world go by."

Hannah nodded into the darkness and conjured up the vision of what he described in her head. It did sound magical. "I definitely want to experience that one day," she said wistfully.

"Traveling is good for the soul. It makes us open our eyes to the way others live and gives us experiences we carry with us forever. There is so much to see, I fear that I will never get to all the places I want to."

They sat quietly for a moment before Hannah prompted Baniti. "And your last choice for your top three?"

"Oh, that is easy. Australia. I have seen parts of the East Coast and I loved it. My long-term plan is to one day join the group of people known as the Grey Nomads."

Hannah laughed. "My mum and dad are Grey Nomads. Dad got an early retirement package, so they took off to see all they could. They love it."

"What about you, Hannah? Where are your favorite places in the world?"

She was grateful for the darkness as she blushed with embarrassment. "I haven't been anywhere exciting. We didn't have a honeymoon because Luke wouldn't take time off as he wanted to make a good impression to get a promotion. He promised that once he made it we would see the world as he would be traveling for business."

"I am sorry if I have made you feel uncomfortable."

"No, no, not your doing at all. I just realize how much I have put on hold while I waited for Luke."

"So, where are your top three places you want to visit?"

"New York, for all the obvious reasons. The United Kingdom; I want to see all the folktale places, like Stonehenge and Lochness." Hannah paused to consider her final choice. She would have normally said Egypt, a cruise down the Nile had always been so romantically appealing but thought this was probably not the best time to bring it up. She didn't want him to think she was implying anything. "Third place would be the Geisha and blossom trees of Japan."

"All great places to visit."

As they drove along the quiet night streets of outer Sydney, Hannah allowed herself a momentary lapse of good judgment and thought about what it would be like to have Baniti as her husband. He was kind to strangers and he didn't roll his eyes and make snarky comments at her music choices. He was encouraging her to think about what she wanted and needed and to take steps to get it. Baniti had been friendly and interested in her thoughts and opinions, unlike Luke who was only interested in people who could help him advance his situation. And to complete the picture, Baniti was far more handsome than Luke, but that could have been the appeal of his personality joined with his accent.

Baniti found a park across from the house and it was only when Hannah went to thank him for the lift that she registered the car in front was Luke's. "What is he doing here?" she blurted out.

"Sorry?"

Hannah gestured to the white Audi in front of them. "That's Luke's car." A sinking feeling began to grow and she almost fought against her head swiveling to see if he was at Amy's house. It was beyond comprehension that he was here, and yet there he stood on the porch talking to her best friend. The betrayal at what she saw was almost as painful as the spiteful words that he had unloaded on her in the restaurant earlier that night.

## Chapter 4

Her pretty friend, Amy, with her Eurasian beauty and outgoing personality, stood on the top step of her porch looking intently as Hannah's soon to be ex-husband, Luke, appeared to be explaining something. Hannah didn't know what to do. Should she get out of the car and demand to know what was happening, or wait and see what occurred next? Her decision was taken away from her as she watched Luke lean in and kiss Amy. Hannah covered her eyes with her hands, not wanting to see any more.

Baniti laughed. Hannah kept her eyes covered, not wanting to see the betrayal of her best friend with her husband. *Why is he laughing?* She was indignant. *Does he not understand the situation or the pain this causes me?*

"Hannah, open your eyes," he spoke softly. "There is nothing to fear and much to be grateful for. Including having a fantastic best friend."

She cracked open her fingers to look and quickly took them away from her face as she watched in wonder as Luke stood in front of Amy, holding the palm of his hand to his cheek. His other arm was being waved wildly and he spoke loudly, but Hannah could only make out sound not what was being spoken. "What happened?"

"She slapped him." Baniti chuckled. "Hard."

"She did?"

"Of course she did! Is she not your best friend?"

Hannah felt guilty. What was she thinking to believe Amy would betray her in that way? She had made it very clear over the years that she tolerated Luke because Hannah loved him. Hannah felt ashamed that she had been so quick to jump to the conclusion that Amy would ever betray her in that fashion.

They both continued to watch as Amy flung her hand out as if telling Luke to stop talking and then gave a shooing motion. It was clear she wanted nothing to do with him and that she would prefer him to leave immediately. Luke spun on his heel and stomped his feet all the way to his car, like a petulant child, not taking any notice of the people parked in the car behind him. He pulled out of the parking space and drove away too quickly.

"Well, that was unexpected," Hannah announced to herself as much as to Baniti.

"Which part?"

"All of it. The whole night, really." Her stomach gurgling interrupted the conversation

"I have just realized that you didn't get to eat tonight. So, you still haven't tried Egyptian cuisine. This will not do," Baniti stated with friendly firmness.

"It's fine. If I stay with Amy for a little while, until I get sorted, I will just pop down to your sister's place and grab some take-way."

"You should come to my parents' home on Sunday for lunch. It is a big family get together and then you can try my mother's and my sister's cooking." He smiled encouragingly at her. "That way you get to taste real Egyptian food, not the stuff we make fancy for the clientele." He pointed to Amy, who stood waiting on the porch. "Bring your friend. Give me your number and I will text you the details." He took out his phone and waited, looking at her expectantly, as if no one would ever say no to giving this handsome man their number. She wasn't going to be the first, she obligingly gave her number.

Hannah stuck out her hand. "Thank you for rescuing me. I think I would have fallen apart if you hadn't have been so kind."

Baniti took her hand and held it for a moment before letting it go. "It was a pleasure to meet you, Hannah. I hope to see you on Sunday. My family always loves having new people to cook for, they appreciate the food more." He winked at her. "Your friend is coming."

Hannah turned to find Amy slowly walking down the front garden path toward them, she had a hesitant smile on her face. Hannah guessed she probably didn't want to intrude but wanted to check on her friend. "I'm going to get out of the car and come around to your side," she told Baniti.

"Okay, no problem."

Grabbing her bag and doing a quick check to make sure she hadn't left anything, Hannah opened the passenger door and got out. Baniti wound down his window and waited for her to come around the car. Amy crossed the road and engulfed Hannah in a strong hug. "Are you okay?" she whispered.

Hannah squeezed her friend and whispered back. "Yeah."

Amy turned to Baniti. "Hi, I'm Amy. Thank you for bringing Hannah home."

"Hi, Amy. I'm Baniti and you are very welcome. She wasn't in any condition to be left alone, so I made her clean dishes."

Hannah laughed and after a startled look so did Amy. "You made her do dishes?"

"Well, yes, how else was she going to pay for her drinks? Isn't that what happens in the movies?" Baniti joked.

Hannah wasn't certain that Amy knew he was joking.

"Well, I should be going and let you two ladies get inside. My father will have the police out soon looking for his precious car." He smiled at Hannah.

"I can't thank you enough for your support tonight. I'm not sure I was in any condition to make it home after all that alcohol and no food."

"Any gentleman would have done the same. I hope to see you on Sunday, I will send you more details once I have them."

"Bye, Baniti." The women waved as he pulled out onto the road and drove away at a much more sedate speed than Luke had.

Amy turned to Hannah. "Sunday?"

"We have been invited to his parents' place for a traditional Egyptian meal."

"We?"

"Yes."

"And you gave him your number?"

"Why not? I am a free woman now." And with those words spoken all of Hannah's bravado fell away and she turned to her friend and collapsed against her shoulder, weeping.

## Chapter 5

Dawn was creeping up fast and Hannah and Amy had not yet gone to bed. Hannah had only managed to stop crying and tell her best friend the whole sordid mess an hour prior. Amy was still incredulous with the callous behavior of Hannah's husband. Not only had he dumped his wife in a crowded restaurant, but he had also left her there to show up at Amy's house and attempt to begin a relationship with her. He had kissed her, which had resulted in a hard slap and him telling her she was as bad as her friend and him storming off. Both women were astounded by the insensitivity and arrogance the man had displayed.

Hannah was exhausted and tired over talking about it. She would need time to process the whole sordid event and four in the morning was not ideal. "I'm starving," she announced, realizing she hadn't eaten since lunchtime yesterday.

"I have leftovers from a great Egyptian takeaway place," Amy said.

Laughter welled up and erupted before Hannah had time to explain the absolute coincidence that it was. It was good to laugh, even if it was for a brief moment. Amy looked at her like she had grown another head.

"You are not going to believe this, but the cute guy that brought me home?"

"Yes?"

"His sister and her family own the restaurant."

"That is one huge chance event." Amy's eyes became suddenly dreamy and she looked over at Hannah with a knowing expression. "Maybe it isn't a coincidence. Perhaps it is fate?"

"Oh please, keep your mumbo jumbo fate and destiny stuff to yourself."

"Are we going on Sunday?"

Hannah feigned surprise. "We?"

"Yes, we. You gotta have a wing woman."

"Seriously. My husband dumps me today and you are already matchmaking."

"So, you aren't going?"

"If, and that is a big *if*, he sends me the invite with details, I will consider it. Have you ever thought he was just being kind to me? After all, I did cry in his bathroom for over an hour and in his car."

"Well, I am not going to let you eat the takeaway; you will have to wait until Sunday now." Amy looked smug. "What about a ham and cheese toasted sandwich?"

"That sounds great," Hannah admitted. She sat in the large, open-style kitchen area—with an alfresco breakfast nook and family living room—and gratefully watched her friend cook for her. "What did you do tonight? I hope I didn't interrupt anything?" Hannah suddenly realized that she had just assumed Amy was free to help her.

"No, all good. I was studying. I am still perfecting the formula for my lip gloss. It is too slippery. And I have an open book exam coming up soon. It's so close I can almost see that Chemistry diploma dangling in front of me."

As the aroma of melting cheese filled the bright, white and blue kitchen, another thought occurred to Hannah. *What was she going to do for work? She would have to pay her bills and find somewhere to live and...* her brain froze with the overload of all the unanswered questions as they jumbled together.

"What's wrong?" Amy asked as she placed the toasted sandwich in front of her.

"I don't have any money. I don't have a job. I don't have anywhere to live. I don't own a car. I don't even have a credit card in my name." She ticked off the things. The magnitude of the situation dawned on her and she began to tremble.

Amy moved around to the other side of the counter and took both her hands. "You need to calm down. I promise everything will work out. Just take a few breaths and let's work through the panic."

Hannah nodded and tried to stop her hands from shaking. Her heart thudded and it felt like she could feel the blood coursing through her as her anxiety grew.

Amy kept speaking in a quiet voice. "Okay, first thing not to worry about is you have somewhere to live. Mum and Dad aren't coming back from Perth for at least another year; Grandma seems to be doing quite well now they are there. I have always wanted to have a roommate and it's not like we don't have the space for you."

Hannah's chest felt tight and she had a sharp pain, she would think it was indigestion if she didn't know better. Hannah nodded her head but continued to focus on just breathing.

"You do own a car. We will go over and pick it up later, once we have slept or I can go with my brother to do it if you aren't ready to see Luke. The car might be in Luke's name but the judge will not look kindly upon a man who treats his wife poorly when it comes to divorce settlements." Amy stood to her full height of five foot three and lifted her head. "I will remind him of that, if necessary." Her brown, almond-shaped eyes full of anger.

The idea was comical, and it made Hannah forget her pounding heart for a moment, or painful chest; she smiled slightly. "I would pay to see that."

"After the slap I just gave him, I don't think he is going to be too quick to mess with me."

Hannah's smile widened.

"We can fix the credit card issue this moment. You just need a credit debit card and you can apply for one of those online right now."

It was a relief to have someone take control. Hannah hadn't had to think for herself for a long time and now it made her nervous when she did. What happened if she made the wrong decision? "Okay, let's do that." She pulled her phone from her pocket and went to hand it to Amy.

Her best friend stood back and held up her hands. "You need to do it. I will walk you through it, but you need to learn to do this."

Hannah was shocked and slightly hurt. "But..."

Amy spoke quietly. "He has taken away your independence and you need to take it back. Do the things you can do to grow your confidence." Amy leaned in, her bright, brown eyes determined. "And you are absolutely capable of creating a bank account."

By the time the bank account was created, Hannah's heart rate had returned to normal and the shaking had ceased. Amy was right; doing such a simple thing had made her feel better about herself.

"Now, the final hurdle for the evening," Amy announced with a flair of the melodramatic.

Hannah groaned. "A job?"

"A job."

"I haven't worked for so long, I am not sure anyone would hire me."

Amy rolled her eyes. "You are not thinking big enough."

"I'm not?"

"No. This is your moment. You are twenty-eight and have the chance to do whatever you want. You have somewhere to live, you are entitled to half the money in your accounts and you have time. You wanted to be a nurse, does that still appeal?" Amy paused and raised a black eyebrow at her.

Hannah waited, not wanting to ruin her friend's overly dramatic moment. Amy grabbed Hannah's shoulders for emphasis. "It is all about *you* now. What do you want?"

## Chapter 6

As she chose a few things from the spectacular array of food on the trestle table, Baniti's mother came by. "No, no, that is not enough food." Hannah thought her accent was as enchanting as her son's. Without asking, the amiable woman picked up the closest tongs and selected several more things for Hannah to sample.

Amy dutifully held out her plate when the woman gave her a scornful look at its meager contents. "I like it here." Amy laughed as she watched her food pile grow.

"Both too skinny," muttered the matronly woman.

Hannah knew Amy was thin because she was one of those women who had a fast metabolism. Her Asian heritage giving her less curves. Hannah was lean for a different reason and it pained her to think about it. She once had curves that would turn a man's head; the classic hourglass figure. Now she was thin and her hip bones and ribs stood out because Luke would look at her with outrage if she did any more than pick at the food on her plate. It had started early in their marriage; they had been out for a company awards night when he had given her a disgusted glare as they ate dinner with his colleagues. On the way home, he had cruelly told her that he was mortified with her eating at dinner. That she had sounded and looked like a cow chewing its cud, and he would appreciate never having to experience that again. Hannah had been humiliated and had quickly learned to appease him by putting little on her plate and just picking at her food in tiny morsels as this would not earn her a look of contempt or revulsion.

The food was now piled on her plate and it made her feel slightly anxious at the thought of being in front of all these people and them watching her eat. She was beginning to panic as Mrs. Salah waited with anticipation for her to sample something on her plate. *What happens if Baniti's family thinks I eat like a cow too?* She didn't want to make them feel turned off when she ate.

Thankfully, Amy, who was always happy to be the center of attention, stepped in and made quite the show of looking at her plate. "I don't know what to try first. What would you recommend, Mrs. Salah?"

"Hawawshi is our oldest family recipe." She pointed at a pastry-filled, round parcel on Amy's plate.

"Then we shall try that one first," Amy announced while nodding encouragingly to Hannah.

Taking a deep, steadying breath, Hannah picked up the Hawawshi. It was a large portion and no one was looking at her now that Amy had spoken up. She took a nibble and the pastry melted in her mouth. The filling was delicious, full of flavor, and at that moment she didn't care what people thought of her as the spices filled her mouth. Once she had finished that one, Hannah greedily picked up another thing on her plate and began to nibble on that.

Baniti came to stand next to her, his own plate full of the fabulous, aromatic food. "What do you think?" he asked in between mouthfuls.

"It is wonderful."

He smiled broadly at her. He didn't seem concerned about the way she was chewing. Hannah had a growing feeling that she was going to have to assess everything she thought about herself and face and discard all the negative things Luke had told her to keep her under control and in her place, just the way he preferred it.

"Thank you for inviting us today."

"I promised that I would. I owed you a meal, after all. Most people don't come to the restaurant, drink, and clean, but not eat."

"Most people don't let someone they don't know cry at their bar, pour them a champagne to celebrate getting dumped, and then make them do dishes as payment," she countered.

He laughed. "Yes, true. It was an eventful night. A first for me."

"For me too." She tried not to sound sad. Today was the first day she hadn't cried; she wanted to keep it that way.

"I want you to meet someone." He waved to a stunning, deep olive-skinned woman, with wavy, dark-brown hair and naturally long-lashed chocolate, colored eyes.

Hannah watched as she nodded politely at the people she was standing with and made her way over to them. Amy joined them as the woman arrived at Baniti's side.

"Hannah, Amy, this is my fiancé, Farida."

"It is a pleasure to meet you," Amy spoke. "I would shake your hand but mine are a bit full at the moment."

Everyone laughed as Amy was juggling her laden plate, wine glass, a serviette, and a half-eaten pastry all at once.

Farida smiled kindly at Hannah and gave her a gentle squeeze. Hannah was careful not to get food on the woman's gorgeous, bright-red dress. "It is lovely to meet you, Hannah. I hope we can be friends."

Hannah noted that Farida accent was much stronger than Baniti's. "I would like to be friends. You are very lucky to have a fiancé like Baniti, he was very kind to me when I needed a friend." Hannah realized she meant it. Hannah had to admit that she had mixed feelings. She was relieved because she wouldn't know what to do if a guy did like her, but also mildly disappointed because now she worried that maybe Luke had been right, and she was lucky to get him. She didn't trust herself anymore to make good decisions. Upon all that consideration, she was not upset to discover that Baniti was engaged. Her marriage had only crumbled the week prior; she had no real intention of getting involved with anyone. He had helped her through the most difficult night of her life, but it had only been a harmless distraction to talk to Amy about how handsome he was.

Farida moved closer to both women and spoke in a conspiritual tone. "Many men don't want their wives to mix with the Australian women. They are frightened your ways will rub off on us and we will begin to take more control and stand up for ourselves and our daughters. Baniti is not like that. He sees the value in people and he thinks you would be good friends to both of us."

Hannah almost choked on that statement. She was probably the worst example of how to not let a man control you. Her whole life had come to revolve around pleasing her husband and she had lost her identity along the way. "Have you ever had a pedicure?" Hannah asked.

"Oh, that is a marvelous idea," chimed in Amy. "We are going to get our feet pampered next Saturday, would you care to join us?"

*thank you* at them from behind his fiancé.

## Chapter 7

Sunday afternoon and Salah's family gathering was still going strong as the sun began to set, and for the first time since that fateful night, Hannah felt content. She had met many of Baniti's family and had spent much time speaking to his fiancé, Farida. She had attempted to help clean up but was firmly escorted from the kitchen and told to mingle. She knew Amy needed to get home to study and Hannah had to admit that all this socializing had made her tired. It was time to leave.

"Baniti, thank you for the wonderful afternoon, but we have to get going."

"Thank you both for coming. And thank you for asking Farida to join you for a pedicure next week. She is very much looking forward to it."

Amy answered. "It was our pleasure. She is so friendly and warm. We are looking forward to it."

Hannah looked around. "Is your mother still inside? I would like to thank her and your father for their hospitality."

"Follow me." Baniti led them back into the well-appointed two-story house and through to the kitchen where several older men sat around the kitchen table while a few older women stood dividing up leftovers into plastic containers. "Omm, Abbi, Hannah, and Amy are leaving and wanted to say goodbye."

"Just in time," his mother announced. She took two leftover filled containers and handed one to each woman.

Hannah took the box and smiled gratefully. "Thank you for inviting us. We had a fantastic time. Your home, family, and food are all wonderful."

"You may bring her back anytime, Bani," his father chimed in from his place at the head of the table.

"What about me?" joked Amy. "I too have had a marvelous time and thank you for the hospitality."

He grinned with a glint in his dark eyes. "Very well, but only if you teach me how to make dumplings at some point."

Everyone laughed. "Abbi, that is not fair. How do you know she makes dumplings?" Baniti protested.

"Because I asked her and she said she was the best at it." The old man looked around the room, eyes wide with feigned innocence. "What? You all know how much I love a dumpling. Amy wasn't upset that I asked her. Why is everyone else?"

No one could argue with that logic and on the promises of returning to make dumplings and giving friendly hugs, Baniti escorted them from the kitchen. Farida joined them as they stood in the well-manicured front yard.

Their goodbyes were interrupted by the sound of thumping music and a loud car engine coming down the road. "Masuda." Both Baniti and Farida laughed at the same time.

"What's a Masuda?" asked Amy.

"Not what, *who*."

A shiny black, large four-wheel-drive utility, with checker plate tool boxes on the back, pulled into the driveway. The car was turned off and the loud music died with the engine. A young man, around twenty-five climbed out of the driver's seat and made his way to the quartet standing on the lawn. Hannah felt a stirring in her stomach that she hadn't felt in years. Masuda was similar in appearance to Baniti—they were obviously related—but where Baniti was clean-cut and perfectly put together, Masuda was the opposite. His olive skin was tanned, giving him a darker appearance and his hair was longer and a little wild, kept in place by the sunglasses on his head. He was of similar height, but his body stronger, shoulders wider. Like Baniti, his face was handsome and friendly.

"Hey," the interloper greeted them as he hugged both Baniti and Farida.

"Masuda, this is Hannah and this is Amy." Baniti introduced them.

"Hannah, Amy, this is Masuda, my cousin."

"Great to meet you both."

Was Hannah mistaken or did his hand linger in her hers a fraction longer than it should have when he shook it? *You need to stop doing this to yourself. Baniti wasn't interested, he was just friendly, and Masuda is probably the same,* she told herself firmly.

"How much trouble am I in from one to ten, do you think?" Masuda asked Baniti.

"Definitely around a seven."

"But I have a great excuse, that should win me some points."

"Okay, let's hear it," Amy spoke up. "Hannah and I will judge your story."

"Fair enough. I was helping Mrs. Nowak, my elderly neighbor," he paused.

"Excellent opening. Good brownie points," noted Hannah.

"Her husband died a few years back and while she has a few friends stop by, I don't think she has a family that visits her. I was leaving and I saw her outside trying to turn off the main water tap in her front yard. I couldn't just leave her there. I have been raised better than that." He stopped and looked at Hannah. "Too much?"

She laughed and said "No."

As Baniti said "Yes."

"I like Hannah's answer better." He continued, his large, brown eyes sparkling with mischief. "I asked Mrs. Nowak if I could help and she explained that there was water going everywhere in her bathroom and she couldn't get the water turned off. So, I turned the water off for her and went into the house to discover that there was, in fact, water everywhere. I couldn't leave her like that and plumber rates on a Sunday are ridiculous."

"You would know." Farida snorted.

Masuda ignored the comment. "I went back to my place, got changed, went back, and fixed her pipes, helped her clean up the water, and made sure she was fine before I left. And here I am, four hours late and looking like I missed out on the best bit of the party: new people." His warm smile melted Hannah's resolve to not jump to conclusions a little.

"I take it you are a plumber?" asked Amy.

"Yes, started my own business about a year ago. So far, so good." He held his arms wide. "Well, does my story hold up?"

Baniti narrowed his eyes. "How much of it is true?"

"All of it."

"Then my guess is yes, you are going to be crowned the hero for saving the old lady. You may even leave here with enough food for you and your neighbor," his cousin said with a hint of disgust.

"Mrs. Nowak would love that."

"Hannah and Amy were just leaving."

"That is a shame."

"I have to study or else we would stay," Amy explained.

"What are you studying?"

"Chemistry. I want to produce my own skincare line."

Masuda whistled. "Impressive." He turned to Hannah. "What do you do, Hannah?"

She knew the question had been coming, she had answered it several times already today, it didn't make her as uncomfortable as it had earlier that day. It appeared the embarrassment had worn off. "I am having a career change and am unsure as to what to do next." It wasn't a lie and it avoided the subject of what she had been doing until now. Most people weren't inquisitive enough to ask anything further.

"Oh… " Masuda began but received a shake of his head from Baniti. Hannah was grateful for the intervention.

"Well, we better get inside with the latecomer. It was great to meet you and I look forward to next week." Farida gave them both a hug.

Everyone said their goodbyes and Hannah couldn't help but wonder what it would be like to be with a man who would help their neighbor without a second thought.

## Chapter 8

Hannah hummed cheerfully as she pushed the food trolley down the nursing home's corridor. She had started her new job two weeks ago and loved it. She was working in the kitchens of a small nursing home and while it didn't take much brainpower, it took a lot of compassion. The week prior she had started a carers course, so she would be able to work within the nursing home in other capacities, but that would take three months to complete, so until then she helped prep, clean, and deliver meals. Delivering morning or afternoon tea to the people that lived there made her day and she took great delight in listening to their stories and helping them with their jigsaws, puzzles, or crafts as she opened packets of biscuits and poured drinks. Hannah watched the nurses and knew that, eventually, she wanted to start her nursing degree, but that would wait until she could support herself and that would only be possible once she had her carers course completed.

Mrs. Jones was secretly her favorite person in the home. A small, quiet lady who carried herself with great dignity, even though her shoulders were hunched and she used a walker. Mrs. Jones spoke in a clipped, British accent, and she never raised her voice; even her laugh was delicate. But she had a sharp mind and a sharper tongue if you didn't do something to her liking. Her biscuit and tea were to be placed just so and her pen for her word puzzle had to be blue. She liked to face the window if the sun was shining in the morning and would ask for her afternoon tea to be brought out to the small, pretty garden in the afternoon on the cool, but sunny days.

"How do you smile and comply with her?" the day manager, Trish, had asked at the beginning of her second week. "She is always so particular in the way she likes things."

Hannah had shrugged. She knew why, but she wasn't going to explain it to Trish. "She is not that bad. Once you know how she likes it and you do it that way, she is quite lovely." Hannah knew that having to appease Luke continually had made her docile and agreeable. In this circumstance, it wasn't a bad thing to be that way. Within marriage it was horrible, and she would never allow that to happen again. She would rather remain single forever than allow herself to be treated like that.

"Would you like to sit outside today, Mrs Jones?" Hannah asked as she wheeled the trolley up to her.

"That would be pleasant."

Hannah held the door open for her before gathering a slice of cake and making a cup of tea and heading out to place it on the white, wrought-iron table next to Mrs. Jones. "Here you are. Can I get anything else for you?"

"Thank you, Hannah. You are most kind. Would you be able to sit and talk for a few moments?" she asked in her quiet, English accent.

"Yes, I can spare a few moments for you without getting into trouble. Is there is anything you would like to talk about?"

"I thought we could talk about you."

"Me?" Hannah was surprised. "I am not interesting at all. I think you would have much more interesting stories to tell than me."

Mrs. Jones gave her a penetrating look, her watery blue eyes told Hannah that she was wrong in her assessment of herself. "I have a feeling you have a tale to tell. No matter how much I bark at you, you don't respond with anything other than servitude. That, my dear, is not a good thing."

Hannah just looked at her feet. She didn't know what to say. Mrs. Jones hadn't asked her a question, so she kept quiet, which she guessed proved Mrs. Jones's point. The sun was warm and soothing on her back and bowed head and the bird calls were pretty in the afternoon stillness.

"Are you married, Hannah?"

"Technically yes, but no, not anymore." Hannah swallowed hard around that statement. It was the first time she had had to say it aloud to someone.

"How long have you been separated?"

"Six weeks." Tears burned her eyes, but she was determined not to let them fall this time.

"It is very new, it will take time."

"It was a shock," Hannah admitted voluntarily.

"I am sorry to learn that."

"I am not sorry it is over, I am more sorry I let myself be treated so poorly for so long." Hannah spoke softly, ashamed to admit her faults. She knew she had many, after all, Luke had been fixated on them for years. "I am struggling to cope with all the changes and to learn to trust myself again. I am useless to everyone." Her voice caught, but the tears didn't fall.

"You are not useless. You make a very fine cup of tea to start with." Mrs. Jones used the gentlest voice Hannah had heard.

Hannah looked up to see one of the older gentlemen ransacking her trolley. She stood to go. "I need to stop Mr. Pygall from stealing all the food."

"Yes, I understand. But one thing more... "

Hannah turned to the old lady.

"Don't let him win. Fight to find yourself again. It will be worth it, I promise." Mrs. Jones's harshness had completely disappeared and had been replaced with a warmth that eclipsed the sun. Just as swiftly, the bristly, proper lady was back. "You had best be off before he absconds with all the goodies." She made a shooing motion toward the door.

Hannah didn't wait around. Mr. Pygall was attempting to stuff several packets of sweet biscuits into his shirt pocket when she arrived. She took those away from him but offered him a large slice of cake and another cup of tea, which appeased him, and he allowed himself to be steered back to a chair in front of the television with *I Love Lucy* reruns showing.

As Hannah steered the trolley back to the kitchen, she made the resolve to take another step forward. She didn't know how she would do it, but it was time to shed another of the learned behaviors Luke had imposed on her. Mrs. Jones was right. She would not let him win.

## Chapter 9

It had been a long week, but Hannah found that she enjoyed the tired feeling at the end of each day. She worked four shifts a week at the nursing home and then two-night classes, but had picked up two extra shifts as someone had been sick. She felt a sense of accomplishment that she hadn't felt in a long time. Living with Amy had also turned out to be enjoyable. They talked and laughed and ate bad food and promised to go to the gym the next day and spent hours dissecting the latest bad Rom-Com on Netflix. And when the dark times descended and Hannah became frightened of all the things she would have to learn to do for herself and was faced with decisions only she could make, Amy was there as a shoulder to cry on and a supportive friend.

As Hannah walked into class, she was about to switch off her phone when it beeped and a text from a number she didn't know popped up. She slid the phone onto silent and put it in her bag. She would deal with the message when the class was over.

The class went well and Hannah felt like she was learning quickly. She had been worried that her ability to learn might have been lost. Like everything else she had experienced since Luke had left her, it hadn't been as scary as she had built it in her mind. The air was cool as she hurried to her car, only remembering that she had a message on her phone when she took it out to take it off silent.

**Hi, it's Masuda. I hope you don't mind me texting you. I have been pestering Bani for your number since I met you but he wouldn't give it to me. He finally explained how you met and that he was concerned about giving it to me. I promised to be extra kind and not ring you to ask you out, but do it over text so you don't feel uncomfortable saying no. I hope it is okay that he gave me your number. M. :-)**

Hannah sat staring at the phone screen. Her heart thudded in her chest as she thought of the gorgeous man she had met seven weeks ago. Her first response was no. How could he possibly want to go out with her? She was a huge disappointment. If she went out with him then he would see all the faults Luke had seen and she didn't think she could handle any rejection at the moment, no matter how small.

Mrs. Jones's voice crept into her head. *Don't let him win, dear.*

Now, Hannah reminded herself that she had made a promise that she would take steps forward. This was not what she had had in mind, but it was what had been placed in front of her.

**H: Hi Masuda, it is great to hear from you. I don't mind that Bani gave you my number.**

Hannah started the car as she waited for a reply. She looked at the time and realized he might be asleep. Tradesmen went to bed early from what she understood. Now she wished she hadn't sent the text for she could have woken him. Hannah fretted the entire twenty minute drive home. As soon as she pulled into the driveway and turned the car off, she grabbed the phone and checked it.

**M: Hey, you didn't answer my question???**

**H: What question was that?**

**M: Would you go out on a date with me?**

**H: I don't know.**

Hannah decided honesty would be crucial for this to have any chance at working.

**M: It would be very casual - nothing too romantic where there is pressure. Something like Luna Park or the zoo, where there is something to do aside from sitting and look at each other. Though I would be happy to look at your face for a full date. Was that too much?**

She laughed. Even in text form he was charming.

**H: Maybe just a hint too much. Can you turn it down a fraction?**

**M: I'll tone it down as much as you need if you just say yes.**

**H: Very casual?**

**M: So casual that to the average observer we will look like friends.**

**H: Okay.**

**M: Okay, yes?**

H: Yes. I will go out somewhere on a very casual date with you.

M: Cool. Is there somewhere you would like to go? How was that for relaxed?

H: Perfect. I think the zoo was a great idea.

M: Favourite animal that you want to see?

H: Otters. I love Alaskan Otters. You?

M: Oh, I think Otters are great too.

H: Ha, ha. No. What will be your go-to animal?

M: Promise no laughing?

The response had Hannah intrigued and she smiled as she hit send on her answer.

H: No laughing. Now you have me very curious.

M: Maybe I should make you wait, so you don't back out of the date.

H: I won't back out. Tell me. Please ;-)

M: Well... maybe I should make you guess.

Hannah groaned. She had hated guessing games as a kid. She looked up to find Amy watching out the lounge room window at her. Grabbing her stuff, she got out of the car and made her way into the house.

"Everything okay?" asked Amy as Hannah dumped her things on the kitchen table.

"Yes, I am making a cuppa, do you want one?" Hannah called out.

Amy wandered into the kitchen, holding a half-filled cup of coffee. "No thanks, I am good."

Hannah's phone pinged. She realized she hadn't answered Masuda. "Pick a random animal you would find at the zoo."

Amy stared at her. "Huh? Um, okay. Red Panda."

Hannah picked up her phone.

M: ??? You scared to guess.

H: Red Panda?

M: Good try. You are in the right area.

"It's not a Red Panda," Hannah told Amy.

"What are you talking about?"

Hannah laughed. "Sorry, I forgot the relevant parts. Now, no freaking out, okay?"

Amy's eyes narrowed. "What did Luke do?"

"No, no. It is good stuff, not bad. Masuda asked me out on a very casual date. We are going to the zoo and I have to guess which animal is his favorite."

Amy squealed and jumped around the kitchen.

"Okay, settle down. You are making me freak out. This is not a big deal, so don't make it one."

"Sorry. Try Wallaby."

**H: How about a Wallaby? They are adorable.**

**M: Australian animal and furry. You are so close.**

Hannah read the answer to Amy. They both stared at each other for a minute before they both spoke in unison. "Koala."

**H: My final guess is koala.**

**M: Yes. They are so damn cute but don't you tell anyone I said that.**

**H: That is very useful information to have if I ever get invited to another Salah family event.**

**M: You wouldn't.**

**H: We shall see how great your casual dating skills are.**

Hannah grinned at Amy as she showed her the texts. She was very much looking forward to the date now.

**Chapter 10**

Hannah discarded another dress as she searched through her closet for the perfect, yet very causal, first date at the zoo outfit. It had been just over two months since Luke had discarded her like the clothing that now lay in a heap on the end of her bed, and with the aid of Amy, they had gone to her marital home and emptied out everything that belonged to her one day while Luke had been at work. They had not bothered to pack it neatly into boxes, they had simply taken her clothes—coat hangers and all—and laid them in the back and boot of Amy's larger car. All of her bathroom products had been swept into plastic bags, as were her shoes that were not boxed. A large garbage bag was used to hold all her handbags and purses and another for all her underwear—including the lingerie she had never liked nor worn, but Luke had continued to buy throughout their marriage.

It had taken surprisingly little time to empty the house of Hannah. Her teddy bears from childhood, photos of her family, mementos from her teen years, all stuffed into bags or laid between items of clothing to be transported to Amy's. There were things she had to leave behind for now. Her craft stuff filled an entire room and would take too long to pack up and would possibly make them have to do a second trip and Hannah had no intention of running into Luke, if at all possible.

They had returned to Amy's and spent the remainder of the day reorganizing the guest bedroom, which had originally been Amy's brothers. In the space of a day, Hannah's life had been changed again and another step had been taken forward and away from her marriage. Today would be an even greater one. As the week went on, she had become less excited and more nervous about the date. It had been so long and it didn't matter how casual it would be, it would still be a date.

Hannah gave up looking for the perfect outfit and decided that she would tackle that once she had had a shower. Stepping under the hot water and letting it wash over her, Hannah found that her mind began to wonder. At first, she thought of nothing of consequence, allowing her mind to flit from thought to thought. Her mother's voice floated into her mind. *Do you think going on a date this soon is wise?* Her mother had always been overly critical, which was probably one of the reasons Hannah hadn't recognized it in Luke until they were married and his resentment and demands grew. But this time maybe her mother was right?

She shaved her legs and armpits, in case she chose something to wear that exposed them. Luke's voice replaced her mother's *Stupid, undesirable, unlovable. Don't speak when we are out with colleagues, your conversation is always dull and witless.* Tears fell and mingled with the water. *Why would Masuda want to go out with me? Maybe he just feels sorry for me.*

Her gentle tears turned to shaking, hunched over bawling. Her control was washed away; raw, naked emotion was exposed. The damage Luke had inflicted would not be fixed with one casual date. Hannah managed to turn the shower off and grab the closest towel before collapsing on the cold, tiled floor and allowing herself to feel everything she had been running from since that night in the Egyptian restaurant. She wept. No gentle sobs. Loud, heart-wrenching gasps shuddered from her. Was she broken? Would she be like this forever? Useless? Her facade had disintegrated and in its place was a terrified woman who didn't know who she was.

A loud knock on the bathroom door interrupted her spiraling thoughts. "Hannah, I am coming in," Amy announced. She didn't wait for an answer, Amy gently opened the door. "Oh, Han." She looked down at Hannah curled up on the floor, wrapped in a towel. Without another word, Amy sat on the floor and gathered her best friend into her arms.

Hannah was grateful for the support of her friend and that Amy not once told her to stop crying or that it would be all right. Amy just held Hannah while she cried, stroking her wet hair and telling her she was sorry she was in so much pain.

The tears eventually stopped flowing and her eyes felt red and raw. She was exhausted and felt paralyzed. Hannah felt stuck; she just wanted to lay on the bathroom floor and hide from the world and all its decisions and emotions. *Why do I always end up on the bathroom floor?* she wondered.

"Hannah, I'm going to get up and grab your phone. Is it in your bedroom?"

"Yes," Hannah's voice was dry and croaky.

With great care, Amy let go of Hannah and let her slide back into a fetal position on the floor. "Try to sit up, if you can," she told her as she left the bathroom.

Hannah lay there for several more moments before she told herself that it was time to move. Slowly, as if she was Sleeping Beauty waking from her slumber, she rose, pushing herself up to a sitting position. She slumped against the cold, beige wall, taking very little notice of the chill that ran through her skin.

Amy returned with Hannah's and her own phone in her hand. She plonked down next to Hannah, ignoring the wet floor mat. "Can you please unlock your phone? I am going to text Masuda and tell him the date is off."

Hannah opened her mouth but was not given the chance to say anything.

"You are not ready. Luke has hurt you beyond imagining. Not only has he destroyed that bright, beautiful woman I met all those years ago, he completed it by humiliating you in public." Amy grimaced at her. "I thought a date might build your self-confidence and Masuda seems like a great guy. I was wrong. You need counseling and time."

Without any argument, because there was nothing to argue about, Hannah unlocked her phone and handed it to Amy. The message was typed and sent without anything being discussed.

"Let's get you to bed. You are freezing." Amy stood and dragged Hannah up with her.

Hannah allowed herself to be escorted to her bedroom and discovered that while Amy had grabbed Hannah's phone she had also taken the pile of clothes off her bed and dumped them on a chair in the corner and pulled back the blanket. "Thank you," she said softly as she pulled the old t-shirt that she used as a nightdress over her head.

As Amy tucked her in, Hannah's phone pinged. Amy fished it out of her pocket and opened it, ignoring the fact that it was an intrusion of privacy. "Masuda answered that he is sorry to hear that you can't make it and that he hopes you are okay. And that if you want to try again just text him."

"What did you tell him?"

"I told him that you couldn't make it because you were feeling unwell and that maybe the timing just wasn't right."

"Oh, okay." Hannah couldn't help but wonder if he was disappointed or relieved that she had called off the date.

"I am going to text Farida and explain too," Amy informed her as she took out her own phone and sent their friend a text. The girls had hit it off when they went out for pedicures and ended up spending the day together and having Baniti join them for dinner. They planned to have a pedicure every month to catch up. "Would you like a cup of tea?"

"Do we have any chamomile?"

Amy went to respond as her phone rang, she looked at the number. "It's Farida. I'll get your tea." She answered the phone as she walked out of the room. Hannah overheard the beginning of the conversation, "Oh, hi, Baniti. Yes, she is okay..."

Hannah turned to face the window, looking out on a bright morning. She felt numb. All the tears and grief had gone and in its place was a vast expanse of emptiness. Would she ever feel again?

## Chapter 11

The weather was too cold to sit outside.

The small garden area that Mrs. Jones liked to occupy with her afternoon tea was flooded. Sydney's weather had been unpredictable all week and while the wind had abated, the intermittent, heavy rain had not. Hannah finished making herself and Mrs. Jones a cup of tea and placed them both at the four-seater, round table, that was tucked into a corner near the small selection of books that passed as a library and as far away from the loud television as possible. She watched the small, fragile woman gingerly take her seat and then moved the walker out of the way. "Would you like a blanket while I get my lunch?"

"A blanket would be most welcome." Mrs Jones smiled.

Hannah took out the playing cards from her pocket and handed them to the old lady. "Can you please shuffle these?"

It took Hannah only a few minutes to collect her lunch box. She quickly put the container in the microwave, and went in search of a warm blanket for Mrs. Jones's knees while her food heated up. She was back at the table with food and blanket in no time.

As she opened the container, Mrs. Jones wrinkled her nose. "What are you eating?"

"Dumplings. My friend Amy is half Chinese and she promised our friend's father that she would teach him to cook dumplings months ago. They had his first lesson last night." Hannah looked at the steaming dumplings and grinned. "Some of them are a little oddly shaped, but he did amazing for his first time."

Mrs. Jones peered into the Tupperware container. "I haven't eaten a lot of different foods, I must admit. My husband would only eat meat and three vegetables." She smiled at Hannah. "The most exotic thing he ever tried was spaghetti. Because he didn't eat it, I didn't eat it. My children are always telling me that I should try new things, that I am missing out."

"Would you like to try a dumpling?"

Mrs. Jones starred at the small, white lumps as if considering a life-changing event. "I think I will."

"Great. I'll get you a plate and fork. We will give chopsticks a miss this time." Hannah clacked her own chopsticks together for emphasis. She stood and quickly hurried to the kitchen; she didn't want Mrs Jones to change her mind. "Here we go." Hannah placed a small plate and fork in front of the old woman and retook her seat. "Pick one."

Mrs. Jones pondered the dumplings for a moment before stabbing one with a fork. Hannah poured a little bit of light soy on the plate and the lid of her container, then chose one for herself. Mrs. Jones watched Hannah dip the dumpling into her sauce and followed suit. Hannah popped the whole dumpling into her mouth and Mrs. Jones's eyebrows rose but she followed Hannah's example. They both sat there chewing and Hannah watched her friend's face closely. There was no screwing up of the nose or downturn in her thin, but still painted pink lips.

"Well?"

"It was not the best thing I have ever eaten, but it was tasty. If your friend makes different varieties I would like to try more."

"I will make sure of it." Hannah finished her dumplings, offering Mrs. Jones another one, which she took. After tidying up and making Mrs. Jones a fresh cup of tea they settled in to play cards.

As Hannah dealt the cards, she had to admit how much she had come to love her Thursday lunch breaks with Mrs. Jones. Sometimes they were joined by other residents of the nursing home and they always attempted to teach her a new card game, that there were now too many rules floating around her head. Today they had resorted to playing Go Fish to give poor Hannah's overloaded mind a rest.

Mrs. Jones seemed to be enjoying the simplicity of the game and had commented that perhaps she could play this when the grandchildren came to visit. "Do you have an ace?"

"Go fish," Mrs. Jones responded.

Being told to "go fish" in a clipped, British accent made Hannah smile every time.

"So, tell me, have you settled into Uni yet? Met any cute boys?"

Hannah had begun her nursing degree the month prior and had found the first few weeks difficult. She had confided to Mrs. Jones that maybe Luke had been right and that she wasn't smart enough to get a degree. In a tone that pulled Hannah out of her wallowing, Mrs. Jones told her to stop feeling so sorry for herself and that she was perfectly capable; she just needed time to adjust. She pointed out that Hannah had already completed a carers course and had been moved into that role at the nursing home because they thought she was competent. Mrs. Jones had then bluntly told her that Luke only wins when Hannah doubts herself.

"You were right, I just needed time. I am loving it. Most of the teachers are great, one man reminds me of Luke. But now that doesn't frighten me; he is just a bully and with my psychologist's help I can handle him."

"That's my girl." She paused and looked at her cards. "Do you have a six?"

Hannah handed over a six.

"What about the man situation? Any cute ones on campus?"

"No, but the majority are younger than me, straight out of high school." Hannah didn't add that since her disastrous almost date with Masuda, she had been deliberately avoiding even thinking about men in that way.

Mrs. Jones didn't push it. Instead, she changed the subject.

"Have you met the new resident yet?" Mrs. Jones paired another card.

"No, I am not assigned to her wing today. I was going to pop in and introduce myself though."

"She seems to be quite lovely. Thought she would have a strong Polish accent with a name like that, but she sounds like the rest of you uncouth lot." She winked to take the sting out of her barb.

Hannah laughed. "Ah, yes, us convicts and our broad Aussie accents."

"What is the new resident's name?"

"Mrs Nowak."

Hannah frowned. A memory tickled the back of her mind. *Why did that name mean something to her?*

## Chapter 12

Hannah tapped politely on the door before entering the room. "Mrs Nowak?"

A heavyset, elderly woman sat in a large, high-backed tapestry covered, well-padded chair. She had a pair of thick, red-rimmed glasses perched on the end of her nose and she looked over them when she looked up from the book she was reading. "Yes?"

"I just wanted to say welcome and to introduce myself. I'm Hannah."

"Hello, Hannah."

"Is there anything I can get you? I am just about to finish up for the day."

"That is kind of you to ask, but I am fine."

Hannah looked around the room. Like most residents, there was a large shelving unit along a wall in her room. This one contained books.

Lots of books. Only one black and white photo in a frame of a man sat on the top shelf and a few ornaments. There was also no television.

"What are you reading?"

"Matthew Reilly. The latest one in the Jack West series."

"He's an Australian author, right?"

"You don't read?" asked Mrs. Nowak.

"I used to, but that was years ago. Now I don't have time. The only things I have been reading of late are textbooks."

"What are you studying?"

"Nursing."

A knock on the door interrupted their conversation. "I hope it is okay for me to visit. I can come back if you need?"

Hannah turned around to explain that she was just introducing herself when the words caught in her throat. Now she remembered why the name of Mrs. Nowak sounded familiar.

"Hannah?"

"Oh, hi." Hannah felt herself flush. He was still as handsome as she remembered. His hazel eyes framed by thick, black eyelashes and heavy dark eyebrows. A mouth that looked like he was always on the verge of smiling and a wealth of slightly unkempt hair, made her recall why she had been willing to go out with him in the first place, even though she had known deep down it was a bad idea. He had obviously come from work as he wore his high vis shirt, canvas blue trousers, and steel capped boots—all typical plumber uniform.

Masuda looked at her, a warm smile spreading across his face. "You look wonderful. You have let your hair grow. It looks great."

Hannah unconsciously lifted her hand up to her hair. Her fire-red hair was pulled back into a low ponytail and now reached her shoulder blades. "There have been a few changes to me."

"Yes, I heard you telling Mrs. Nowak that you are studying nursing. I think that is amazing. Congratulations." He sounded so genuine.

Masuda walked into the room and kissed his old neighbor on the cheek. "How are you today? Settling in yet? Made any friends?"

Mrs. Nowak looked over her glasses at Masuda. "It's not my first week of primary school."

Masuda laughed, not in the slightest bit upset at the chastisement of treating her like a child.

"Well, I will get going and let you and Masuda chat. I just wanted to say hello and invite you to our card games on a Thursday. I play with Mrs. Jones every Thursday on my lunch break. Sometimes the other residents play with us, you are most welcome to join us anytime." Hannah turned to Masuda and tried to look calm when inside her body was responding to his in a way it hadn't done to anyone else's. She was surprised and a little fearful of the instant want she had for the man. "It was great to see you again. I finish in half an hour and need to get ready to handover to the next shift."

Hannah left the room and made her way back to the nurse's station where she needed to focus on writing up her notes and giving them to the nurses and carers who would take over. *Sometimes timing sucks,* she thought to herself as she searched for a pen. She was always losing pens.

Shunting Masuda and his caring, hazel eyes out of her head, she finished up her paperwork and did one final check of her patients for the day and made a last cup of tea for Mrs. Jones and Mr. Pygall.

"I see Mrs. Nowak has a visitor," commented Mrs. Jones as she took the cup of tea.

"Yes."

"He was quite handsome."

Hannah stood there smiling at Mrs. Jones, while she surreptitiously looked down the corridor towards Mrs. Nowak's room. "Are you trying to play matchmaker?"

"You have been single for quite some time and I think it just might be time to get back out there." Mrs. Jones held up her gnarled hand.

"Now, I know you had that one terrible near date, but that was a long time ago and you have come so far."

Hannah laughed and bent down so only Mrs. Jones could hear her. "He was that one terrible, near date."

"No?" Mrs. Jones was shocked.

"Yes. So, there is no point in playing matchmaker. I am sure he will stay well away from me now." Hannah didn't have any reason to still be at work, but she continued to linger in the hopes of seeing him without it seeming contrived. It looked like that wasn't going to happen. She would have liked to apologize in person for what had happened. "I will see you tomorrow," she told Mrs. Jones. "Have a good night."

As Hannah collected her bag and signed out, she checked her phone for the time and knew Amy would be sitting at home, working on her marketing for her soon to be released cosmetic line, as she had completed her degree a few months prior. She sent a text to Amy.

**H: You are not going to believe who our new resident is.**

Amy responded immediately.

**A: You found Elvis?**

**H: Very funny. No. Mrs. Nowak is our latest member.**

Hannah waited to see if Amy remembered where she had heard the name.

**A: Not ringing any bells. Should I know her?**

**H: We know her neighbor.**

**A: We do? You are being very cryptic today.**

**H: He helps her out with plumbing issues and is late to parties because of it.**

Hannah smiled and waited for her to finally figure it out. She pushed open the door and checked to make sure it locked behind her. They didn't need any escapees. Hannah was grateful that the rain had stopped as she made her way to the car. She hated driving in the rain.

**A: NOOOOOOOOOO**

**H: Yes! And he was visiting her today when I dropped by to introduce myself.**

**A: Did you talk?**

**H: He told me my hair looked great.**

**A: That's it?**

**H: We were in Mrs. Nowak's room. Should I go back and find him and apologize?**

**A: Do what you want to do. Whatever you feel will make you happy. I gotta go. We will chat when you get home. Xox**

**H: K xoxo**

Hannah stopped next to her driver's door and frowned at the now blank phone screen. Should she go back in or just leave it alone?

"HELLO, HANNAH." A MALE voice said with forced civility.

Hannah's head snapped up from the phone screen she had been staring at, considering if she should go talk to Masuda or just let things be. "Luke." She blinked. She was more surprised to see him there than she had been to find Masuda visiting someone in the facility. "What are you doing here?" Hannah gathered her coat around her like armor, not to guard her against the biting chill in the late afternoon air, but from the man that stood before her.

"I thought I would see where you worked." He moved to close off any escape for her. She was now trapped between her car and another one, with large thick bushes in front of the parked cars.

"Why do you care where I work?" Hannah tried to keep her voice light.

"Can't I be interested in what you are doing?"

"Sure. I just don't know why you would be. You made it pretty clear how you feel about me."

"Oh, come on. You make it sound worse than it is." He scoffed. "People get divorced all the time and manage to remain civil." Luke was at his most charming.

He was speaking as if what he said was quite reasonable and he hadn't treated her appallingly year after year, culminating with breaking off their six-year marriage in a restaurant. Everything through the divorce process had so far been handled by lawyers, with very little contact between the two of them. Hannah had been hoping for it to stay that way. Her life had started to feel like her own and she didn't need Luke interfering and making her doubt her choices.

"Yes, some people manage to remain civil." Hannah was doubtful that Luke understood what it meant to be truly civil to her. The last time he had been civil, without him wanting something that Hannah could recall, had been a year into their marriage. Over time he had learned to manipulate her emotionally, to the point she didn't trust herself or her decisions and she had tried so hard to please him. It sickened her to think of herself in that way now.

"How have you been?" Luke asked in what he probably thought was a friendly tone.

"Fine." Hannah just wanted him to go. She didn't care why he was there; he just needed to leave.

Silence descended on them as Luke waited for Hannah to return the question. The silence grew ominous and Hannah decided it wasn't worth aggravating him further. "How have you been, Luke?"

"I have been well. Thank you."

The dead air stretched between them again as Hannah pulled her coat tighter. The air grew cooler as the afternoon gave way to early evening. "What do you really want, Luke?"

"You remember my brother?"

Hannah refrained from rolling her eyes at his words. Of course she remembered his brother. She remembered his entire family. She had been part of it for eight years, after all. "Yes."

"It's his wedding in two weeks."

"Yes, I hadn't forgotten. I was planning on sending a gift and card."

"We RSVP'd to go together."

"That was before," she pointed out, wondering where this was heading.

"I think we should still go together."

Hannah was dumbfounded. "You do?"

"Yes. I think it is a sensible thing to do."

"I think that is not a good idea." Hannah looked at the man she had loved, worshiped even, and felt nothing. His large, gray eyes had always made her forgive him anything. Now they just made her sad. To think she spent so much time twisting herself into something she wasn't for a man who had never appreciated who she was. He had cruelly told her that he had never truly loved her on the night he had discarded her. Hannah would never forgive him for the pain he had caused.

"I think it is the right thing to do." Luke smiled at her.

Hannah could feel the falseness. It made her skin crawl. She remained silent, hoping he would understand through her muteness.

"Will you go with me?"

"No." She began to dig around in her bag, looking for her keys.

"What are you doing?"

"I am leaving now."

"We haven't finished talking."

"Yes, we have. Or did you want a tour of where I work?" Hannah wanted to end this and hoped calling his bluff would do that.

"I don't have time today, maybe another time," he answered blandly.

"Great, can't wait," she muttered sarcastically. Her hand finally found the keys in her handbag and she clicked the button. It was time to get away from Luke.

"Hannah, you should reconsider."

She acted dumb, hoping to discourage him that way. "Reconsider what?"

"I think it is important that you come with me to my brother's wedding. You know I wouldn't be here asking if it wasn't."

"I don't think I can make it any clearer. I am not going to your brother's wedding with you. I don't need all those people looking at me and gossiping about us."

"I think you should reconsider." Luke took a threatening step toward her, yet he kept the fake smile plastered across his face. She didn't flinch. He had never touched her physically; all his abuse had been mental.

Hannah held her ground and looked him square in the face. The work she had done with her psychologist had helped immensely and at that moment she felt all those hours of crying and being vulnerable about her situation had brought her to this point. She needed to take her power back and this was the time. Luke needed to see her for who she was, not what he thought she was.

"No."

"What?" Luke stood there, astounded by her audacity.

Hannah closed her eyes against his glare and planted her feet like she was ready to fight. She opened her eyes and spoke firmly.

## Chapter 13

"N. O." She spelled it, slowly and loudly. Hannah waited for the explosion. He didn't disappoint.

"I beg your pardon? No? After all I have done for you, you deny me this?" He glowered at her, his voice rising with every question. "How ungrateful you have become. I gave you everything. It is not my fault you could not reach my expectations."

"I don't think belittling me further is going to get me to agree to go with you." Hannah was amazed at how calm her voice sounded. Inside she could feel her control slipping, but she had worked so hard, she was not going to let him intimidate her.

Luke looked taken aback, he placed his hand on his chest. "I am not belittling you. I am simply speaking the truth."

"You are trying to bully and manipulate me into doing what you want." She stood her ground; it was an amazing feeling.

"You are right and I am sorry."

Hannah waited. She knew it was a ploy. It wasn't the first time she heard him say those words, but he never meant them. It was just a different way for him to get what he wanted.

"I haven't told my parents that we have separated. They love you so much and I just couldn't hurt them when this is such an important occasion for them."

Hannah was incredulous. "You what?" Luke's parents lived overseas and they never had a great relationship with their son so Hannah never had the opportunity to get close to them. This was why she had not been surprised they hadn't contacted her when Luke had discarded her, but now she knew that it was because they didn't know.

"It just seemed easier to take you and then have the both of us explain that it wasn't working between us and that we had separated."

"You want me to lie to them and tell them that it was mutual, when in reality you abandoned me while I was crying in a restaurant bathroom?" Hannah was beyond shocked. Luke knew no boundaries and would do or say anything to get his way. She had had enough. "Why don't you take your ruthless dream girl? The one that will suit your needs better. I am certain a family wedding wouldn't be difficult for her to network at."

"Don't be nasty."

Hannah laughed as she finally understood. She crossed her arms and leaned back against her car, suddenly far more comfortable with the situation. "There is no dream girl, is there? No one but me would put up with your demands? Or what? You couldn't train anyone to replace me in time?" She pushed him. She had never done it before. It felt great.

"So, you won't go with me?"

"For the final time. No."

Luke rubbed his head and the pleasant look he had been wearing slid off his good-looking face. Alarm bells went off in Hannah's mind. He slowly looked her up and down and sneered. His true nature finally making its appearance. "Probably for the best. You have let yourself go I see. I doubt you would be able to fit into any of those expensive dresses that I bought you."

Hannah said nothing. The spiteful comment hurt, but it wasn't untrue. All the take-away and indulging with Amy, Baniti, and Farida had made her go up a dress size. Her curves had returned and she had embraced them, until now.

They stood staring at each other as Trish, the day manager, walked by Hannah's car. "Great work today, Hannah," she called as she walked by.

Hannah smiled, thrilled at the compliment. "Thanks, Trish."

As Trish climbed into her car Luke mimicked Hannah. "Thanks, Trish."

Hannah felt her face redden.

"This is what you want to do now? Wipe old people's arses and spittle off their chins? Feed them and shower them? I couldn't think of anything more revolting." He shrugged as if he didn't care. "It's probably all you are good for. By Trish's words, it seems that are you good at it. Must be finally nice to know that you are good at something. Everything else you ever did you were terrible at." The words cut, but

Hannah was concentrating on remembering all the good things about herself. Listing them in her mind as she and Amy had practiced.

He went on. "I shouldn't have been so generous with the settlement, my lawyer warned me not to be. After all, you sat at home and did nothing, while I was out working and earning us enough to be comfortable and you were always ungrateful. You couldn't even keep the beautiful house I provided you clean. Never wearing the clothes I chose. When I think about the amount of money I spent on designer lingerie and high heels for you and you just complained that they weren't your style. I am your husband, you should do what you are told and wear what pleases me."

"Was," her voice was barely above a whisper as she corrected him. All her fight was slowly seeping away.

"What?"

"Was. You were my husband. All the financial side is done, you have no hold over me. In five months I can file for divorce and you won't be able to stop it."

"You unworthy piece of trash. You were lucky to have me, no one will ever want you. You are used goods and fat. You chew like a cow and have no spark to you. You are repulsive." Each of Luke's words came out hard and harsh, piling on top of her until she felt like she was suffocating. She sagged under the weight of his horrid words. Hannah studied her shoes, hoping to control the tears that threatened to spill down her cheeks.

"A man will only sleep with you once and then they will not stay. They will leave just like I did. You are terrible in bed. Prim and proper, no lingerie for the lady. It was like sleeping with a frigid virgin every time."

"I think that will do," a voice spoke behind Luke.

Masuda stood there, his arms crossed over his chest and a look of fury on his face.

# Chapter 14

Masuda stood there, looking furious.

"Mind your own business," Luke told him bluntly.

"This is my business. You don't speak to women like that."

"I will speak to her how I wish, she is my wife."

Masuda barked out a laugh. "No, she isn't."

Hannah noted that Luke flexed his fists but didn't say anything. She wanted them both to go away so she could climb into her car and cry. She wondered if Masuda could see how shaken she was or had simply stepped in because it was the right thing to do.

Masuda moved to one side to allow Luke an exit. "I think you have said all you ever need to say to Hannah." He smiled encouragingly at her, completely ignoring the glowering man between them.

The beautiful, open smile gave her the few ounces of courage she needed to speak, "Goodbye, Luke. Please don't contact me again."

Luke looked to Masuda and then back at Hannah, realization dawned on his face. "Oh, you two…"

Masuda cut him off, "Don't say it." He warned. "You think you know, but you don't. Now, the lady has asked you to leave her alone. Do we need to call the police for you to do it?"

Hannah held her breath. She didn't know what Luke would do. He was used to bullying her. She was smaller and mentally fragile after his years of torment; Masuda was strong and not going to be intimidated.

Luke turned to her. "Always remember that I got rid of you because you weren't good enough."

And with those parting words, he turned and walked past Masuda. They both watched as he climbed into his car, pulled out of his parking spot too quickly, and sped off. His driving was still reckless.

Hannah stared at her feet. She needed Masuda to leave, she didn't want him to see her broken. All the hard work of the last seven months had been shattered by the cruel words. *Why does Luke still have that power over me?* she asked herself. Hannah clutched the door handle behind her back and willed herself not to cry.

"Hannah?"

"Thank you for that. I need to go now." She couldn't look at him.

"Hannah?" his voice was soft and sweet.

"I bet you are grateful now that I didn't go out with you all those months ago, after hearing what he had to say about me?"

Masuda's shoes appeared in her field of vision. He moved to stand in front of her. "Hannah?" he repeated.

"Masuda?"

"I am going to hug you and I am not going to let go until you pull away. Would that be okay?"

A tear slid down her face, but she didn't lift her head as she whispered "Yes."

Masuda's arms wrapped tightly around Hannah. At first, she tensed; he was the first man to touch her aside from Luke in nine years, then she felt the comfort being offered and she turned her face and placed it on his chest, tucking her arms into her chest and allowed herself the freedom to cry. He did nothing but hold her.

Emotions tumbled through her mind as she fought for balance. Fought for the control she had gained and the confidence she had slowly been building. She was determined that Luke would not do that to her again. Hannah would no longer be the girl in a blubbering mess on the bathroom floor because of him. The whole thing had been horrid, but he had said much worse things to her over their time together. She remembered Mrs. Jones's words and repeated them to herself as she stood being comforted by a kind, generous man, who had a great heart. *I will not let him win.*

As Hannah's tears eventually ran out, she became more aware of the feel of Masuda's arms around her and how safe she felt. He smelled good too. She supposed it wouldn't be fair to make him stand there holding her forever, but it would be lovely. Hannah didn't pull away as she finally spoke, instead, she inched her arms out from being tucked in between them and slowly moved them to around his waist. "Thank you."

"I came out, hoping to catch you before you left."

"You were looking for me?"

"Yes. But now I don't think would be the right time to talk about it."

"Masuda, is there ever a right time?"

"Well," he paused and she felt him gently stroke her hair. "I was going to ask you out again, but after witnessing that, I can see why you wouldn't be ready to trust anyone."

"Mmmm," she couldn't disagree with him.

"Now, I know why Baniti was so reluctant to give me your number in the first place. And why you backed out of the date."

"It is difficult to trust, but I think you should," she spoke cryptically. She pulled her head away from his chest and looked up at him, but made sure to not loosen her arms from around his waist.

A look of confusion crossed Masuda's face. "What or who should I be trusting?"

"I think you should trust your first instinct from earlier today." She squeezed him gently, hoping to make him understand that she was stronger now. He had given her the support and time she needed to gather herself.

Comprehension dawned and a silly, happy face followed. "Hannah?"

"Yes?"

"Would you be interested in going out on a date with me? Very casual, of course."

"Is your favorite animal still the koala?"

"You remembered." His handsome features showed how pleased that made him.

"Yes. I did want to go out with you that day, but I just couldn't. I didn't realize how much damage he had done until I was getting ready that morning. I am sorry if I hurt your feelings."

"Oh, don't be sorry about me. I felt horrible for pushing you when Baniti had warned me."

Hannah smiled warmly at him and finally let go of him. Masuda immediately did what he had promised and removed his arms from around her. She suddenly wanted them back. "Okay, so we are both sorry."

"Would you consider joining me, Bani, and Farida for a visit to the zoo? I hear the Alaskan Otters are wonderful."

Hannah liked the sound of that. It was casual and would give her the chance to learn more about Masuda without the pressure of a real date. "I wonder what Bani's and Farida's favorite animals are?"

# Chapter 15

"Frogs?" Hannah laughed. "Well, that is not one I thought you would say."

Baniti held his hands up to stop all three of them laughing. "Let me state my case."

"Very well."

The four of them stood at the entrance to the Sydney Zoo, Farida and Masuda held visitor maps as they discussed what they would like to see.

Bani began to tick off all the things he loved with his hands. "Did you know that some frogs have no tongues? Each species has a different sounding croak and there are over five thousand species." He paused to wait as if he expected them to be astounded with this. Hannah had to admit that it was an incredible fact. He continued his list ticking. "And my favorite is that some frogs swallow their food using their eyes," Baniti finished triumphantly.

"Ewwww," Farida looked at her fiancé.

"Okay, then what is your favorite?" he challenged her.

"The giraffe," she stated as if it was the most obvious choice in the world. "They have amazing patterns in their fur and look gentle and graceful." She grinned at her fiancé. "And my favorite thing is they have the most gorgeous eyelashes."

"Eyelashes?" he scoffed. "Now I am intrigued and need to get a better look at these eyelashes you speak of."

Hannah watched the easy way the two of them interacted and teased each other. That was what she had hoped for in her marriage, not the belittling nastiness she had received.

Masuda was concentrating on reading the map. "Looks like you are out of luck, Bani. No frogs here. Do you have a second favorite animal?"

"Yes, the penguin."

"You are in luck, they have those."

"Why the penguin?" Hannah wanted to know.

Baniti shrugged and grinned at them all. "Because they are so cute and funny." No one could disagree with that statement. "So, what is your animal of choice?" Baniti asked her.

Masuda interrupted. "Bugger, they don't have them here, but they do have something similar." He looked up at her and smiled. "Asian small-clawed otter is all they have."

Her heart jumped and she shyly smiled back. "That's okay. I love all otters."

"Otters are adorable," Farida chimed in.

Hannah looked at Masuda and gave him an innocent, wide-eyed stare. "And do they have your animal?"

Masuda's hazel eyes returned the stare, with an equally innocent one of his own. He made quite the show of looking at the map. "Yes, they have lions here."

Hannah laughed, "Coward."

"Lions are majestic and live in packs and take care of each other. All very appealing." Masuda made his case for the lion.

"Yes, lions are magnificent creatures, but are they your absolute favorite?" Hannah goaded him. Then instantly felt ill and regretted what she had done. She was nervous that she had pushed him and made him reveal something he truly didn't want to. Would he punish her for that by sulking, or being spiteful? She looked at the map in Farida's hands rather than look at him as she waited for the repercussions of her provoking him into revealing the truth when he had warned her not to.

"What aren't you telling us?" Bani needled his younger cousin.

Masuda laughed. "I may have another animal that I think is awesome."

Bani narrowed his brown eyes at Masuda. "Okay, give up the secret. Obviously Hannah knows and now I want to know."

"Oh, I want to know too," said Farida. "Give it up, Mas."

Masuda folded up the map and put it in his pocket. "I'll make you a deal. We do a lap of the zoo and check out all the animals. My favorite is here and if either of you two guess it by the end, I will buy you both an ice-cream. *But* if you don't guess it, you owe Hannah and I an ice-cream each."

"We will need to consult about this," Baniti declared and pulled Farida aside.

Masuda took Hannah's hand and she waited for him to be angry with her. Instead, he kissed her knuckles and gave them a seductive nip. "You, my dear, are a traitor. Hopefully, the promise of ice-cream will bribe you to stay quiet."

"I do like ice-cream," she admitted. "I might be able to help you out."

He winked at her and released her hand as Baniti and Farida returned. "You have a deal."

"Great. Let's go."

Farida still held her map open. "If we head that way we go to the koalas."

Hannah made sure that she didn't make eye contact with Masuda as they headed toward the koala enclosure. Instead, as they drew closer she linked her arm with Farida's and engaged her in conversation. "You were saying at our last pedicure that your cousin was insisting she be included in the wedding party. Is that still going on or have you managed to resolve it?"

"Baniti came up with a great solution to make her feel included but not put her in the party," Farida beamed at her fiancé.

They stood in front of the enclosure and watched the koala's slumbering in the Eucalyptus trees. There was a handler there, holding one and allowing people to touch the back of the docile animal. As they joined the queue, Hannah watched Masuda grin at her and then resume his interested face in the conversation. "So what idea did Bani come up with?"

"We asked her to help my mum with all the lists and doing table arrangements." Farida turned to Hannah. "My mum has pretty bad arthritis in her hands and struggles to write for any length of time. This way the cousin is helpful and Mum doesn't push herself."

"That is a great idea." Hannah complimented Baniti.

"You all don't need to sound so surprised," he complained as they moved up the line.

Everyone laughed as they took it in turns to touch the soft grey fur on the koala. Hannah smiled to herself as she heard Masuda talk to the koala when it was his turn. "Hey, buddy, how you doing?"

"And how is the dress shopping going? You finally settled whether you are going traditional?" Hannah attempted to keep the distractions going.

"I have decided to disappoint everyone and not have what anyone wants but me. All I can say is it is white with a Cleopatra feel."

Baniti put his arm around Farida and kissed her. "And I don't care what she wears as long as she turns up and marries me. She will look beautiful in anything she chooses."

"Well, that was fun," Masuda announced as he joined the group. "Where to now Map Lady?"

They moved away from the enclosure to allow others to get in to see the animals. "Mmmm... that way." Farida pointed to the right. "And by the way, I love chocolate ice-cream."

"Huh?" Masuda did a double-take, while Hannah had to stop herself from laughing.

"You sure, Honey?" Baniti asked his fiancé.

"Oh, yeah. Did you not see his adorable face?"

"The koala was pretty adorable," agreed Hannah.

"I'm not talking about the koala. I am talking about Mas. He was captivated while he chatted with his *buddy*."

Bani grinned at his cousin. "If Farida is calling it, then I am backing her. Masuda, is your favorite animal the koala?"

Masuda groaned and looked to Hannah with mock anger. "This is all your fault. My reputation will be ruined."

Hannah patted him on the arm with pity. "What reputation? You rescue old ladies and young women. I think your reputation was tarnished a while ago."

"Well, when you put it like that."

"I just have one question."

"What's that?"

"Why the koala?"

HANNAH LOOKED UP FROM the biology book that she was studying as Amy came into the kitchen. "Hey, how was work?"

"Some people are just so rude," Amy sat down at the table and pulled off her shoes and undid her shiny, black hair from the high ponytail she always wore. She yanked the blue top of her chemist assistant uniform over her head, revealing a black tank top.

"What happened?"

"Just some woman who insisted that she get her things as we were closing and took forever, like I spend my life waiting to serve her." Amy blew out her breath, letting her frustration go. "Want a cuppa?" She stood up to fill the kettle up and turn it on.

"Sure, that would be great."

"How was your day at the zoo?"

"Really good." Hannah went back to her studying.

"Seriously? That is all you are giving me?"

Hannah looked up and shrugged. "I don't know what you want me to say. It was fun. Masuda is wonderful, funny, sweet, kind, generous."

Amy took out two mugs and the milk as she waited for the water to boil. "You make it all sound like it is a bad thing."

"I don't know if it is or not," Hannah said. She had sat there staring at the biology book since she had returned from the double date and had battled with the idea of what to do about Masuda. "He is everything I could ever ask for, but am I ready for all of that?"

"All of what? Don't you think you are jumping ahead just a fraction?"

"It is perfectly obvious that he likes me and wants more and it is intoxicating, but that is how I felt about Luke. Today Masuda did and said all the right things, as did Luke when we first went out."

"And you don't think you can trust yourself to make the right decision on this?" Amy guessed as she poured the boiled water into the cups.

"What happens if I am wrong about him?"

"What happens if you are not wrong and he treats you the way you deserve and you end up being blissfully happy for the remainder of your life?" Amy put the tea in front of Hannah and resumed her seat at the kitchen table. "You are never going to date again because the guy might be horrid?"

"I had considered it."

"That is a lonely way to live."

Hannah barked out a laugh. "Ha! Says the hermit who never dates."

Amy poked her tongue out at her best friend. "I don't date because I don't want to, not because I am scared to. When the right guy comes along I will be ready, but I am in no rush for it to happen."

"I am in no hurry either," said Hannah.

"I get that, but when the good guy comes along you shouldn't run in the opposite direction without at least going out on one date with him."

"What happens if I fall for him and he ends up the same as Luke?"

Amy took her hand and looked at her seriously, all flippancy was gone. "That won't happen. Masuda may not be the right guy for you, but he won't be like Luke either. You know what to look for. You know the warning signs better than most women. It won't happen to you because this time I won't stand idly by while you claim that everything is fine. It will never get that far."

Hannah thought about what Amy had just said. *You know she is right. You know the warning signs, the subtle things they start with. The first signs of manipulation. The shock they display when called out on their behavior.* She knew that all of it was true and she knew after seeing Luke in the car park and refusing to accompany him to his brother's wedding and not feeling guilty about it later that she had finally broken free of his grasp. *You are stronger than you think you are.*

"I do like him," admitted Hannah.

Amy let go of Hannah and picked up her mug, taking a sip of her coffee. "If you took your fear out of the equation would you see him again?"

"Yes." Hannah didn't have to think about it. She was attracted to him on every level and spending more time with him was appealing. She had thought about him frequently over the intervening months since the original disastrous near-date. Wondered what he had been doing and anytime he had been mentioned when they had been out for dinner with Baniti and Farida or getting their monthly pedicure with Farida she had stayed quiet, but hopeful that they would speak about him so she could learn more. And since the incident in her work car park, she had thought about him constantly.

"You know one date with the guy is not going to break you? You have done the work with your psychologist. Now it is time you need and self-belief that you are not the things Luke said you were. Masuda can't hurt you like Luke did unless you let him and I can't ever see you letting another man do that to you."

"But... "

"But nothing. You go out and it doesn't work out then you may get hurt, but that is a normal hurt that we all experience, not the pain you were put through to be molded to what he wanted. Don't confuse the two."

Hannah sipped her tea. "When did you get so smart about relationships?"

"I have no clue, but you have to trust me on this one. Just agree to one real date with him."

"If he asks me."

"If he asks you."

Hannah's eyes twinkled at Amy. "He is hot, isn't he?"

"Um, hello. Yes, he is. I don't even know why you are hesitating. Don't you want to see him without a shirt on?"

"Amy, don't say that."

"Why? It's true."

"Because now all I will think about is Masuda without his shirt on."

## Chapter 16

Hannah sat down in the seat that Masuda had pulled out for her. As she sat, she tugged down the short dress Amy had insisted she wear for the occasion. It was her favorite dress and Hannah had been surprised that she could still get it on over her hips now she was eating normally again. She had been amazed by how flattering the dress had become with the curves she now carried. The dress was something she had always felt self-conscious wearing, worrying about if Luke would think it appropriate. Now it was something she didn't have to worry about. It was made from black velvet and had a scalloped, low, round neckline, and no sleeves. When she was standing the dress sat mid-thigh, which was the shortest thing she owned and she had forgotten how much it rode up until she had sat in the front seat of Masuda's truck. She had teamed the dress with black, strappy sandals and had, with Amy's insistence, slathered her body in fake tan, so her naturally pale legs didn't glow in the dark.

They were out for dinner at a tiny, stunning restaurant that sat on an esplanade with other tiny eateries that all had the best view overlooking the beach. Hannah could see an ancient wooden pier, with old fashion lights lighting up a small portion of the inky sea to either side of it. The moon was high and full casting a romantic glow on everything, or that's what she thought in her current mood.

She took the proffered menu while ordering champagne.

"Do you mind sharing food with someone or are you the type to just order your own? Either way is fine with me," asked Masuda.

"I am happy to share if you have something in mind, otherwise I can just order my own."

"I am told the Seafood platter is amazing here, but it is for two."

"I love all seafood, so am happy to have that."

The waiter came over and took their order, while the drinks waiter delivered their drinks. Masuda held up his drink in a toast. Hannah followed suit with her champagne, remembering Baniti doing the same thing the night Luke had left her in his restaurant. "To fresh starts and happy endings."

"Corny, but cute." Hannah clinked her glass against his. As she took a sip she looked out the window, watching the people walk up and down the esplanade and out onto the pier.

"You are very quiet." He moved his chair closer to hers, but not close enough that she would feel crowded. "How do I get to know you if you don't talk to me?"

"Ask me a question then." Hannah looked back at him and waited for a question.

"I don't know which one I want to ask first. I want to know every-thing I can about you."

Hannah felt a little more confident to banter with him now so took a chance and smiled cheekily at him. "Ask me what you ask all your dates that you have been set up with over the past few months."

"You know about those?"

"Yes, I know about every one of them." She didn't admit how much it had twisted her up inside and confused her when she had listened to Farida and Baniti talk about them with Amy.

"My mother has tried to set me up several times with girls with similar ethnicity to me, but I never find common ground with them, especially ones that are only new to Australia. I know they have opinions and wants, but they just don't speak up. I am positive over time that I could get them to trust me but none of them have been interesting enough to wait that long." He stopped talking and smiled politely as the waiter placed their three-tiered tray of seafood in the center of the table.

They both murmured their thank yous as he took his leave. Hannah took a prawn and placed it on her plate and began to eat it, only to receive a look of scorn from Masuda. Her heart started beating faster and her palms went sweaty as she tried to figure out why he had given her such a look. She had not filled her plate up. And then it dawned on her and she tested out her theory. Hannah took up the tongs and took several more items from the piles of food before her. The more she put on her plate the more satisfied Masuda looked. Hannah relaxed as she placed the tongs on the edge of the bottom tray and again picked up her knife and fork. Masuda smiled at her as he took a bite from a crayfish tail.

"Go on with what you were saying," Hannah urged, interested to know what he was looking for in a woman.

"I have been surrounded by Aussie girls who know what they want, as I did all my schooling through the local public school and we arrived when I was just starting school. It must have rubbed off on me because I find Western women appealing. And it turns out I have a thing for redheads. Not too many natural redheads in Egypt."

Hannah blushed as he pretended to leer at her. "Behave," she chided coyly, enjoying the flirtation.

"I like it when you tell me what to do. We shall have to see where that leads one day." He winked at her most charmingly before he sat back in his chair to catch the attention of the waiter as if he hadn't just set her mind racing with pictures of him without his shirt on. *Damn you, Amy.*

He ordered another drink for both of them before he turned to her with a more serious expression across his handsome face. "Do you know what you want, Hannah?" he asked.

For the first time in years, she could answer honestly. "Yes," she reached across the table and took his hand. "There are so many things I want, but let's start here."

THE WAVES WERE SOOTHING as they rolled onto the sandy beach. It was a beautiful night with many people taking the opportunity to walk along the wooden pier after their meal. Masuda offered her his jacket as the night air had cooled and she had left hers in the car. He gently placed it over her shoulders and took her hand in his as they had left the restaurant.

"Would you like to take a walk along the pier?" she asked.

They slowly made their way up to the end and stood, silently watching the sea make its way back to the shore. A lone light gave off a soft glow and Hannah spent the majority of the time pretending to look out at the water when in reality she was admiring the side profile of Masuda. She marveled at how perfectly her hand fit into his.

Once they had returned to the esplanade, Hannah didn't want it to end but was too nervous to speak up. After all, she had already prolonged the date by asking if he wanted to go for a walk. She was surprised at herself for being so clear about how much she had enjoyed herself and wanted to stay here with him.

"Do you need to be home yet?" Masuda asked her.

"No."

"Would you like to sit down with me?"

"Yes. Very much."

They sat down a little distance away from the pier, in a small rotunda with a stunning vista of the water and full moon. He let her hand go to help her put his jacket on properly, rather than be draped over her shoulders. She noted that he didn't retake her hand as they sat there.

"Thank you for dinner, it was delicious." Hannah put her hand over her stomach. "I think I might split my dress when I climb back into the car after all that crayfish."

"You are welcome." He reached over and tucked a stray strand of her red hair back behind her ear.

Hannah wanted him to put his arm around her, but also knew that he probably would have by now if she were anyone else. He was being overly cautious and she appreciated it, but on the other hand, she didn't want to be treated like fragile glass that could easily shatter. They would have to find common ground somehow.

"Can I ask you a question that might make you feel a little uncomfortable?" Masuda intruded on her thoughts.

"Yes." Automatically her shoulders tensed.

"At the zoo, when you teased me and made Bani and Farida aware that I may have misled them regarding my animal, what did you think I was going to do to you?" he asked her. He didn't turn to face her, he kept watching the night sky, giving her space and time to answer the question.

"I didn't know what you would do. We had joked over text, but I had never done it in person." She took his hand and snuggled in closer to his side, resting her head on his shoulder. She thought about it and decided that if this was ever going to work she would need to be honest with Masuda about her feelings so he could understand her reactions and help her move through them. "I was scared and was anticipating some form of negative reaction," she admitted.

"Hannah."

She loved the way he spoke her name. It was like a caress, always soft and tender.

"You need never fear me. I may get angry with you, but never over something so silly, and I will never call you names or make you feel bad about yourself. I will raise my voice at some point when I get frustrated, but it will never be at you, just at the situation. And I expect the same courtesies from you."

Masuda reached across and lifted her chin, while he turned to face her. He gently kissed her on each cheek and the tip of her nose. "I don't want to frighten you by coming on too strong, but I think I have made myself clear in my intentions. I want to cherish you and show you how a real man cares for someone. And I want you to always be honest so we can work through your issues together." He voiced the words she had been thinking. He kissed her forehead. "I did some research and now understand that it may take you a long time to learn to be you again." He kissed the side of her mouth. "I want to help you find you." Masuda kissed the other side of her mouth. "Let me help you."

Hannah looked into his eyes and saw understanding and desire. Her heart sang for the understanding being offered and her groin tightened with the thought of Masuda slowly undressing her and discovering her body. She pushed the momentary appearance of Luke's cruel comments about her being frigid away and tried to stay in the moment. "Kiss me," it came out as a whisper.

She closed her eyes as his lips touched hers. The kiss was full of promise and her body responded. She reached for the front of his shirt and pulled him in closer, while their kiss grew in strength and want. It was the perfect kiss and as they pulled apart she saw that he felt the same way.

He leaned down and nibbled on her earlobe and whispered. "You are impressive."

"I think I'd like you to kiss me again."

"You think?" he joked. "I'm wounded."

"Somehow, I doubt it."

"Well, I did say I would enjoy you telling me what to do, it appears you have taken to the idea quite quickly."

"Would you stop talking?"

"Your wish is my command."

"Masuda," she threatened.

"Hannah." He caressed her face and then did what he was told and kissed her.

## Epilogue

Hannah felt beautiful in her new navy-blue, halter top dress with its collar covered in sparkling silver diamantes. Her hair was now long enough to be swept up in a messy bun and she had allowed Amy to apply her make-up heavier than normal, complete with fake eyelashes. "You are the most gorgeous woman here," Masuda whispered in her ear, before kissing just below her lobe and sending a thrill down her spine.

They moved slowly around the dance floor to the only slow song, aside from the bridal waltz that had been played for the evening. The day had been perfect. The weather was not too hot nor too cold. The venue was divine, an oasis of lush green land filled with trees and flowers in full bloom. A tiny stream ran through the center of the gardens and there were several ornate white bridges that you could use to cross to either side.

The ceremony had been magical and nothing like Hannah had experienced before. Farida had thrown tradition to the wind with her wedding gown and it was spectacular. The dress was white, full length, and had an expansive, rounded collar just like the dresses Cleopatra had worn. The gold and silver sequined collar had a matching wide belt that drew in her pleated, chiffon-layered dress to accentuate her waist. Her long, thick, dark hair had been pulled back into a tight braid that wound its way down her back; gold and silver wire was threaded through the braid. The look was striking.

"Oh, I think Farida has me beat. She is glowing." Hannah looked over to her friend, dancing with her new husband.

Masuda held Hannah a little tighter and lightly pressed his hips against hers. "I promise to make you glow later."

Hannah giggled and kissed him softly on the lips. "I'll hold you to that promise and I might return the favor as I am liking you in that suit."

"Do you think we could leave now then?" Masuda joked.

"Can I interrupt and have this dance?" Baniti and Farida had appeared next to them. Hannah had been so caught up in flirting with Masuda that she hadn't noticed them. She hoped they hadn't heard their banter.

Masuda stepped away from Hannah. "Of course, but only if I can borrow your bride in return?"

"That was the plan," said Farida as she held out her arms to Masuda.

Baniti took Hannah into his arms and spun her around before steering them further onto the dance floor. He was a better dancer than Masuda, who just moved from side to side and occasionally turned around in a circle, but she would never tell either of them that. "Are you enjoying yourself?" Baniti asked her.

"Very much so. I am thrilled that I could celebrate this day with both of you."

They moved past Amy and Baniti's father who were supposed to be dancing but had come to a halt in the middle of the dance floor to discuss the merits of what type of dumplings she would teach him to make next. They were told off by Mrs. Salah, Baniti's mother, who spun by them in a mass of teal satin with magnificently embroidered designs of gold throughout the incredible material. "Dance with the girl instead of arguing with her and she might make you what you want."

Everyone within earshot of the conversation laughed and agreed with the sentiment as they all moved slowly away to the beat of the music.

Hannah cleared her throat and looked at Baniti and marveled again at how different her life was now, after being thrown away in an Egyptian restaurant and how this man's kindness had led to all of this. She willed herself not to cry as she had been thinking about what she wanted to say to him for a while if given the opportunity. "I want to thank you."

"You don't need to thank me for anything."

"But I do. You were generous and compassionate when you had no cause to be and you have welcomed Amy and me into your circle of friends and family."

Baniti smiled at her. "You are both wonderful friends. I am glad I had the chance to meet you and you have been amazing with including Farida, which you didn't have to do. So, it turns out you are just as kind as me."

She felt the tears form. "I am not sure I would have done so well without you that night. You gave me that hint of hope when I thought the world had ended."

"There is always hope."

A tear rolled down her cheek, which she swiped away.

"I do have something to apologize for." Baniti scrunched up his nose at her. "No matter how hard I tried I couldn't keep Masuda away from you."

Hannah couldn't help it she laughed loudly, drawing stares from several wedding guests. The song finished and Masuda came to join them.

"What was so funny?" Masuda started to ask, but he stopped. "What did you do? You made my girl cry." Masuda frowned, only half jesting at the situation as he saw the unshed tears in Hannah's green eyes.

"He didn't make me cry. I made me cry," Hannah attempted to explain.

"Okay." Masuda looked no less confused.

"Don't worry about it. I will explain later." She grabbed his tie and slowly pulled him closer until she was looking up into his perfect hazel eyes. "I do have something to discuss with you though."

"Sure, what is it?"

"What did you mean by *your girl*?"

Masuda kissed her on her forehead and held both her upper arms. "That should be obvious. We have been dating for three months and I think it is clear to everyone here that I am yours for as long as you want me to be."

Hannah tugged on his tie and brought his face closer to her own, his warm breath mingled with hers. There was no fear, no dark voice calling her names or making her doubt her choices as she spoke the words, "Would forever be okay with you?"

"Forever is exactly what I had in mind."

# SAMANTHA

Reflections of Love Novella Collection

Book Two

## TAYA RUNE

# Samantha

### Chapter 1

### Samantha

Samantha stared at the photo frame, a much younger, carefree version of herself smiled back. The image in the frame had long, dark blonde dreadlocks, green eyes, and very little life experience. She wore a white t-shirt with fluorescent green Go-Go written on it and over-sized denim overalls. The image that now reflected in the large mirror—that stood on its stand in the corner of the room—was very different. All grown up and successful. The dreadlocks abandoned when they became an impediment to moving forward in her career. Samantha's hair was still long and dark blonde, but now it came from a bottle to hide the ever-encroaching grey. She still liked to wear over-sized clothing but had swapped the overalls to pretty maxi dresses and brightly colored kaftans. Today, those had been put aside for a more traditional simple black dress and tailored jacket. With the frame still in hand, she sat down on her old teenage bed and looked around her childhood bedroom, surprised that even after thirty years it still felt safe and just like home.

The noise from her father's wake drifted up the stairs and into the attic bedroom. People chatting, dishes clattering, and mobiles ringing with their personalized ring tones all fought for dominance in the silence of her room. Her eyes slowly swept around the bedroom and fell on memories everywhere. Trophies from tennis playing days, pictures of her group of girlfriends that she had shared her firsts with, tubs of cosmetics and nail polishes, all old and cracked. Samantha knew her father had been the one to not allow her mother to clean out her room when Samantha had left to follow her dreams. Though Samantha had been home for visits over the intervening years, she always felt it wasn't necessary to change the room as her father was obviously attached to it, probably far more than she had ever been.

Finally, her eyes came to rest on the large wooden workbench that sat under the huge bay window that she had stared out and day-dreamed from in her entire youth. The wooden workbench was covered in scorch marks and scratches, just like the ones in her workshops in New York and Paris. A pile of old, well-loved tools sat in a cluttered heap in the corner of the bench, as if she had only used them yesterday instead of thirty years ago.

Her open suitcase sat on the end of the bed. Her current tools—just as well-loved as the ones on the workbench lay—still wrapped in the center of the case, having been protected by a layer of clothes surrounding it. Samantha traveled everywhere with a basic tool set and sketch pad, as she never knew when an idea would strike.

She was exhausted but knew that even if there were no wake going on downstairs there would be no way she could sleep. Jet lag killed her. No matter how long she had been traveling the globe, her body somehow never adjusted to it. It was her own personal kryptonite.

A photo of her father and herself standing at the peak of one of the nearby mountains caught her attention amongst the other photos pinned to the photo board. She would have been no more than ten, but still remembered the day clearly. They had packed their lunch and left early to avoid the crowds and heat. Her parents had always been hikers and introduced Samantha to it early, slowly building up her stamina and strength. That day had been the culmination of years of training and she had finally reached the summit. It was a day to celebrate and the photo would now return to New York with her.

Samantha put the photo she was holding back on her bedside table and tried to relax her shoulders. It had been a chaotic few days and everything had not been processed. It still felt like her father was going to walk through her door at any moment and ask her if she was ready to go. She had been prepared for this moment a long time, but now it was here she found she was not ready at all. He had been diagnosed with cancer years prior and told he had no more than a few years to live. Yet, not only did he live, he had thrived; throwing all the doctors' predictions away and taking each day as a gift. After the initial shock—with Samantha returning from Paris, where she had been working, while living in Sydney—he underwent his first rounds of chemo. After that, they settled into a pattern of her returning twice a year when her business brought her closer to Australia or Australia itself. He had looked great and still healthy the last time she had been to visit—just four months ago—but cancer does that sometimes. One minute you are well, amazing the doctors with your resilience, and the next minute the fight is lost and it is time to go.

The phone call had come in the early hours of the morning while she was in a small village in the middle of Chile, on a research holiday. It had been difficult to find flights to get home to Australia on such short notice from the remote location. It had taken four flights of ever-increasing size of plane and distance traveled before she had returned to Sydney airport, to then face the drive out to the Blue Mountains. At one point, she wasn't sure if she would make the funeral.

The service had been held in her father's favorite gardens rather than a church, and the celebrant was an old family friend who had cried with the rest of them as they celebrated his life, while saying goodbye. Her father had come from Irish stock so the wake was expected to be rousing and long-lasting, and the tight-knit community was doing their best to honor that. They were heading into their fifth hour, which was why Samantha had decided to come up to her bedroom for a little respite before going back to help her mother.

A cough interrupted her thoughts. Samantha turned to find the last person she would have expected to be standing in her house. Three decades after she had walked out of his life, her stomach filled with butterflies and her heart quickened. Andrew was still able to take her breath away.

"I thought I might find you here."

His voice brought back memories.

## Chapter 2

### Samantha

Sam checked her reflection in the rearview mirror to make certain all the sunscreen had been rubbed into her high forehead and straight nose. She pulled on her well-worn baseball cap and adjusted the long ponytail to fit more comfortably. With practiced efficiency she checked her backpack for her full water flask, first aid kit, light-weight windbreaker, a small tube of sunscreen, a few protein bars, and most importantly, a compass.

Slamming the old car door hard to make certain it closed, she made her way to the group gathering in front of the policeman. She stood slightly to one side of the crowd and waited for the chattering volunteers to settle.

"Hi," a deep male voice spoke beside her.

She turned to her right to find a broad expanse of muscular shoulders at her eye level. "Hi," she responded as her head moved upwards to take in a friendly smile, dimpled chin, and shaggy hair that reminded her of Jon Bon Jovi.

"I'm Andy."

"Samantha."

"Excuse me, can I have everyone's attention please?" the officer called through his megaphone. The crowd instantly quietened and gave him their full attention.

"Firstly, I want to take this opportunity to thank all of you for coming out and volunteering your time. The parents are extremely grateful and we are hoping with so many experienced locals on board we can find the missing boy quickly. However, for the search to go smoothly we need everyone to be honest about their abilities and knowledge of the area.

"We are searching for a nine-year-old boy, dark hair, thin build, about 136cm tall. He is wearing white Volley sneakers, red board shorts, and a white Duran Duran t-shirt. His name is Steven, but he will also answer to Stevie.

"He has been missing for about four hours since wandering off from his parents as they were walking one of the trails. He is not a local and has no experience, so we can't be certain if he will remain in one place or keep walking to try to find his way out.

"Now, I want you to report to this officer, who will take your name and experience level and put you into groups."

Samantha was always surprised at how swiftly these things could be organized when needed. This would be the third search she had participated in over the years. Without fuss, everyone was allotted a group leader and section to search and were sent on their ways. She was put in charge of a quadrant and six people because she was a local and had been hiking the harder tails alone for the last several years.

As she waited for her fellow searchers to gather around she was silently thrilled to have Andy join her group.

"Hi, again," he greeted her.

She smiled before turning to welcome the whole group and quickly read out the instructions she had been handed. It turned out they had a fifteen minute walk before they reached their assigned area. Several of the group took out Walkmans and put on headphones, while one man seemed to not want to chat and moved to the back of the group, leaving Sam and Andy to talk.

"So, how old are you?" Andy opened the conversation.

"Twenty."

Andy whistled, "And they put you in charge of one of the harder tracks."

Samantha shrugged. She wasn't certain if he was being deliberately insulting, misogynistic, or just trying to make conversation and was really bad at it.

They walked in awkward silence for several minutes before she decided to rescue him. "How old are you?"

"Twenty-three."

"Is this your first time visiting the Blue Mountains?"

"How do you know I am not a local?"

"Because I have never seen you before and I have lived here my whole life." Sam didn't add that if she had seen him before she would have remembered him.

"Yes, I have been here for about three weeks. It's an incredible place filled with beautiful things."

She ignored his clumsy flattery. "What do you do?"

"I have just finished a Bachelor in Environmental Science and I've been studying Chinese at night school so I can be a tour guide," he explained enthusiastically.

Samantha was impressed. "That is terrific. Where are you planning to work?"

"I am thinking around here, I see a lot of potential." He smiled at her and her heart fluttered just a little. "Do you think after we have found Steve that you would have dinner with me? I'd like to run some ideas by someone with local knowledge," his voice had turned serious.

Sam resisted the urge to straighten her top or tidy her hair. She hadn't been on a date in six months and the thought sent her into a mild panic. She had been spending all of her spare time at her workbench, perfecting her skills as a jeweler and working on new designs. "I'd like that."

They spent the next several hours slowly and meticulously searching their section of trail and the surrounding bushland for Steven. The sun grew hotter as the late afternoon cleared the blue sky of all clouds, and Sam made certain that everyone had water and they stopped to rest under the shade of the ginormous Mountain Blue gum trees frequently. The protein bars she had brought with her went to her, the man who was still keeping very much to himself, and the final one to Andy. It was just after five when word reached them, via the walkie talkie she had been issued, that Steven had been found. Andy had scooped Sam up into a celebratory hug and she had revelled in his strong arms. She was certainly looking forward to their dinner plans and what might happen later. His strength was definitely a turn on.

# Chapter 3

## Andy

It was a perfect day and he felt jubilant as he held open the door for Sam. They had spent the day going from hotel to hotel in the Blue Mountains area. Handing out his newly created brochures that were the culmination of a year of hard work. The summer tourist season was about to begin, and hopefully he would start to see bookings from the pamphlets—explaining his different tour options—through the booking desks at the larger hotels.

"Thanks for helping me out today." He gave Sam a quick peck on the lips, knowing that if he gave her a softer kiss he would want to take her back to his place rather than go onto the last hotel on their list.

"It's been great. I am so happy for you." She returned his kiss and walked around to the passenger side of his truck. "You have worked so hard for this."

Sam happily ticked another name off their list and announced their final destination. She wound her window down and let the cool mountain air fill the cabin and her lungs.

Andy watched her for a moment, mesmerized by her beauty, and even after a year still wondering how he got lucky enough that she chose to be with him. He pulled out of the gravel car park and out onto the winding road that ran through this section of the mountains. Dappled sunlight broke through in places and he loved the feeling of peace that driving through this area always brought him.

It didn't take long for them to arrive at the last hotel. A huge, swanky building with a broad driveway, plenty of parking, and a huge open lawn area—where children were running and laughing, getting out their energy while their parents checked in or out of the hotel. Andy gathered up the last of the brightly printed brochures and smiled at Sam. "Wish me luck." She walked him to the front door and held the door open for him as his hands were full.

"You don't need it, but good luck."

He watched her look around the crowded reception area. "You want to wait outside? Doesn't seem anywhere for you to sit."

"Great idea. I have my sketch pad in the truck, I'll grab that and see if inspiration comes." She dug the keys out of his back pocket and gave his ass a sneaky pinch while she was at it.

"Hey, no fair. I got my hands full."

"Really? I didn't notice." Her gorgeous green eyes were full of false innocence. "Love you." She smiled and breezed back out the door.

Andy walked into the noisy lobby and brought his thoughts back to what he was doing there. He had been rehearsing the speech for so long he no longer got nervous, he just needed to get the first line out. As he approached the reception desk he was stopped by a voice, "Andy?"

He turned to find a striking brunette with a hint too much exposed flesh for the uniform she wore. Jennifer was a friend of Samantha's, through playing tennis, and they quite often crossed paths at parties and dinners out. "Hey, Jenny. I didn't know you worked here."

"Just got my hospitality certificate. I am learning the front desk at the moment, been here about a month. What are you doing here?"

Andy held up the brochures. "I was hoping to speak to whoever is in charge of the tour desk. I am up and running and wanted to put my pamphlets here and run a few offers I have at the moment and incentives for the tour desks that give me great business." He gave her his most charming smile. "Could you help me out?"

"Sure thing, come this way. Troy is great and free at the moment to chat, by the looks of it." Jenny walked him over to a large, dark wood desk, that had three phones, a booking duplicate form, a credit card swipe machine, a large yearly dairy, and a monthly diary. "Troy, this is my friend Andy, he wants to talk to you about a few things, have you got time?"

Andy watched with appreciation as Jenny leaned over the desk, exposing her breasts a little more for Troy's benefit. Sam would never have done that, she didn't flirt with anyone but him. She was a different type of girl.

Troy stood and held his hand out to Andy. "Hi, I've got time now if you want to sit down?"

"Thanks, Troy." Jenny straightened up and smiled at both of them. "Good luck, Andy. Say hey to Sam for me."

The meeting went smoothly and by the end, Troy had readily agreed to promote Andy's tour company, and if he booked enough tours the perks Andy was offering were enticing enough. Andy left the meeting feeling like he was starting to get somewhere. He had spent the past year learning as much as he could about the area and what was available and finding a niche that no one was offering at the time. Having Sam with him, who was a local and expert hiker helped immensely, and they had created a wonderful, new product for the tourists.

He walked over to his truck to see if she was near it, but as he approached he spotted her sitting on a bench, head down, her blonde hair—now dread-locked—shielding her beautiful face. He knew her face so well and knew she would have a crease between her brows and her bottom lip caught between her teeth as she concentrated on letting the idea escape from her mind and onto the paper, where it would sit until she got home and created a unique piece of jewelry. Her creativity was something he greatly admired, having very little himself, but it came with a drive that almost obliterated all other thought, and sometimes he had to reign in his wants as she became lost in her ideas.

Andy was driven too, but not to the same extent. He wanted to build a company that would do well and afford him the luxuries to help him raise a family as he saw fit, but never at the expense of everything else. He strived for balance while it appeared that Sam strived for perfection.

"Hey, babe." He sat down next to her.

"Hey, how did it go?" She didn't look up, instead she added a few more strokes with her charcoal pencil before closing her sketch pad.

"Just as great as the others. Did you know Jenny worked here?"

"I had heard about that but must have forgotten. You obviously saw her."

"Yeah, she introduced me to the Tour Desk Manager."

"That was good of her."

Andy watched as children played around them, laughing and occasionally yelling as a sibling didn't play fair. A couple intervened and began to play catch with the kids. "That will be us one day." He couldn't help it. The words tumbled out of his mouth before he had a chance to think it through. Usually, a comment like that elicited an exasperated sigh from Sam and a reminder that he knew she didn't want to have children. This time, nothing. He looked over to find her lost in thought with her holding a fern leaf out to catch the sunlight. "Babe?"

"Mhmm?" She wasn't listening to him.

"Love you."

Sam looked away from the leaf and snuggled into his side as he lifted his arm around her. "I love you, Andy."

## Chapter 4

### Samantha

No, no, no, Samantha wailed in her head as she watched Andy take a small velvet box from the picnic basket and kneel on one knee. Her suspicions had been growing all afternoon as he had brought champagne rather than his usual beer, and taken more time with his appearance. They had chatted about nothing of consequence and she had watched him watch young families with a wistful expression. Alarm bells started to ring as he began to tell her just how much he cared for her and how he was thankful every day she had seen through his poor attempts at flirtation at their first meeting and had agreed to have dinner with him. She quickly looked around to see if there was anyone within hearing distance. Thankfully, everyone was engaged in their own day and taking no notice of the young couple under the large gum tree.

She felt her panic grow and the heat rise in her face as she floundered for the right words. She closed her eyes against his love-filled deep blue eyes and tried to figure out what to do. She yearned to say yes, every fiber of her being was connected to him but knew that in the end that would be the wrong choice for her. Instead, she opened her eyes and just stared at him.

"Will you marry me?" Andy repeated the question.

"No," she whispered, "I can't." Samantha was relieved he had chosen a park rather than a crowded restaurant so there were no witnesses for the conversation they were about to have.

Andy's face paled and his lips thinned as they always did when he tried to stop a quick, usually hurtful, retort from slipping out. "Why?"

Sam moved onto her knees and leaned forward, closing her hands over the box that held an elegant solitaire cut diamond in a yellow-gold setting. She softly closed the box that was still in his hands, and gently kissed him. "I love you. God, I love you, but you have always known my plans." She sat back on her heels. "I'm twenty-two. I want to travel. I want to learn from the best in Europe and the States." She stopped and took a deep breath. "You want to stay here and grow your touring company."

He watched her, his eyes begging her to change her mind.

She went on. "And I don't want children, and you do."

"But I love you." He put the ring box down and took her hands. "I am certain that you will want them when you are older. So many women change their mind."

She held onto his strong hands, knowing that this would be the final time she could do it. "What happens if I don't change my mind? Should I bring children into this world and all the responsibility of being a great parent just to make you happy?" He frowned at her. "Or maybe you shouldn't have them to make me happy?"

She couldn't stop the tears that leaked from her green eyes. She knew this had been coming. The relationship had to end, but she had been avoiding it as she loved him deeply and completely. "It's impossible. Both of us want to do great things, but one requires me to give up my dreams to keep you, and the other means you have to give up your dreams to be with me."

They sat there, both lost in their personal misery. His eyes glittered with unshed tears.

"I love you, Samantha. I don't want you to leave. Stay with me, create a beautiful family here in these gorgeous mountains. Can't you study here? Your jewelry already sells well, isn't that enough?"

Sam removed her hands, stung that he would ask her to give up all her dreams while he offered to compromise nothing. She felt her temper rise. "You haven't heard me at all these past two years. I don't want children," she said forcefully.

"I heard you, I just assumed you meant you didn't want children until you were older. I am willing to wait." He tried to retake her hands.

"And all my talk of traveling and living overseas and working for some of the big names was also just talk?" She gritted her teeth in an effort not to raise her voice. Sam was astounded that they were even having this conversation. She had been open from the beginning about her career plans and her ideas of not wanting children to tie her down. He always acted like he had heard and understood. It had always been assumed, on her behalf, that while he continued to grow his business here she would embark on her training overseas. Now she realized he had simply thought she would change her mind because she was young and loved him. Did he know her at all?

"You are twisting my words."

"No, I think I am hearing you just fine. You want me to marry you and give up on all my life goals and settle down here, without ever going anywhere and have children I don't want, because it will make you happy." Her voice had grown cold and she stood as she spoke. Her self-preservation had kicked in.

"This is all getting mixed up. I think I said everything wrong." He scrambled to his feet.

"Nope, I am fairly certain you have said exactly what you meant. Can you please take me home now?" Sam swallowed her tears of pain and anger at his arrogance and stalked over to his car.

Without asking for help, he gathered up the remnants of the picnic and put the velvet box in the basket. Stowing the basket in the back seat, he didn't say anything as he started the engine.

The trip home was agonizingly slow as she tried not to look at him. Her anger was dissipating rapidly and she knew that once they reached her house she would have to say goodbye to him forever. It had been a beautiful two years, but it was over and the only thing that lay ahead was heartbreak.

## Andy

THE HOUSE WAS A mess. Every room that Andy walked into was filled with party paraphernalia. Balloons in a multitude of colors hovered off the floor, their colorful ribbons trailed behind like sad, tired tails. Plastic glasses, empty or still half full of punch, were crowded on many surfaces. Food bowls with crumbs in the bottom sat piled next to the sink in an attempt from someone to help clean up, and a few jackets were strewn around the place as people had left them behind the night before. From what he remembered of the night before, it had been a successful New Year's Eve party.

"Good morning," a female voice called from the front door as he heard it open and close.

"In the kitchen," he answered the voice. Andy only then realized he had pulled on a pair of shorts—when he had finally stumbled out of bed—but nothing else. He was just heading into his bedroom as Jenny entered the kitchen area. "Just getting dressed, I'll be right out," he said as he closed the door.

"Don't get dressed on my account," she joked through the door.

He could hear her in the kitchen, she was filling the sink up with water. Jenny had been amazing since Samantha had left ten months ago. At first, everyone had rallied around him, though he had told no one that she had turned down his proposal, only that they had broken up. But time had moved on and people went back to their concerns and Andy had felt more isolated and alone. Jenny had made certain he was invited to parties and outings with their friends. Friends that had originally been Sam's, but now that she was gone they still included him, thanks in part to Jenny.

He grabbed a tank top and pulled it on, quickly brushed his teeth and hair before coming back out to find Jenny emptying drinks down the second sink. "You don't need to do that."

"Oh, I don't mind. I helped make the mess, after all, the party was technically my idea."

Andy grabbed a garbage bag and began filling it with empty glasses, napkins, the dregs of food from the bowls, and assorted streamers. He carried a pair of scissors so he could pop the balloons as they floated into his path. "Did you have a good night?"

"Yes, you were the perfect host. I think your party will be the talk of the town for a few months. People are already hoping you are planning another one next year."

"Ughh, the pressure," he groaned good-naturedly.

"Put a record on. I find music helps cleaning go quicker."

"Sure, any preferences?"

"No, just something upbeat."

Andy pulled out one of the compilation albums he owned and put it on the turntable. By the time both sides of the record had played the cleaning was complete. He had enjoyed listening to Jenny sing as she cleaned the kitchen, washed dishes, and swept the floor. She was a woman who wore her sexuality for the world to admire and she pranced around the kitchen to the Go-Go's in her crop top and denim shorts, exposing her perfectly tanned and toned stomach.

"Thank you so much for helping," Andy clinked his coke glass against hers as they both stood on his decking area, overlooking a small brook that ran through the back of his property.

"Any time."

"Did you get a midnight kiss last night? I was so busy shaking hands and kissing cheeks as the host that I didn't get to say Happy New Year to you."

"No, no kiss last night. I have been hoping that a guy I am interested in would find me, but he is a little slow at getting the hint. I may have to work harder and make him understand I am interested in being more than a friend."

"Some men can be a little slow," Andy admitted.

"Especially you," Jenny put her glass on the outdoor table and then reached for his.

"Me?"

"Yes, you."

It took Andy's brain a few minutes to catch up with Jenny. He watched as Jenny placed his glass next to hers and moved to stand exceptionally close to face him. She looked up into his face and he noticed for the first time how pretty her eyes were. Soft cornflower blue, but there were no innocent looks there, rather a woman who knew what she wanted and how to get it.

"Happy New Year, Andy. I hope this year brings you all you desire," it was a clear invitation.

He responded by instinct, lowering his lips to hers. He moved his hand up into her auburn hair and brought his other arm around her waist, pulling her into him. His mind told him that this was not Sam, but his want over-rode it and he deepened the kiss.

*She is not Sam.*

*No, Sam didn't want you, remember?*

*But I still love Sam.*

*Time to move on, buddy. Jenny is hot, here, and fun.*

*I am not sure this is a good idea.*

*Just go with it, it's not like you are going to marry her. She is just saying that she likes you.*

As Andy argued with himself, Jenny had inched her hands under his tank top, now she drew her nails slowly down his back. Her hands came to rest on his ass and she pulled him toward her. She finished the kiss and took a step back, a glint of mischief in her light blue eyes. Andy licked his lips but remained silent as he watched her slowly pull her crop top up over her head to reveal a lacy black bra. Without pausing, she then undid her denim shorts and inched them over her hips to reveal matching lace panties. By the looks of it, Jenny had come prepared to seduce him, and she was doing a marvelous job so far.

Andy pulled his own top off and discarded his shorts with less flair than she had. "Happy New Year, Jenny," his voice had grown husky.

"Oh, I think it is going to be an amazing year." Jenny's grin was wicked.

## Chapter 5

## Samantha

The exquisite tiara glinted in the darkened room of the Tower of London. Its superbly crafted diamonds and drop pearls were known to be Diana's, Princess of Wales, favorite. Samantha walked around the large glass case that showed off the magnificent piece and imagined the hours it had taken to craft such a masterpiece. She took notes and ignored the curious glances of a couple, who watched her as she bent to get a view of the back. As she studied the tiara, she also acknowledged that sadly, Diana would probably never have the opportunity to wear it again as only weeks prior the palace had announced that the Princess and Prince Charles had separated. No one had been surprised, but many had been saddened. Coming from Australia, Samantha had had no concept of how loved the royals were, especially Diana, until she arrived in London two months ago.

A bell dinged, followed by an announcement that the exhibit of the Crown Jewels would be closing for the day in fifteen minutes and to please start making your way to the exit. Samantha quickly finished her note-taking and made her way with the small crowd to the exit and out onto the bustling streets of London. The weather was growing colder as winter rapidly approached, and she knew it would be time to get her parents to send over her cold climate clothing. She had not needed in the past three years as she had been living in Italy. Though the weather had been cold, it had never been brittle and brutal like the winter she could feel coming.

Samantha stopped at her favorite fish and chip shop after getting off at the South Kensington tube station, on her way home to her tiny apartment near her school, the Royal College of Arts. She tore open the top of the wrapped food and burnt her mouth as she popped a salty chip in. She knew it would happen, but couldn't help herself. Salty hot chips were divine.

Her phone began to ring as she put her key in the door, juggling her package of fish and chips, handbag, and sketch pad. Just as she got inside her phone stopped. Samantha's answering machine kicked in and soon her voice announced who they had rung and that she would call them back. "Sam? Are you there?" her mother's voice filled the tiny apartment and Sam quickly grabbed the phone off its cradle and through a mouthful of chips answered, while turning the machine off.

"Oh, Sammy, it's so good to hear your voice."

Sam dumped her bag and pad on the bed and sat on the side, using her bedside table as a table for her fish and chips. "Mum, how are you?"

There was a delay and Sam took advantage of it to rip open the paper to reveal the delicious golden, crispy fish inside.

"Everyone is well here. I tried to clean out your bedroom a little, but your father insisted I leave it as is. What have you been up to? How did you leave things with Antony? Have you settled well into London?"

Antony was a guy Samantha had been seeing the last six months she had been in Italy. The grandson of the man who had given her her first chance and the equivalent of an apprenticeship. It had been a huge learning curve to be away from home for the first time, and to learn a new language and a new skill set. Not only had she honed her crafting skills, but he had also taught her much about stones—precious, and semi-precious. After three years, he had one day announced he could no longer teach her anything more and that she needed to develop her sketching skills further and had recommended a short year course at the Royal College of Arts in London to round out her skill set. Not having had her grandparents around her growing up, Samantha had cherished the old man and was sad to have to say goodbye.

"Tony and I ended on better terms than Andy and I did." It still hurt to think about Andy and the profound heartbreak she had felt after saying no to his proposal. "Tony always knew I wasn't going to stay and he listened." Sam shrugged to herself. "It was a much lighter relationship, I never loved him." Sam wanted to change the subject. "Is there anything exciting going on back home?"

"Um, nothing too interesting," her mother answered vaguely.

"Mum?" Sam finished off her fish and starting picking at her last few chips.

"I am not sure if it is something you want to know…"

Her mother trailed off and with the delay over the phone line, it felt like forever. "It's about Andy, isn't it?"

"Yes."

Sam sat still for a moment and stared at the hideous fleur de lis style wallpaper and tried to decide if she wanted to know or not. In the end, she figured it was probably best to know rather than let her imagination run wild once she got off the phone with her mother. "Okay, tell me. I am a big girl. I can handle it."

"Andy is getting married next weekend. I only just found out myself." Her mother hesitated for a moment. "I am sorry, Sammy."

"Don't be sorry, Mum, I am the one that made the decision." Sam hated herself for asking, but she needed to know. "Do you know who he is marrying?"

The delay stretched her mother's pause and made Sam feel like she was bracing for the worst.

"Jenny. Your friend from tennis and school."

A few unkind thoughts floated through Sam's head, though she didn't voice them to her mum. "She will make a beautiful bride. I hope she gives him everything he wants." Sam attempted to sound gracious.

It must have been enough to fool her mother. "That is very kind of you. I will pass on your best wishes if I run into him." Sam could hear some mumbling in the background and assumed it was her father. "Sammy, I have to go. Dad says I have been on the phone long enough." Her mother's voice broke as it always did when it was time to say goodbye.

"I miss you, Mum. Tell Dad I miss and love him too."

"I will talk to you in a few weeks, hopefully, you will have good news about a job by then."

"Okay, bye, Mum." Sam hung up the phone and the tears she had been holding back began to fall. Sam blamed it on missing her parents and being homesick as she settled into a new country, but deep in her heart, she knew it was for another reason.

### Andy

THE EMERALD GREEN POCKET kerchief would not sit straight, regardless of how many times he adjusted it. His hands fumbled as he tried to get it to sit like anything other than a limp lettuce leaf. "Here, let me," Jenny's brother, Michael, told him.

Michael had the same auburn toned hair as his sister, and wore his hair long and blow waved like a Rock Star from the band Van Halen. He and the other two groomsmen, Geoff from Andy's high school years, and Russell, who was his first employee four years ago, wore black tuxedos, brocaded vests, and emerald cravats that matched the offending pocket kerchiefs. Andy wore the same, except he wore tails instead of the tux jacket. Thankfully it was a cool spring day in the Blue Mountains and he and the groomsmen would not overheat in the full three-piece suits.

The kerchief issue was rectified and suddenly Andy felt overwhelmed. There was nothing left to worry about. Everything had been organized with very little input from him as Jenny had a clear vision in her head of what her perfect wedding would look like, and he was far more interested in the being married and having children part than the wedding. As the men joked around, Andy's mother and father walked in and everyone instantly settled down. "Would you fine gentlemen escort me downstairs, please? John would like a word with Andrew before we begin."

The three groomsmen responded immediately with formal bows and began to squabble over who would do the official escorting. Judith, Andy's mum, solved the problem by taking Geoff's proffered arm and she ordered Russell to get the door while Michael was to bring her a glass of champagne. The room became quiet as the door closed and it was just Andy and his father, John, left. John raised his beer glass and Andy picked up his water and they clinked glasses. "To your happiness," John toasted.

"Thanks, Dad."

John moved to the third-floor window and looked out, Andy came to stand beside him. Below were the wedding guests, all chatting and sipping flutes of champagne as they milled around the rows of white folding chairs that stood at the ready on either side of an aisle created out of colored petals. At the end of the aisle stood an arch with soft colored flowers entwined around the white painted wood. A photographer mingled with the guests, taking snapshots as he waited for the main event. Everything appeared to be just how Jenny had planned it. Judith appeared below, still escorted by Geoff, and guests took that as a sign that they needed to begin to find seats.

"I am going to say this and I want you to not overreact but to think about it for a moment before you answer. Can you do that for me?" John looked at Andy, his expression grave. Making his already wrinkled face worse.

Andy nodded. "Okay."

"I know that everyone is here and this is a huge day. Something you have always wanted." He smiled fondly at his son. "But if something doesn't feel right or if you don't want to go through with it then just don't. Your mother can handle the guests and you and I can just leave."

"You're serious?" Andy blinked rapidly, trying to digest what his father had offered. "You don't think I should marry Jenny?"

"I didn't say that. It is not my place to say who you should or should not marry, I need you to know if you are having second thoughts, don't go through with it and your mother and I will deal with the immediate fallout."

Andy looked out the window. Everyone was seated and the groomsmen were standing near the arch, next to the celebrant. Usually the bride held everyone up, but this time it was the groom. *Do I have doubts?* he asked himself. *Hell yeah, you do. One person for the rest of your life is a big ask. Is it enough to make you not want to marry Jen?* His first instinct was no; he wanted to marry Jen. He loved her, she made him happy and they had a great time together. They both wanted a family and shared dreams of building a house overlooking the sunsets of the area and raising the kids in the beautiful countryside that was the Blue Mountains. His second instinct gave him pause for a second as a face with long blonde hair and wide lips that always smiled at him in a way that made him want to hold her forever came into view. Samantha. She would have made a beautiful bride. Andy shunted the image away. *Sam didn't want to marry you, Jenny does. Stop being an idiot and marry the girl.*

"Thanks, Dad, for the offer of helping me with an escape if needed, but I am good. I want to marry Jenny."

"That's what I was hoping to hear, but needed to make it clear that there was no pressure to go through with it." John hugged him, a rare occurrence. "Let's go get you married before she changes her mind."

In all his thoughts, that was one Andy hadn't considered. "Best I do not keep her waiting any longer then."

It didn't take long to reach the gathered guests and take his place at the front. Within moments the opening chords of *If You Asked Me To* by Celine Dion began and all the guests stood and turned to face the first bridesmaid as she walked down the aisle of petals. In quick succession, the other two followed before Jenny and her father appeared.

Jenny was a vision of white satin puffiness and lace. A creation to rival any gown seen on the current soapies, such as Days of Our

Lives or General Hospital. As she appeared to float toward him, Andy smiled and any uncertainties vanished as he looked at the woman he would spend the rest of his life with.

## Chapter 6

### Samantha

It doesn't matter how often you wear high heels, they kill your feet. The balls of your feet burn and your toes begin to curl in on themselves. And if you are unlucky, your lower back will also begin to ache. Samantha was grateful to get into her hotel room and remove the offending gold shoes, flinging them into a corner in an act of defiance. She flopped down on the couch and laid her head back, looking up at the fancy ceiling, still a little in awe of the evening she had just experienced. Her head had stopped buzzing from the small amount of cocaine she had done earlier that night and she felt better for it. Sam wasn't sure that the music industry was quite her scene.

Her boyfriend, BT, flopped down next to her and held out a wrist. "Can you give me a hand? These cufflinks are great, but I can't get out of them."

Sam had designed the cufflinks on a whim several years prior as she created her first design range for a small fashion house. They had been the biggest selling item and had set her on a path for designing men's jewelry, something she hadn't thought about as an option up until that point. Over the next few years, she had then created exclusive men's ranges for some of the fashion industry's biggest male lines, including Hugo Boss and Armani. Sam had met BT as she was leaving a meeting and he was coming in for a fitting. She was instantly attracted to him. He was twenty-nine, only a year younger than her, and a talented musician, who had just hit the big time. Her heart had thudded in her chest so loudly that she thought everyone in the shop had heard it.

Six months later and she found herself sitting in an extravagantly expensive hotel room, paid for by BT's record label, exhausted after attending the Grammys and an after-party that felt like it would last an eternity. She helped him out of the cufflinks and undid the buttons on his shirt cuffs for good measure before grabbing the remote and clicking on the TV. He quickly divested himself of his shirt and sat on the couch next to her with just his trousers on. They looked quite the pair. Sam barefooted, but still wearing a gold, skin-tight dress, hair swept up to reveal huge gold earrings that twisted in intricate patterns. BT shirtless, tiger tattoo on his chest revealed but he still had on his black leather pants and socks and shoes.

"I am starving," he announced. "Do you want anything?"

"It's five in the morning, they will be making breakfast. I don't know if the kitchen will be open."

BT looked at her, his glassy, bloodshot eyes showing how silly he thought she was sometimes. "They will make you whatever I want."

"I don't want to be a pain," Sam insisted.

"What do you want to eat?" he moved closer to her and kissed her shoulder.

"I want a cheeseburger."

"I think I have changed my mind." BT nibbled her ear. "I think I am hungry for something else."

"I have a plan." Sam moved to kneel in between his legs. "You order the food and then we can get busy while we wait."

"You are so clever sometimes."

BT dialed room service and placed their order, while Sam began to unlace his shoes. The TV droned on in the background, the beginning of a morning show announcing that they had all the highlights from last night's Grammys caught her attention. She finished taking off his shoes and socks as he got off the phone. The morning show came back from their ad break and began their segment about the Grammys, they began with the red carpet. Sam moved back up onto the couch, she wanted to see this.

"Hey," protested BT.

"In a minute, I want to watch this." She waved him away with her hands.

BT stuck out his adorable bottom lip and pouted. He stood up and put his hand in his pants' pocket and pulled out a small bag of white powder. Sam chose not to say anything as she watched the beautiful people being interviewed on the TV, the same people she had mixed with the night before. BT proceeded to line up several small rows of snow with a coaster.

"You want some?" He held out a tiny silver straw he carried for such occasions.

Sam began to decline when BT and herself appeared on the TV. "Look, it's us." Sam found the remote and turned up the volume. BT was talking about his upcoming, much anticipated first album as his first two singles had hit number one within a week of release. The camera moved in for a close up of his face, and Sam appreciated just how hot the man sniffing cocaine on the coffee table in front of her was, though she doubted the parents of all the teen girls would agree.

She watched as BT put his arm around her on the screen and waited for the TV to move onto another star, but instead the interview continued. Sam held her breath, hoping that the next section would be played out. She watched with growing wonder as BT introduced her to the interviewer, and in essence the world, as his girlfriend. And when asked how they met, explained that she was a jewelry designer. The interviewer had gone on to ask Sam about the earrings she was wearing and the camera had moved in to a close up of her face. The TV went back to the morning studio presenter and the lady commented on how gorgeous those earrings were and that they would be back after a short break with all the winners of the night.

It was difficult to decide what to do first. Jump up and down, ring her Mum and Dad, squeal with delight, or a combination of all three. She turned to celebrate with BT but he now lay on the couch, with his eyes closed. He was either out of it or asleep, but either way, he was in no condition to share in her moment. The hotel phone rang and she checked the time, it was five-thirty in the morning. It was probably room service regarding their food. She picked up the phone. "Hello?"

"Hello, this is Randall Matting, could I please speak to Samantha Rawn?" A deep voice with a strong Southern drawl spoke.

"This is she."

"I represent Sascha Peak."

"The actress?" Sam clarified.

"Yes, Ma'am. I apologize for the early morning phone call, but she was up getting her make-up done and saw your walk on the red carpet. Things move quickly and she didn't want anyone else snapping you up first." Randall went on.

"Ah, okay. Snap me up for what?"

"Sascha wants you to create a necklace and earrings for her appearance at the Oscars."

Sam swallowed a yell of exuberance and put on her professional voice and grabbed a nearby pen and notepad. "When are the Oscars?"

"March 24th."

"That's a month away," she told him as if he wasn't already aware of it.

"Yes, is that a problem?"

Sam fought the moment of panic and answered. "Not at all. I will just need to meet with Sascha and see her chosen outfit within the next few days. Where exactly is she filming?"

"On one of the lots at Universal studios. She can meet you today if that is possible?"

"That would be perfect. I was planning on flying back to Paris tomorrow, which is where I am currently based." Sam took down the time and details of where to meet the famous actress and hung up the phone.

The doorbell rang and a waiter announced that it was room service. Sam quickly took a blanket from the side of the lounge chair and draped it over BT, so he looked like he was sleeping rather than passed out on drugs, and went to get her cheeseburger. Sam skipped to the door, like a happy school girl.

## Andy

THE FOYER OF THE hospital was crowded as he made his way through the main doors and over to the elevator. Andy carried an overnight bag and pink roses in one hand and held his son, Thomas's, small hand in his other. Thomas held a large pink, plush rabbit for his newly arrived sister, Kate. They made their way up to the maternity ward and were intercepted by a nurse who told them that the doctor was just checking on Jenny and that perhaps it was best to wait in the small maternity waiting room until he was done. She gave Andy a meaningful look and nodded toward Thomas.

Jenny's birth had been difficult and she had ended up having emergency surgery after it, as she had torn the uterus and they couldn't stop the bleeding. Hence the overnight bag he carried as she had needed more clothes; she wouldn't be coming home as soon as planned.

"Sure thing. Will you let us know when we can go in?"

"Yes, I'll come and get you, or I will let your wife know and maybe she can come out here with the baby so he can play."

Andy went to the small waiting room, which was filled with a toy chest in one corner, several comfortable lounges, a coffee table filled with bundles of pamphlets regarding breastfeeding and other things baby related, and a small wet area with tea and coffee making facilities. The TV was in the corner, high enough that children couldn't reach it.

Andy checked his watch, it was three in the afternoon, and Play School would be on for Thomas to watch. He switched on the TV to have Samantha's face fill the screen—his throat grew dry and his stomach gained instant butterflies. She smiled at the camera, she was wearing a gorgeous gold dress and her blonde dreadlocks were gone, replaced by a messy top knot. They were talking about the earrings she wore and the guy standing next to her was telling everyone how wonderful and talented she was. He heard Jenny's voice, cooing at Kate, coming down the corridor and he felt instantly guilty as if he was caught doing something wrong. Andy flicked the channel to the opening sequence to the children's program he had originally been looking for and turned to his son. "Tommy, Mummy is coming. You got the rabbit ready for your little sister?"

The chubby-faced, almost three-year-old nodded seriously and clutched the plush toy. Andy ruffled his light brown curls and his heart felt like it would burst with love at the sight of his son. This was what he had always wanted and now he had achieved it. He had the family he had hoped and dreamed of. Marriage to Jenny was more difficult than he thought it would be, there was far more compromise than he had expected, but he loved her and she him, and they made it work. Tommy was a wonderful, easy baby and had grown into a toddler that could melt anyone's heart. And now Andy had a daughter to hold and cherish and raise to be as strong and fierce as her mother.

Jenny came in and smiled wanly at the two males in the room. "Here are our beautiful boys," she announced gently to the baby in her arms. There was a tension in her voice that Andy hadn't heard until now.

Andy helped her settle into a chair and helped Tommy present his sister with the pink bunny he had chosen. After being allowed to kiss

Kate's forehead, Thomas lost interest and went to play with the toys in the toy box.

"How are you? What did the doctor say?" Andy asked as soon as his son was occupied.

"Kate is latching on well and they are happy with her weight and feeding." Jenny's light blue eyes filled with tears.

Andy became alarmed. "What aren't you telling me?"

"The doctor advises against us having any more children. He is not sure my uterus will be capable of carrying another child full term."

"Oh, Jen." Andy was stunned, this was not the type of news you could ever prepare for and they had already begun discussing having a third.

"I am so sorry."

"What do you have to be sorry for? It's not your fault, you didn't make this happen." He felt the tears burn in the back of his throat but didn't cry. She needed him to be strong, this was the time to step up and comfort her, not fall apart.

He sat in the chair next to hers and watched their baby girl sleep. Her tiny, wrinkled hands clutched the edge of the blanket. She was perfect. "You know we are lucky. Some people never get to have a child and we got two beautiful, healthy babies. I know this is difficult because it's not our choice, but I think we have to look at our blessings." It was unusual for him to talk about blessings, but he felt strongly that his children were a gift that he should never take for granted and this was the universe reminding him of that.

Kate yawned and snuggled deeper into her blanket. Andy's heart was full, but he knew he would need to be careful how he said things to Jen, as he wasn't the one who had been told it was their fault they couldn't have any more children. He reached over and tucked a long piece of auburn hair behind Jen's ear and cupped her face. "Your body has created two babies. That is enough. Our family is more than complete. Let it rest and heal and be thankful it will not need further surgery."

"I love you, Andrew Hammond. Sometimes you know exactly what to say to make me feel better." Jen smiled at him, putting on a brave face. "Would you like to hold your daughter before I have to feed her?"

"I thought you weren't going to let her go for a minute there."

"I am just storing up on hugs because we both know that this girl is going to be a Daddy's girl and have you wrapped around her little finger by the end of next week."

Andy took Kate and kissed her cute, button nose. "I think it is already too late."

## Chapter 7

### Andy

The sick feeling didn't go away, no matter how much Andy wished for it. He had asked the question after overhearing two women gossiping in the supermarket behind him but had not seriously considered that what he'd heard she would confirm. "Is it still going on?" he asked, though he wasn't sure he wanted to know.

Jenny sat across the square kitchen table from him, crying. Andy felt nothing but anger and nausea. The tears had no effect, he didn't care that she was sorry. "No."

"How long?"

"That it's been over?" Jenny stood up, went and picked up a box of tissues, and moved to sit next to him.

"Don't come near me," he barked at her. Usually, he kept his temper in check; today he didn't care how aggressive he came across. The kids were at school and she had betrayed him.

Jenny meekly went back to her seat on the other side of the table and dabbed her eyes with a tissue. The tears continued to flow as she quietly sobbed. He looked away from her in disgust and instead stared upwards and concentrated on the slowly spinning ceiling fan.

"How long was it going on and how long has it been over?" He spat the words out, anger punctuating each one.

"I ended it about a month ago. It only happened a few times over the course of a few months."

"Who?"

"It doesn't matter. I ended it and he left the area."

"And I am just supposed to believe you?" He closed his eyes and fought for control of his emotions. "Why?"

"He made me feel what you don't," she spoke softly.

"Great, now it's my fault you had an affair." He blew out his breath and looked at his wife of ten years, it was like he didn't recognize her.

"No, it's not your fault, but..." she trailed off.

"But, nothing. You flirt with everyone, I always thought that it was just who you are and that you never meant anything by it. I was obviously wrong. Did the flirting get out of hand this time? Have you had more than this affair?" As he spoke the words he felt like he would vomit. Until that moment, his thoughts hadn't gone down that path, but now it was filled with ideas that she could have been doing this the whole time they were married and everyone had been laughing behind his back. He felt humiliated. *How many people know about this?*

"No, it was just this one time. He made me feel heard and wanted, but I knew it was wrong the moment it happened."

"And yet, you still carried it on for several more months before finally ending it." Andy was not going to let her off the hook that easily.

Jenny began to cry harder as she tried to explain through her tears. "You don't let me in. There is a piece of you that you hold back. I know you love me and want to be married, but I always feel like I am not getting all of you."

Andy frowned, he had no clue to what she was talking about. He worked hard for his family, he was committed to giving them his time and being a hands-on dad. He loved his children and didn't look at his role around the house as helping her out. They were his children and he did as much for them as Jenny did, especially as she worked full time as a manager at the hotel and his business, with the magical new thing called the internet, could be run more from home. "I am always here for you, in what way am I holding back?"

"You give the give kids one hundred percent, you are an amazing father and I couldn't think of a more caring, considerate, and patient person I would want to raise my children with. I am not talking about our family, as such. I am talking only about our relationship."

"So, we are back to blaming me for you screwing someone else?"

Jenny blew her nose into another tissue and tossed it onto the growing pile on the table. "No, I take full responsibility for my choices and I did the wrong thing. It is on me." Her cornflower blue eyes were red-rimmed and puffy from all the crying and they looked at him beseechingly. "What I am trying to do is make you understand that I didn't just go out and randomly do it, I have always felt that you have never given your whole self to me and I am even more aware of it now as I watch you with the kids and how much love you pour into them. You hold nothing back with them."

"You are jealous of the love I give our children?" None of this made sense to him.

"If I am honest, yes, I am a little jealous."

"You light up when they walk into a room, when they call you for help, when they achieve anything."

Andy just didn't get it. "Should I not feel that way?"

"Of course you should. I just want you to feel that way about me." She smiled a tiny sad smile at him.

"I celebrate your achievements, I am always there when you call for help—in any capacity you need. And I love it when you get home."

Jenny sighed the sigh of someone resigned to a situation. "She took something of you when she left and you are frightened to ever feel that pain again so you hold back with me. After thirteen years I thought you would have been over it, but I think I came to the realization that you will never get over it wholly and I went looking for comfort elsewhere."

Andy didn't have to ask who "she" was. "Don't bring her into it. I moved on from her and I am fully committed to you and I don't want to ever hear you use her as an excuse for your bad choices. She left, but she was honest about who she was. You have betrayed me, you threw our marriage away, you put everything we have worked towards in jeopardy and you dare to blame her for it." He was furious. Andy felt that he needed to get out, he couldn't be around Jenny at the moment. The pain he felt was becoming too hard to deal with and he felt caged. "I am going out, I need time."

"Will you come back?" Jenny stood and followed him as he collected his keys, wallet, and mobile. "I am sorry, I made a mistake. I want to be with you, only you." Her tears had started again.

"I just don't know." Andy walked out the door and closed it against her crying and pleading eyes.

## Samantha

The three-carat, emerald cut diamond engagement ring sat in its display box, mocking her. Sam scowled at the pretty ring and snapped the Tiffany blue box shut. She ticked the corresponding item on her inventory sheet to mark that she had inspected the final piece and it was ready for the launch. Six boxes to go. This should have been one of the most exciting moments in her life, but as she gazed at the line of twelve engagements rings, all she felt was envy for those who had a loved one who cherished them enough to buy them such a ring as those she had designed for the exclusive launch.

Sam's love life was a disaster of epic proportions and it had become something of a joke amongst her close friends to hear her tales of woe when she stumbled through one hideous date to the next. It had started with BT and his spiraling alcohol and cocaine addiction that had ended up taking his career and almost his life. She had then dated Joe, a magazine reporter, who had only been after an inside scoop of BT, and when she had told him that that conversation was always going to be off-limits, he broke up with her. Then she had been with James, who had ended up being too needy and always wanted to hold her hand and touch her. Though appealing at first, it soon became more alarming when he wanted to hold her hand while she ate and then had to be reassured that she still cared for him when she told him she needed two hands to eat her food. Sam quickly extracted herself from that relationship. It had been six months since her last date and she had no plans on dating for the foreseeable future.

The next Tiffany's box sat there, waiting for her final inspection and she begrudgingly picked it up. Sam looked at the name of the design and corresponding number on the sheet as she opened the lid to reveal the engagement ring inside. This one was her favorite and yet the one that filled her with her angst. It was a beautiful solitaire diamond; simple, elegant, and it reminded her of another ring. This was her personal homage to the man she still thought about when she thought she was unlovable or worried that there were no good men out there. Sam had named the ring Forever Yours.

"You are taking forever. Is everything in order?" Henry, her assistant, walked carefully through the doors of her personal workspace carrying a tray filled with a fine china tea set that she had been developing for Wedgewood. He placed the tray on her desk and came over to the large table where she worked. He leaned over her shoulder and looked at the ring she held. "The least flashy of all the rings you designed, but it appeals to me."

"It is a perfect diamond." She held it up to the light and admired the clarity. Sam checked the claw and the actual gold ring before returning it to the box.

Henry picked up the sheet she had been marking and ticked the box before he announced the next ring. With Henry there to keep her on track and not reflecting on what could have been, Sam got through the final five rings and helped him place them all in a box to be delivered to Tiffany's for their final inspection and approval.

"No rest for the wicked," Henry announced as he placed the packed box to one side and brought the china tea set over to the work table.

Sam smiled at Henry as he bowed, as if he were a butler serving her afternoon tea. "Thank you, Jeeves." She tried an English accent but failed miserably. They both laughed at the attempt.

"I just heard back from Prada, they want to know if you are interested in collaborating on a sunglasses line. They heard you were working with Tiffanys and I think are hoping to jump on your ever-rising star."

"Let's hope I don't crash and burn." Sam was feeling greater pressure every time a new opportunity presented itself. From the moment the actress, Sascha Peak, had worn Sam's custom made necklace that had plunged just far enough into her decolletage to draw attention but was still perceived as sexy rather than trashy, she had become a sought after jewelry designer amongst the stars of the world. That had led to recognition with her peers, and offers from bigger brands came after.

Sam hadn't had any huge setbacks in her career and she wanted to keep it that way so she put her personal life aside, like she usually did, and worked twice as hard as everyone else. The Sam who was trying to prove her worth at twenty-two by walking away from the man she loved was still on the same path she had chosen for herself, and most of the time she was happy with it. Just on occasion, she wished she had someone special to share these moments with.

Henry waved his dark hand in front of her face. "Hello? What is wrong with you? I just told you Prada wants you and there is no celebratory jumping?"

"Sorry, Henry, just having an off day. Can't seem to get my head out of the past."

He narrowed his huge brown eyes at her and puckered his lips. "Mmmm… I think it is time to go out and party tonight. Too much work is making you a dull boss and we simply cannot have that."

"I don't know." Sam didn't feel like partying.

"You dragged me halfway around the world to live in New York and we have been here four months and not even started to experience the party scene."

"Henry, I am thirty-five, the party scene might just be behind me. I have always been much more of an outdoors, camping type girl." She spread her arms wide. "Look at me." Sam wore a white, over-sized t-shirt that hung off one shoulder and military green cargo pants, with platform flip-flops. A white bandana covered her straight blonde hair and she wore little make-up.

"You aren't getting out of it that easily. I am well aware of the many party dresses you have in your wardrobe and I am happy to go out with an old woman."

"I am not that old," she protested.

"Ah-ha. So you can still party."

"No fair, you tricked me."

"Stop whining and let's get on with it so we can go drink champagne and celebrate the Tiffany's launch and that Prada now wants you."

"Do I have any choice in this?" She tried one more time to get out of it, but the more she thought about the idea of letting her hair down and dancing the night away with Henry, the more appealing it became.

"None. Tonight we party." Henry twirled her around. "Tonight, you might even find Mr. Right."

### Andy

ANDY CRIED. THE SILENT cry of someone trying to fight for control. Mouth closed, chest heaving, noise in the back of his throat, eyes screwed tight type of crying. Where the tears didn't flow freely, they escaped through the cracks. He cried for his children and how their lives would change if their parents broke up. He cried for the situation he found himself in. He cried for the change in his and Jenny's relationship—even if they remained together, it would never be the same. But most of all he cried because he knew she was right. Sam was always there, in the back of his mind. Taking a place in his heart that Jenny could never fill and Andy didn't know if he wanted that to change. Could he ever completely let go?

He looked out the car window and had to admit that he still cared for Sam. She still influenced his decisions, even to the place he had chosen to escape and think was in connection to Sam and his past, not his wife and their relationship. He watched a group of small children play around the tree that he had asked Sam to marry him. Where his life had taken a huge, unexpected turn because he hadn't listened. He laughed bitterly at the irony of the moment. He now sat in the same area and his life had taken another huge turn he hadn't anticipated but had precipitated by not hearing those around him.

Jenny had been asking him for years to talk more to her, to let her into his thoughts. He had been evasive, denying that he wasn't completely open with her. Now he thought about it in the light of Jenny's blunt admission and he knew he had been afraid to let her in because those thoughts and spaces held Sam. Was he prepared to put Samantha Rawn behind him to save his marriage? Did he want to do the work on himself to fix the problem? Yes, Jenny was the one who had cheated and the thought of it made bile rise from his gut and settle with a bitter taste in his mouth, but had he been cheating on her in a different way by never letting go of the image of his planned life with Sam and putting that expectation on Jenny?

It was uncomfortable to think about these things and usually, he would have shoved them deep down and just got on with it. This time he couldn't, there was too much at stake. Andy took the keys out of the ignition but left his phone behind. He didn't want to be disturbed by work, Russell would just have to deal with things without him. He got out of his ute and locked the door before heading onto the path that would take him through the parkland.

Andy drew in the fresh, crisp spring air and admired the tall gum trees that lined the path. He walked slowly, hoping the serene lake that came into view would calm his own thoughts and feelings so he could think rather than react. The first thing he needed to acknowledge was that he clearly still loved Jenny as the thought of her under another man made him feel possessive and like he wanted to punch something. His stomach clenched at the idea and the nausea returned.

By the time he had done a full lap of the lake and had meandered along several paths, he was no closer to a decision than before. He loved her, he didn't want to break up the family and not see his children every day, but could he ever forgive her? Yes, he had things he needed to fix and face but she had cheated. It was a thing he didn't know if he could get passed.

After an hour or so of wandering, he decided he was thirsty and needed to get a drink from the kiosk, but had left his wallet in the car with his phone. As he opened his car door he noticed his phone screen lit up. He glanced at the screen as he picked up his wallet and saw that it was the school calling him. He pressed the button to return the call without bothering to listen to the message.

"Hi, this is Andrew Hammond, I am just returning a call from the school."

"Hello, Mr Hammond, I was ringing to let you know that Kate was playing on the monkey bars at lunchtime and had a bit of a tumble, she has bumped her head."

"Is she okay?"

"Oh yes, just a little lump on her forehead, she has an icepack on it. School policy is we must contact a parent when a child receives a knock to the head," explained the office clerk.

"I think I will come down and check on her. She can stay if she likes, but I want to make sure she is fine."

"No problem. I will see you soon then."

They hung up and Andy turned the car on, drink forgotten, and pulled out of the car park. All his worries now focused on his five-year-old daughter, who could warm his heart with one tiny giggle.

It took him only ten minutes to arrive at the school. As he pulled into a car park and made his way up the path to the school office building, he heard another car pull into the car park. He didn't look behind him, he just wanted to get to Kate to reassure her and himself that she was fine. As he walked by a doorway a small voice called out, "Daddy?"

Andy stopped and went to the doorway, there was his little girl, bravely holding a huge icepack to her head and sitting on the side of the school sick bay bed, swinging her legs as they were nowhere near the floor. "Hey, bunny, how is the head?" He took the pack away to reveal a small lump. He was relieved to see the skin wasn't broken.

"Cold head," she grimaced at him.

He laughed. "Okay, you can take the pack off now. I think you will be fine."

"Why you here?"

That was his Kate, even at five she got straight to the point. "The school rang and I just wanted to check on my bunny's head."

"Can I go back to class? We are painting today."

"Sure." He helped her down off the high bed and walked her out into the hallway to run straight into Jenny.

"Mum, I hit my head." Kate pointed to the lump.

"I can see that."

Andy let go of Kate's hand and stood back as Jenny inspected their daughter's head. His heart hurt as it fought with itself. He loved the concern she displayed for their children. She was a wonderful mother, but at the moment he just couldn't think of anything else but her kissing another man.

"Dad said I can go back to class."

"If you want to go to class you can. I will come back and pick you up at the end of the day as we planned. But if it starts hurting you need to tell your teacher."

Kate moved from foot to foot and Andy knew she was impatient to get back to class as she didn't want to miss out on the painting. "Promise."

Jenny straightened up and looked at Andy for the first time. There was a plea in her blue eyes that he ignored. "You take her to class and I will let the office lady know what is happening," he said.

"Bye, Dad," Kate called happily as she skipped next to her mother as they walked down the corridor. Andy watched them go, coming to terms with the fact that he would do almost anything to not break apart his family. But could he forgive Jenny?

# Chapter 8

## Samantha

Richard smiled at her from the deck chair next to hers on their private balcony as they basked in the Mediterranean sun from the luxurious cabin on the Greek Island hopping cruise.

"What?" Sam asked as she lowered her sketch pad. The twinkling of the sunlight across the gentle waves of the turquoise bay had given her inspiration on a new bracelet and she wanted to get the idea sketched before it slipped away.

"Nothing. I am admiring you." Richard wiggled his eyebrows at her.

"You have seen me draw before."

"It never gets old. And you are so cute when you bite your bottom lip when deciding on something. It is rare to find someone so passionate about what they do."

Sam reached across, offering him her hand. Richard took it.

"It is rare to find a man willing to accept me this way. Most want me to be successful as long as it suits their life. Only you have been willing to come halfway."

He rubbed his thumb over her knuckles, which sent a thrill down her spine. "I couldn't imagine you any other way."

"I love you," Sam spoke quietly.

Richard smiled his lopsided smile, which to Sam made him even more handsome. He was fifty, ten years older than her, and worked out a few times a week to keep himself in shape. Though he had tried to keep up with her when she had gone on her last hike, she had had to slow down for him. He was tanned, bald, and as financially settled as she was. They had met through mutual friends at a fundraising function and had started dating immediately. "Have you finished? I didn't mean to interrupt you."

"Give me five and I am all yours."

"Sounds great. Would you like another drink?"

"A martini would be fabulous, thank you."

Richard got up and pulled a shirt on over his head as he walked into the cabin. Sam settled back into the deck chair, smiled at the vista before her, and took up her sketch pad again. It didn't take long to finish the basic sketch of a bracelet and she had the chance to simply lay back and relax with the warm sun just touching her toes.

Sam must have fallen asleep as the next thing she knew a voice was calling her. "Sam, honey?"

"Mmmm, do I have to wake up?" she asked, keeping her eyes closed.

"Well, no, but your martini is ready."

She lifted one eyelid and looked at him. He held up the martini glass. "I guess I can wake up for a Richard-made martini."

He waited while she sat up straighter before handing her the drink. "I got generous and gave you a few olives." He sat on the deck chair but didn't swing his legs around to lie down, instead he sat there looking at her.

"Thank you." Sam took the small wooden pick that held the olives in the glass and pulled it out, ready to take a bite when something caught her eye. Slowly she put the olive laden wooden stick on the small table beside her and looked more carefully at the ring at the bottom of her glass. "There seems to be something in my glass." It was difficult to get the words out. She struggled with unwanted memories.

As she lifted her head, Richard slid onto one knee. "Samantha, please let me be the one for the rest of our lives. I adore you. I love you. I worship you. The thought of you not being in my life makes me weep." He looked at her and she was surprised to see a single tear upon his cheek. "You have brought me back to life."

Sam put her pinkie finger into the bottom of the glass and carefully pulled out the engagement ring. The ring was huge and in the latest design. A halo ring, with a large round diamond in the center, surrounded by smaller pink diamonds in an octagonal shape around the edge. Seven diamonds, diminishing in size were on each side of the platinum band. It was stunning and nothing like the twelve rings she had created for Tiffany. Sam had never had the want to design another engagement ring after those twelve. They had been a success and had led to other collections but never engagement rings. "It's stunning."

"That's not an answer." Richard took the ring from her and held it out. "Will you marry me?"

"Yes," Sam whispered, not wanting to break the spell of the moment. "I couldn't think of a more perfect man for me to marry." She didn't know why she chose those exact words but knew it was time to put aside Andy. To finally let go of the past and move forward with this man, who accepted her and her wants, desires, and needs without wanting anything but love from her.

Richard slipped the ring onto her finger and they both stood. Sam looked up into his brown eyes, lifted her hand, and cupped the back of his neck. She drew his head down to hers and kissed him with passion and a greater understanding of love than she had experienced before. Sam was finally capable and willing to appreciate what a man like Richard had to offer. Strength, stability, acceptance, and confidence in his own worth that she didn't need to continually focus on making him happy, as he knew that was his job.

As they broke apart, Richard kissed her softly on the forehead. "You are so beautiful. You will make the most gorgeous bride." He slowly began to tug on the tie that held her bikini top in place. "I do have one problem though."

Sam trailed a hand down his chest and began to undo his shirt buttons. "What seems to be the problem?"

"I am going to need the most amazing wedding ring, do you happen to know a jewelry designer that could help a guy out?"

"I have one in mind, but she might need some convincing."

Richard lifted Sam into his strong arms and carried her into the cabin. "I know a few things that might help convince her."

## Andy

THE CAKE WAS PINK, three-tiered, and filled with layers of vanilla sponge and chocolate ganache. It was decadent and over the top, but Kate had insisted that's what she had needed to make her tenth birthday complete. The cake sat on the trestle table, as the party swirled around it, half-eaten and mostly forgotten. What had been a simple child's birthday party had turned into an all night event as the parents had arrived to collect their children. The ones who were good friends of Andy and Jenny's had been invited to stay on for a few late afternoon drinks that had turned into pizza for dinner and more drinks.

Andy cut a small slice of cake and nibbled at it. He had had too much to drink and was hungry and the cake was the easiest thing to grab, as he didn't want to walk up the stairs to the kitchen. Most of the adults and children were gathered on the flat, lush green lawn dancing to Gwen Stefani's *The Sweet Escape* and laughing. Andy stood there and grinned like a fool as he took in the scene; this is what he had pictured his life to be like. Surrounded by family and friends in his own home, all enjoying themselves.

Life was not perfect, but for the most part, he loved it.

A tall, raven-haired woman with curves and an inviting smile came to stand next to him. Jessica was one of the two women he had overheard discussing Jenny's affair in the supermarket five years ago. She had been Jenny's best friend at the time and had broken her confidence to speak to the other woman about it. Jen had called her out on the situation and had stopped speaking to her for several years. Jessica had continued to try to apologize for her lack of good judgment and her betrayal of trust and Jenny had only last year accepted the woman's words and they had slowly begun to rebuild the friendship. Andy had held his peace, though he was astounded that Jenny could be such a hypocrite about betrayal and wanting forgiveness and trust from him but couldn't move on from her friend's betrayal.

"Hey, Andy. Having fun?" Jess almost purred at him. She stood a little closer than she should and swayed slightly on her feet. It was obvious to Andy that she had had too much to drink too.

"Yeah, it's great. I love having everyone here."

"I have missed these impromptu get togethers. You guys have always known how to throw a party." Jess finished her drink and hiccuped, which brought on a giggle from her. "Ooops."

Andy smirked but said nothing.

"I haven't had the chance to speak to you privately, but I wanted to apologize in person for my part in the mess all those years ago. I should have kept my mouth shut."

"If you didn't keep your mouth shut I may never have known about it, so don't be sorry to me. I am glad you decided to talk about it in the wrong place to the wrong person." He finished his cake and put the plate down and looked at her. "You and I didn't do anything wrong. If Jenny hadn't had the affair there wouldn't have been anything to hide."

Jess provocatively ran her finger through a layer of cream on the cake and licked it off. "You do know I would be happy to help you with a little revenge affair."

Andy didn't respond because he didn't know what to say.

Jess laughed and placed her hand on his forearm. "I am joking," she stopped and winked at him, "unless you want me not to be."

The idea was appealing for a few fleeting seconds, but revenge had never been Andy's style. "I appreciate the offer, but I think I will leave the past behind me. We have moved forward and have found a good place, I want to keep it that way."

"Oh, well, you can't blame a girl for trying. We were all jealous when Jenny snagged you, we all thought you would pine for Samantha forever at one point."

Andy's body reacted strongly to her name. No one ever mentioned Sam, though many had been her friend. He had always had a suspicion that it was because none of them wanted to incur the wrath of Jenny's glare. Jenny was safely on the dance floor and Jessica had already brought up the affair so he guessed she was trying to push his buttons. Though for what purpose, he didn't know. Maybe to cause trouble between him and Jenny for being excluded for those few years.

"Have you ever run into her or spoken to her since she left?" Jessica pushed.

"No." Andy noted Jenny look over at the two of them, her eyebrows raised. He smiled mildly as if everything were okay.

"I catch up with her when she comes to town."

"You do?" Andy tried to sound interested without sounding eager. It was a difficult combination to pull off.

"Yes. She is still the same Sam. Driven and willing to give up love to attain her goals. Though it looks like she has finally found someone willing to be with her and not change her."

"I am happy for her. We all deserve to find that special someone." Andy half meant it. He needed to get away from Jessica before he began questioning her more about Sam. They had been apart eighteen years and he needed to keep that out of his head. No, daydreaming of what could have been… it was too dangerous for his marriage.

Kate, his beautiful daughter, saved him from himself. "Daddy, come and dance with me. Mum promised to put my favorite song on next and cause it's my birthday you have to do what I wish." She looked adorable in her cute, pink fairy costume, she waved her sparkly wand, with its huge shiny star around imperiously.

He bowed to her. "Yes, my fairy princess. Your wish is my command, but only for today remember." He turned to Jessica. "It was great catching up, but now I must dance with the birthday girl."

## Chapter 9

### Samantha

SAM PUT THE IPHONE down and closed her eyes and rested her head in her hands as she sat at the kitchen table in her rented Sydney apartment. She was expecting a phone call from a journalist at an Australian newspaper but was in no mood to be polite and talk about her triumphs. This year had started with an air of excitement as she had announced the impending launch of her first full range under her own label. Richard had been supportive all the way through the process and never complained about how much time it took her away from him.

Her phone began to ring and she picked it up. "Hello."

"Samantha Rawn? This is Todd Aves from the newspaper."

"Hello, Todd, how are you today?" Sam thought Todd sounded no more than fifteen and was still waiting for his voice to drop.

"I am well. Thank you for agreeing to speak to me today."

"I am looking forward to it."

"Can I begin by saying congratulations on the upcoming launch?"

"Thank you."

"And I would like to add my condolences for the loss of your husband earlier this year. It must have been devastating for you?"

"And still is." Sam swallowed hard on the lump that formed in her throat and pushed the memory of the boating accident as far away from her as her mind would allow. Each day her life after Richard grew a little easier, but she was far from healed and most days wondered if she would ever feel normal again.

"Can we talk about the collection and why you chose to launch with an Australian theme? And from my understanding, you are only using Australian precious and semi-precious stones as well as gold sourced locally?"

"I have always been inspired by the places I travel and the cultures I meet, but my first place of inspiration came from the Blue Mountains and I wanted to pay homage to that and the magnificent country I come from. I live overseas and only come back for short visits but there is no place like Australia."

"Can you give us any hints to what we will see in the collection?"

"South Australian musgravites, Cooper Pedy opals, and the very rarest sapphires with coloring that can only be found here. I have taken ideas from the barrier reef to Uluru, from the gum trees unique to our land and the wonderful tales of the Indigenous people who were here before us."

"It sounds sensational. When and where will the world be able to see these creations?"

"I am opening a store in several places across the world and everything will, of course, be online. But there will be a few exclusive pieces you will only find in store."

Sam answered a few more of Todd's questions, including things about her favorite memories growing up in the Blue Mountains and who did she study under, and for anyone wanting to follow in her footsteps how do they begin. She was grateful when the interview was over and she could hang up from the cheerful man.

A reminder on her iPhone flashed up and she got up to tidy the small kitchen area of the apartment and to make sure everything was clean. This had become her weekly ritual on a Thursday as she waited for her father and mother to arrive from his chemotherapy session. He would come in and go straight to sleep for several hours while Sam took the chance to chat and comfort her mother. Her father's chemo would last four months and Sam had committed to staying in Sydney and being available to help for that time. After a small bite to eat, her father would go back to sleep for the evening and both he and her mother would go back home on the Friday before coming back into the city the following Wednesday to start the process again.

She looked at her watch, she had just enough time to jump into a quick shower before her parents arrived. Sam undressed and had a hot shower, wishing that the apartment had a bath. As she got out of the shower and dried herself she looked at her reflection in the harsh bathroom light and was shocked by what she saw. Her cheeks were hollow, permanent dark circles had seemed to have taken up residence under her green eyes and she had a haunted look to her. Her forty-five-year-old face looked ancient. The impact of losing Richard so suddenly, combined with the knowledge that her father had terminal cancer all occurring within six months and the pressure of the launch that she could not postpone because she would lose momentum was weighing heavily on her and the people who typically supported her were either gone or she needed to support them. Sam felt adrift and alone.

After getting dressed in a lavender silk kaftan style dress, she took the chance to lie down on the couch. She was exhausted, overwhelmed, and running on empty. This time in her career was supposed to be a momentous achievement, a celebration of her hard work, determination, and sacrifices and at the moment all she felt was dread. She had hoped to bury herself in her work when Richard had died, but her father's diagnosis had pulled her out of her workshop and into the harsh reality of life all over again. Her mother and father were both strong and coping well, but both leaned on her for support as they didn't want to burden each other, neither realizing that Sam was barely holding on and that she was struggling to keep it all together.

Before darker thoughts could creep in, Sam got off the couch and got out her sketch pad. If nothing else, all the emotion she was feeling usually lent itself to some form of creation. But as she began to draw, not taking much notice of her conscious thought and drawing without really seeing, a face appeared on the page before her. He was just the way she remembered him the day she had said goodbye in her driveway. Shaggy blond hair, chiseled jaw, and caring eyes that had always loved her. At that moment she would swap all the success she had ever achieved to be safe in Andy's arms. She always found it odd that when her soul reached out for someone it was always him, even after Richard, it was still him.

## Andy

THE SMELL OF BUTTERED toast and cooked bacon filled the air and Andy heaved a sigh of satisfaction as he picked up the newspaper that was placed next to his plate of bacon and eggs. Sunday morning breakfast with his kids was the highlight of his week most of the time. And now his kids were almost grown, they had finally achieved mastery in the kitchen and he no longer had to pretend that the watery scrambled eggs or lumpy pancake batter were delicious. Both Thomas and Kate were great at preparing almost any breakfast he requested. As he sipped his coffee and watched several birds fly lazily around the sky from the exquisite view of his balcony that led from the kitchen, he listened to his children bicker about who would clean up in the background. Andy chose to ignore the bickering and opened his newspaper; he loved reading it from beginning to end on a Sunday morning, but only on a Sunday, every other day he was too busy.

He devoured his yummy breakfast and asked for a refill of the coffee as he made his way through the paper. Both teenagers sat with him at the large kitchen table completing their homework. September school holidays were almost over and then only a few short weeks and Thomas would be preparing for his final school exams. They all sat in silence, enjoying the sounds of nature through the open glass sliding doors on the balcony.

Jenny had worked late the night before at the hotel, helping host a fundraiser and co-ordinating with the events manager that had been hired. She finally joined them in the kitchen about mid-morning, after having a sleep-in. As she made herself a cup of coffee she scowled at Andy and his newspaper. "Will she ever stop haunting me?"

"Sorry, Jen? Who?" Andy asked he was confused by her frown.

"Don't worry about it." She plastered a fake smile on her face. "How are you doing, guys? Need any help with your homework?"

Both children told her they were fine.

"What's your plans for the day?" she asked, her voice held a certain edge to it.

Andy looked over the top of his paper; he knew that voice well. He watched as his children stopped reading and note-taking to look at their mother; they obviously recognized the voice too.

Thomas was the first to answer. "I have to work this afternoon. Now I have my license, Dad offered me the chance to run the tour by myself, earn a bit of extra money for when I go to Uni."

"That's great, Tommy." Her tone said otherwise.

Andy watched as their more defiant daughter spoke. "Dad said it would be okay if I went to Milly's after I finished my study for the day and when my room was clean. He said he would take me after lunch."

"Is that what Dad said?" Jenny lifted an eyebrow at him.

"She goes back to school next week and won't get a chance to hang out as much once the school year is over as she wants to start working for the company as Tom won't be there for much longer." Andy kept his voice light, he pressed his lips together so as not to say something that would cause an argument.

"Great. You do know you don't have to work for Dad, you can always come and work with me?"

"Thanks, Mum, but I like being outside." Kate smiled.

Jenny drained the last of her coffee and stood up, again scowling at the newspaper in Andy's hands. "It looks like Dad has your day covered and I am not needed. Good time to get the house cleaned without you underfoot." She put her cup in the dishwasher and left the room.

Andy wondered if it was on purpose or whether she just didn't care enough to ask what he had planned for the day. He had been thinking of staying at home and working on the garden, but now he thought after dropping Kate off at Milly's he might head into the office to get a start on his latest plans to promote the company. It was time to get a website.

"Dad?" said Tom. "Do you know a Samantha Rawn?"

Andy's mouth went dry and his heart slammed into his rib cage as it began to beat quicker. How can a name have such power over someone after twenty-three years? "Why do you ask?"

"Mum kept glaring at the back of your paper and I just read a little bit. It's about a woman, Samantha Rawn, who comes from around here."

Trying to look casual, Andy turned the newspaper to the last page, and there, staring back at him was Sam. His Sam. The woman he still dreamt of. The iconic one that got away. "Yes, I knew her." He smiled at his kids. "Sam is actually the one that introduced me to your mum."

"Why doesn't Mum like her?" Kate was always quick to catch on.

"I went out with Sam before I started dating your mother. It was a very long time ago." He looked at the headline and smiled.

**Local girl made good.**

She had done what she had set out to accomplish and he was happy for her. Truly happy for her. Andy looked at his beautiful children and knew that he would never wish for anything to be different, he adored them and couldn't imagine his life without them. He loved being a father; it was something he gained great enjoyment from and his children were amazing people to be around. But he now understood that the level of commitment it took to be a great parent should not be taken lightly and was not for everyone. When Sam had broken up with him, he had been certain she was wrong about not wanting children, but now after eighteen years of parenting, he understood she had seen that far more clearly than he had. She had simply wanted different things than him. And he should never have asked her to give up her dreams for him; it was one of his biggest regrets in life. He wished he had the chance to fix it.

"That doesn't really explain why Mum doesn't like her. Everyone has past partners," Kate pushed the issue.

Andy thought about how to respond. He didn't want the children thinking bad of their mother but needed them to understand who Sam was to him. They were both old enough to know the truth. He tried not to look overly cautious as he leaned back in his chair to make sure Jenny wasn't around. Andy lowered his voice. "Samantha Rawn was the first woman I loved. I asked her to marry me, but she didn't want to stay here and have children, she wanted to travel the world and create jewelry. She broke my heart when she said no, but I healed and fell in love with your mother."

Thomas nodded, his kind face full of understanding. He currently had a serious girlfriend this final year of school and would need to leave her to go to the University of his choice. He was struggling to come to terms with it because they loved each other deeply. "Life choices are hard."

"The important ones are," agreed Andy.

"By the back of the paper, it looks like Sam reached her dream goals." Kate moved one arm in a wide movement, gesturing at the view from their balcony. "You reached yours too. Great wife, successful business, the home of your dreams already paid off and in an amazing location and most of all, perfect kids."

Andy laughed. "Yes, I worked hard and achieved all I had hoped for." He didn't add the sacrifices of self he had had to make to keep the family together as he and Jenny grew further apart, and that this time he wasn't sure he wanted to work so hard to get it back on track.

## Chapter 10

### Andy

Andy stood at the door of Sam's old bedroom and looked at the first woman he had loved. She sat forlornly on the edge of her bed, staring at a photo on her bedside table. An open suitcase sat next to her, a few clothes were in a heap beside it. The room was how he remembered it, down to the workbench in the corner and the same colored sheet set.

"I thought I might find you here," he tried to make it sound light.

Sam turned her head and he noted that her green eyes grew wide, he didn't know if that was a good sign or not. He didn't know what he was expecting, nor wanting. He just knew that once he had found that she was in town for her father's funeral he had had to come and pay his respects and see her. He had no reason to stay away and it became a need that he couldn't ignore. She was as breathtakingly beautiful as he remembered. The long blonde hair was still there and her skin had that sun-kissed tan she always had because of her love of hiking and being outdoors. Her figure was a little fuller, but so was his, and he found the fuller breasts and rounded hips were just as appealing as her younger, thinner self.

"Andy, thank you for coming." Sam stood and moved toward him.

"I came to check on you."

She was so close to him that he just stopped thinking and pulled her into his arms; it felt completely natural, the twenty-eight years since the last time he did it all falling away as if it were a dream. She fit under his chin, just like he remembered and he kissed the top of her head by instinct, rather than conscious thought. "I am so sorry about your dad. He was a good man."

"Thank you."

He noticed her voice catch and he felt her shoulders start to shake. He just stood there, marveling at the feel of her in his arms after all that time, and allowed her the freedom to mourn. He had lost his father two years prior and it had been a terrible experience that he was only now recovering from. It had also given him the final push to think about how short life was and that sometimes you needed to take a risk and make sure you knew what made you happy.

"I've missed you," he breathed softly into her hair.

Her arms held him tightly around his waist and she leaned her face against his shirt. "I missed you too." Sam sniffed as her tears subsided.

He knew he should probably let her go, but could not bring himself to do it. As he held her, he looked up at the photo board to see a younger, naive version of himself smiling back. He noted that there were several photos of them together still pinned on the board. "Your bedroom hasn't changed at all," he commented.

"Dad wouldn't let Mum touch it, even though I told them several times they could pack up the room. I came home a few years ago when he first got sick and tried to clean it but he just looked so sad that I wanted to pack it up that I ended up leaving it."

He waited for her to break the contact. "What will you do now?"

Sam continued to hold him around the waist but she lifted her head to look at him. "I might stay for six months, make sure Mum is okay and take care of everything."

He tried to ignore the undercurrent that was flowing between them. He wanted to bend down and kiss her, but it was her father's funeral. He didn't stop her as she pulled away from him, a small frown crossing her face.

Sam moved to lean against the workbench. "I can create and work from here." She knocked on the worn wooden top. "I might even find new inspiration."

Andy found himself taking a step toward her when she picked up a book and started fanning herself. He grinned at her.

She laughed. "Don't flatter yourself. I am having a hot flash."

He moved to take the book from her. "Let me help you."

Another frown crossed her face. "How is your wife?"

He noted that she didn't say, Jenny. He spoke plainly, not wanting to give her any other impression except that his marriage was finished. "Remarried and living in Melbourne. Our daughter, Kate, is studying in Sydney, and our son, Thomas, is living in London. We realized that we had nothing in common but the kids." It didn't pain him to speak about it. The marriage had ended without a fuss as if it had run it's course and had fizzled out. He looked at her seriously. "I have always wanted to know, did you make the right choice?"

Sam's face grew softer, her guard came down and the tension that he hadn't realized was there until now disappeared. "Yes. It hurt so much to leave you," her voice was quiet. "I never had children and I never regretted it. I did exactly what I wanted to do and studied under the best. And now I have the complete freedom to create and travel as I wish." She held out her hand and he took it, a charge of heat running between them. "Though I never managed to replace you in my heart, it was the right thing to do for both of us."

He knew it was the wrong time to discuss such things, but the heart did what it wanted. It was her father's wake, but he knew all her father had ever wished for was for her to be happy and Andy knew that now they were finally on the right path at the right time and he could make her and himself deliriously happy. He pulled her to him with the hand he held and kissed her once, as if to seal their fate.

"I am ready to explore the world in about six months." He kissed her again. "Would you know anyone willing to be my tour guide?"

## Epilogue

### Samantha

The French Alps were everything she had hoped and more. It was exhilarating to be out in the open air, free from the cities she lived in and the chaos that surrounded them. Free of the smog and the beeping car horns. Free from the demands of running a successful company.

Sam sat back against her large backpack and soaked in the view before her. Her husband stood, shielding his eyes against the late afternoon glare of the Fall sun, looking out over the mountain range that they had been talking about hiking since they had first met, thirty-five years ago. Andy had announced that for their fifth wedding anniversary they would be traveling to France, and Sam had assumed he wanted to see all the usual tourist things, which he had, but his real plan had been to hike with her through the Alps, away from their busy lives and cell reception.

Being married to Andy was how she had imagined it would be, and spending every night in his bed brought her comfort and joy in equal measure. She only hoped she made him as happy as he made her.

Their reunion had caused less friction within his family than they had thought it would. Thomas and Kate had been accepting of her, especially Thomas who had explained about a high school sweetheart he had left behind, and when they caught up, he always thought about what could have been. Kate had taken a little longer to come around as she had been torn between being happy for her father, but feeling loyalty toward her mother. Jenny had surprisingly been the one to step in and explain to Kate that Sam and Andy were doing nothing wrong. Jenny had moved on and Andy deserved happiness with the woman he was always meant to be with.

Sam had, with bittersweet emotions, finally cleaned out her bedroom in the six months she had taken off to help her Mum heal and cope with her father's death. Her mother had been happy to sell the house and move in with her sister, whose husband had been placed into a nursing home the year before.

Andy had wasted no time and within three months had asked Sam to marry him and they had married soon after that. He still had his tour company business, but only checked in once a week to make sure it was running well. They now split their time between her New York home and office and her London one. Traveling back to Australia at least every four months to visit with everyone. Sam had never needed to settle and have one home and even more so now she didn't feel that need.

Andy turned back to face her and beamed. "Why don't you sketch while I set up the tent? I don't need your help and I bet your fingers are itching to draw something while you are surrounded by all this beauty."

"Do you mind?"

"I knew it. No, I don't mind. I am happy to be your tent provider." He winked.

"You know me so well." Sam unzipped her pack and pulled out a sketch pad, it was an old one and she hadn't opened it in forever. She often did that. Sometimes she would put a pad aside for years only to go back and rediscover something she could work with. The wind caught it and it sailed out of her hand to land at Andy's feet. He bent down and picked it up and instead of handing it back to her, he stared at the open page.

"Sam, when did you draw this?"

She moved to stand next to him and was surprised to see a drawing of his face. "I wondered where that had got to."

She went to take the sketch pad and he held it away from her, a slow, sexy grin played across his face. "When did you draw this? I haven't looked like this for a long time."

"Around ten years ago," she confessed. There was still much they hadn't discussed regarding their previous lives and this was one of them. Sam had never admitted how much she had pined for him over their twenty-eight-year separation.

The sexy grin disappeared and as always, he understood the undertone before she had to say anything. "Why then?"

"Richard had died six months earlier and Dad was on his first rounds of chemo. I was trying to cope and I had my brand to launch. I was overwhelmed and drowning in darkness, your face helped me remember the light." Her voice sounded small and wounded to her own ears. Even now those days brought her great sorrow.

Andy did what he always did best, he held Sam in his arms and radiated the love he had for her. "I am sorry you had no one there for you at that time. I can't change it, but I can promise that you need never face anything alone again." He bent down and kissed her. "I have a confession to make. No matter how hard I tried I couldn't stop loving you. And at one point, I did try to put you behind me. It was affecting my marriage and my ability to commit fully to Jen, but I can't be sure I ever really could do it. I put you as far back in my mind as I could, but you always managed to appear when I didn't guard my thoughts."

Sam put her hands on his broad shoulders and slowly trailed her hands along them and down his arms. "I never let you go. You were the ideal that I held everyone else up to. There were times I wished I had wanted to children just so I could be with you, but I always knew the decision I had made was the right one for us. I wouldn't change it, but there were days my heart ached for you but you were no longer a part of my life and only a memory I carried in my heart."

They kissed the sweet kiss of acceptance and love and understanding of moments that can't be changed.

Her hands found his hands and she pulled him down to her height. She nipped his earlobe before whispering. "How quickly do you think you can get that tent up?"

"I am fairly certain I can set a new world record if I put my mind to it."

"Hop to it then."

He kissed her and her body responded immediately. "Maybe I should help you."

Andy laughed and Sam knew that as long as he was beside her, home was wherever they were.

# OLIVIA

Reflections of Love Novella Collection

Book Three

# TAYA RUNE

# Olivia

## Chapter 1

THE CRYSTAL-CUT CHAMPAGNE GLASS was raised high in a toast to her best friend, Peyton, and her new husband, Thad. Olivia caught a glimpse of her own long face with its round brown eyes and prominent cheekbones, all fractured against the planes as she brought the glass to her lips. She took a sip and tried not to screw up her face as she swallowed the dry brut. Ollie placed the glass back on the table, never understanding why anyone would drink the stuff willingly, and retrieved her own Coke Zero. Growing up with a volatile, alcoholic mother had given her the desire to rarely drink and champagne she thought was made to confirm her choices.

Ollie grinned as she watched Peyton and Thad kiss after the conclusion of his speech, which of course brought a cheer from the assembled wedding guests. They were her two dearest friends, and she couldn't be happier for them.

Peyton and Ollie had met on the first day of high school and had bonded over their difficult mothers. Ollie's mother had been too hungover to make the effort to accompany her daughter to her first day at a new school, so Ollie had had to face the challenge of walking into the school gates alone. While Peyton's mother had cried hysterically at the gates, wringing her hands and telling Peyton that she didn't know how she would get through the day without her precious daughter.

Peyton had quietly but firmly told her mother she had managed to get through every day while she was at primary school, and high school would be no different. Kissing her mother on the cheek, she had quickly walked away and straight into Ollie, who had been trying to move around the two without looking like she could hear what was happening.

"Oh, my goodness, I'm sorry," Peyton had exclaimed as she had taken a step back.

Ollie had laughed. "All good. I'm Olivia. My first day today too."

"Peyton. What home group you in?"

That's where the friendship had started and twelve years later they were still the best of friends.

Ollie watched as Peyton leaned in and whispered something into Thad's ear, he kissed her softly on the cheek and winked at her before turning to thank the waitress for the dessert she placed in front of him. Every so often Ollie wondered what would have happened if she had not been with her ex-boyfriend when she had met Thad at University. Instead, she had stayed in a boring relationship with Tyler the Twerp while she introduced Thad to her best friend, Peyton. Though, if she was honest with herself, she knew her and Thad would never have worked as they were too similar and driven, but it was harmless to reflect about what could have been on those rare occasions when she fleetingly thought about being in a relationship. Most didn't believe her, but she was content and happy being alone. Her life was full and she enjoyed doing what she wanted when she wanted. Being able to make all her life choices without considering another was appealing. Ollie doubted there was a man out there who would change her mind.

Peyton rose, adjusting her sweetheart neckline bridal gown as she did. She was striking. Her dress was stunning in a heavy, pure-white brocade with a panel of royal purple in the back. She was as tall as her husband, which was why she had chosen to forgo an upswept hairstyle and tiara and wore sneakers under her exquisite gown, that and she wanted to be comfortable—no one would know. Her overbearing mother thought she had pretty, sparkling ballet slippers on.

Ollie envied those sneakers at the moment. Her strappy silver stilettos looked gorgeous on her small feet, but after hours of standing for the ceremony, the photos, and already having spent a bit of time on the dance floor her feet were protesting.

"Come with me,"—Peyton held out her hand—"there is someone I want you to meet."

Ollie held up her hands in protest. "You know I am happy being single. You and Thad both promised no trying to set me up unless I got desperate and asked."

Taking one of Ollie's protesting hands, Peyton pulled Ollie to her feet. "Stop being silly. It's not like that, I just want you to meet someone."

Ollie noted as she stood that even in her high heels she was still short compared to Peyton. While she muttered under her breath that she didn't want to be set up, she quickly snuck a peek in the mirror on the far wall as they wound their way through the hundreds of wedding guests. Her normally long, frizzy, always unruly, chocolate-brown hair had been back-combed, curled and hair sprayed, so even if a hurricane hit it wouldn't move. She surreptitiously adjusted the off the shoulder straps of her royal-purple, form-fitting slip dress.

Peyton smiled knowingly.

"Not what you think," laughed Ollie. "I'm more than happy to just find someone for tonight, a girl needs a little action every now and then."

They came to an abrupt halt at Thad's main family table. Ollie waited patiently as Peyton was swamped with people welcoming her to the family and expressing their delight at how wonderful the service had been. Two of Thad's sisters took the time to question her sanity for marrying their younger brother, but it was all done with warmth and humor. Ollie liked Thad's sisters; there were three in total and they had always been kind and welcoming. She knew he had an older brother too, but he lived in America. Ollie smiled and greeted the sisters as they moved away from the table, allowing Peyton to get to whomever it was she wanted Olivia to meet. It was silly but being forced to stand there had made her nervous and butterflies now filled her stomach as she waited. She was going to strangle both Peyton and Thad if they thought this a great time to set her up with someone, though they had both made promises not to, she didn't entirely trust them when it came to her love life.

"Mrs. Adimari, I would like you to meet Olivia," Peyton stepped aside to reveal a beautiful elderly woman.

OLLIE SMILED WARMLY AND took the proffered hand of the older lady, relieved that her best friends had kept their word and not tried to be sneaky about introducing her to someone. "It is wonderful to meet you, Mrs. Adimari."

The woman had medium-length, silver hair that was combed to one side and held in place with a stunning comb of pearls and crystals. She wore a lilac skirt suit with embroidered cuffs and lapels and sat straight and poised. The woman oozed elegance.

"Both of you may call me Mariella or Nona, Mrs. Adimari makes me feel old. I have told you this before, Peyton."

"You have to excuse Peyton, she can be a little uptight with the manners thing. I am pretty sure it comes from her mother," Ollie grinned at the woman and held out her hand.

Mariella raised perfectly groomed eyebrows at her. "Well, yes, that would be easy to understand." She glanced at the bride. "Your mother is wound a tad tight."

"Nona, you have no idea," admitted Peyton. She was rewarded with a satisfied nod at the use of the name.

Mariella took the proffered hand and held it warmly for several moments. Ollie refrained from saying anything further; Peyton didn't need any more reminding about how difficult her mother could be. Mariella looked at Ollie. "May I say that you have the most beautiful skin tone, my dear."

"My mother is Dutch, while my father is Aboriginal," Ollie explained.

Mariella's violet eyes glinted. "Well, they have produced a beautiful daughter." Thad's grandmother turned back to Peyton. "I have something for you, but I don't want to pin it to that gorgeous dress." She reached into her silk clutch and took out an envelope.

Ollie knew the enveloped contained money and that while Thad's family had insisted they continue the tradition, Peyton had felt uncomfortable about it. It had been discussed several times, but the tradition of pinning money to the bride would be followed if anyone cared to at the wedding.

Handing it over, Mariella spoke, "Enjoy your honeymoon in Rome."

Ollie couldn't help herself, "It would seem that all roads do lead to—"

A friendly baritone interrupted her. "Yes, but just remember that when in Rome... well, you know what to do..."

"Yes. We all know what to do in Rome, whatever they are doing," Ollie completed his thought.

"True, but it might take you some time to get to Rome, because as you know..." he plunged on.

"I am aware that Rome wasn't built in a day."

They both began to laugh and Ollie noticed immediately that his laugh was almost worse than hers. She grinned.

He bent down to kiss Mrs. Adimari. "Nona, you look marvelous."

"You were always my favorite, Remy."

He smiled and laughed his loud guffaw. Ollie found it immensely attractive.

"Where have you been, my gorgeous boy?"

He winked at Olivia, including her in the conversation. "I have been fiddling while Rome burns."

Ollie couldn't help it. She snorted loudly as she laughed. Horrified she covered her mouth. This made him laugh louder, accentuating his own blow horn sound. He arched a heavy brow at her. "Finally, a woman who can match my quips and hideous, socially unacceptable laugh."

She gave him a wicked grin and took a moment to appreciate the man before her. He was about five foot nine, making him still taller than her—even in her heels—and clean-shaven. He had close-cropped, dark hair and a straight, strong nose. Full eyebrows, that were obviously kept under control and hazel eyes that were sparkling with mirth which made her think naughty thoughts. His unusual accent gave her a clue as well as him calling Mariella Nona as to who he was.

Remy placed his hand on his Nona's shoulder and looked at the bride. "You look amazing, Peyton, and I wanted to welcome you to the family, but could you perhaps introduce me to your friend?"

Peyton didn't hide her delight as she turned to Ollie. "Remy, this is my dearest friend and the one who introduced me to Thad. This is Olivia."

Remy bowed formally as if they were at a ball in far off England rather than a reception center in Melbourne, Australia. "It is my pleasure to make your acquaintance."

Ollie giggled but curtsied in return to his bow. This man was fun and becoming more interesting by the second. "Olivia, are your dance moves as good as your quips and laugh?"

"You would have to dance with me to unearth that information."

"Well, that appears to be an invitation I cannot resist." Remy turned to Peyton and Mariella. "Ladies, would you excuse us?"

"It was lovely to meet you, Mariella."

"You too, my dear. Come back when Remy lets you go and we shall chat."

Remy held out his elbow as a proper gentleman would and Ollie took it, attempting to be as elegant as he was. Her snort of laughter at his gesture didn't help.

Ollie felt a tingle of electricity as he put his hand on her middle back and held her close. She placed her hand on his shoulder and was impressed with the fine material of his charcoal suit. It was expensive, like thousand thread Egyptian cotton sheets. "So, you are Remy, Thad's older brother?" Olivia guessed.

"Clever girl. Even half my family members can't figure that out."

"You look enough like him and you have an odd accent, mostly Aussie but with a twang of American in there. I am not surprised half of them don't know you... look how many of you there are." Ollie let go of his hand to make a sweeping gesture to the four hundred wedding guests. He caught her hand and spun her around before drawing her back to him.

"Olivia, do you have a boyfriend, husband, partner?"

"Call me Ollie, and no I don't." She almost added that she was not looking for one either but that sometimes came across as too aggressive and man-hating when that wasn't the case. "Do you?"

Remy smiled down at her with a sly grin. "Do I what?"

Ollie returned the smirk. "Do you have a boyfriend, husband, partner?"

The sound of Remy's loud, fabulously bad laugh filled the dance floor.

## Chapter 2

Ollie looked at her hair in the bathroom mirror and was horrified by what she saw—the brush she held limply in her hand was not going to save her. Her hair was beyond description. She had given it no thought as she and Remy tumbled into her bed last night and had later fallen asleep satiated. It wasn't until she had woken a few minutes ago with something poking painfully into her head that she realized she had not removed any pins and taken down her hair. Her frizzy, dark-brown hair had always been the bane of her existence and now it was beyond salvageable and Ollie felt betrayed as she would have liked to entice Remy into one more tryst before she politely asked him to leave.

"Ahem," Remy cleared his throat and Ollie spun to find she hadn't closed the bathroom door when she had come in. He stood there in his tight boxers; his trim, toned body looking glorious in the morning sunshine. "You need some help?"

Ollie's hardened heart melted a fraction. "I don't even know where to begin," she admitted.

"Are there pins in there?" His face was serious and she appreciated that he wasn't making fun of her horrid hair.

"Yes, tons. My hair can be wild so the hairdresser used every trick she had to get it to stay controlled for the night."

Remy walked into the bathroom and kissed the back of her neck. "I don't think she planned for our antics last night." He winked at her in the mirror.

Ollie snorted as she attempted to ignore her body's instant response to his kiss.

"Sit on the side of the bath, feet in the tub," he instructed.

She did what she was told, and he carefully began to gently tug the pins out of her hair and drop them into the palm of her hand. Ollie found the experience more intimate than she had expected, with him brushing against her back. Only her thin, red satin kimono type dressing gown and his tight boxers between them. Remy meticulously searched through the mass of her over-teased, hair-sprayed mess until every pin was uncovered. "Brush," he held out his hand expectantly. Ollie handed it over without protest.

Remy was incredibly gentle as he started on the ends of her hair and worked his way up, separating and sectioning to make it easier. "How do you know how to do this?" she asked.

"I do have many sisters, remember? And they would only play with me if I played dolls. It was my job to brush Barbie's hair out after they had created some masterpiece. I was so relieved when Thad was born." He paused as he pulled a knotty section apart with his fingers before he began to brush it again.

"Where do you fit in the birth order? All I know is that Thad is the baby."

"Marie is the eldest and definitely the most assertive. You want something done, give it to her. I never knew how together she was until I got back. All those kids, a full-time, high-pressure job and she manages to volunteer for several committees at the kid's school. She makes me exhausted," he joked.

Ollie's heart thawed a tad more at the statement. Usually, men were quick to label women like that as bossy; it was wonderful to hear a brother call his sister assertive.

"Ella is next and then me. We are so close together in age that many people thought us twins growing up. She was born in January and I am the same year in December."

"Wow, that was fast work."

"I think after taking them four years to conceive Ella after Marie they just didn't expect for me to come along so quickly. And then there is Viv and Thad, who are also close together in age—it seems they didn't learn their lesson." Remy continued to untangle her hair and

Ollie was finding the experience soothing. No one ever played with her hair, she hated the sight of it and kept it tied up as much as possible.

"Do you want to hear the gross reason why I have this skill?" He waved the hairbrush around.

Olivia was intrigued. "Definitely."

"You know I went to America to go to university and study forensics, right?"

"I vaguely remember being told something about it."

"Well, part of their university program was we had to collect samples off dead bodies. That included learning how to comb matted hair in the hope you could find evidence."

"That is fascinating and disturbing all at once."

"All done." He ran his fingers through her hair a few times and handed Ollie the brush. He helped her out of the tub and pulled her to him as she stood up.

Olivia wound her arms around his waist, enjoying the feel of his naked, smooth back. "Thank you for that. I think I would have been here all day trying to untangle that mess."

He kissed her lightly. "Any time." Remy studied her, his perfect hazel eyes looked grave. "Now, I have a serious question for you."

Instantly Ollie felt her shoulders tighten and she pulled back, he loosened his grip and let her go, though his handsome face clearly showed he was confused by the response. "I don't do serious. Serious leads to complications and hurt feelings when I am after fun and simple."

"Ah," Remy nodded. "I didn't mean to give you the impression that I was about to ask you to meet my family. Though, that would be pointless as you have spent more time with them than I have over the last five years from what I understand."

She laughed, trying to keep the snorting down to a minimum, and relaxed a little. "What was your 'serious' question?"

"What do you want first? Breakfast or sex?"

Ollie was relieved. Remy had been amazing in bed and had been fun to party with at the reception last night, but she was too busy and not interested in giving up her freedom for any man. It was the perfect situation. He would be heading back to America at some point, and until he did she would have someone to play with all the while knowing he had to leave so no serious attachments could be formed to complicate things. "I have another option if you are interested to hear?" She moved closer and hooked her finger into the band of his boxers.

Remy looked down at her finger and back up at her, he lifted an eyebrow. "I am all ears."

She let go of his briefs with a snap and undid the tie on her short dressing gown. "Well, I need to have a shower and thought I might get a bit lonely, would you care to join me?" She let the gown slide down her shoulders, revealing her nakedness.

He laughed his beautiful, hideous laugh. "Your option sounds like the beginning of a wonderful morning."

## Chapter 3

The week had been almost perfect. Work had been great, they had won their netball game, and although she missed Peyton and their almost daily Messenger conversations, she had been keeping up with her and Thad's goings-on with the few pictures the newlyweds had posted on Facebook. Olivia had spent Friday night at a local bar with a few girlfriends, where she had danced and flirted with a few cute guys but had declined to go home with any of them. Now she enjoyed a splendid Saturday morning sitting on her tiny apartment patio, surrounded by her few potted plants, wrapped in a mohair blanket, drinking tea, scrolling through her various news feeds, and reading gossip on her tablet.

As she scrolled through her Instagram account a picture of the Trevi Fountain caught her eye and Ollie clicked on it. It was gorgeous and Ollie was envious that Peyton and Thad were experiencing the incredible country of Italy while she remained at home. Olivia had plans to travel, but setting herself up financially and professionally had been far more important to achieve first. The traveling would come, but it still didn't stop her from admitting that she too longed for adventure in the great wide world. *Oh, stop that,* she told herself, *you sound like Belle from Beauty and the Beast.*

Ollie stared at the magnificent fountain and wondered what she would wish for if she tossed a coin in it. She had got out of the habit of wishing for things when she realized they never came true, even when you didn't share them. Her last real wish attempt had been at her thirteenth birthday party when she had blown out the candles and silently sent out into the universe her desire for her mother not to get drunk and ruin her birthday party. The universe had not seen fit to fulfill her wish and Ollie could still feel the looks of disgust at her mother or pity for herself as parents came to collect their children and her mother slurred farewells from the front door. It had been humiliating and the last time Ollie had had a party with her mother in attendance. Her sixteenth, eighteenth, and twenty-first were all celebrated with her friends and shared with Peyton, as they were both born in August, at venues without both of their mothers' knowledge. As far as their parents were concerned, they had spent their birthdays celebrating with a quiet dinner at home.

She took a sip of her tea and pulled a face as she discovered it had gone cold. It was time to make a new pot. She stood and collected the tray with her tea for one tea set on it and walked back into her tiny, quaint kitchen. As Ollie waited for the kettle to boil, she continued to ponder the wish dilemma. She supposed she could be magnanimous in her wish, such as hoping for world peace or a cure for all the horrendous diseases of the world. As for personal wishes she had no clue.

The kettle whistled and she refilled the pot and carried the restocked tray back out into the bright, late spring morning and let it sit there, the leaves steeping just like her thoughts. What could she possibly wish for that didn't sound greedy or conceited?

Her tablet buzzed as she poured her tea and Ollie was thrilled to see that Peyton had sent her a message.

**Peyton: Ciao O.**

**Ollie: OMG! Ciao P.**

**Peyton: What time is it there? I can't figure it out anymore.**

**Ollie: About 9:30am here, Saturday morning. You?**

**Peyton: 11:30pm, Friday night here.**

**Ollie: How's married life treating you?**

**Peyton: Loving it and loving Italy. It is simply glorious to eat all this wonderful pizza and pasta, though I doubt my clothes will fit when I get home.**

**Ollie: Now I want pizza. Saw your pic of the Trevi Fountain—did you make a wish?**

**Peyton: Sure did. Thad made one too, but he won't tell me what it is. You been up to anything interesting?**

**Ollie: Nope, nothing to report. We won netball, even though we missed your height we managed to get by. Went out with work girls last night. You gonna tell me what you wished for?**

**Peyton: You know what I wished for. I have been talking about it from the moment I got engaged.**

Ollie did know what Peyton would have wished for... getting pregnant on her honeymoon. Peyton couldn't wait to be a mother. Thad's larger, loving family with its less controlling matriarch was all Peyton had ever wanted to grow up in and she wanted to bring lots of children into the world to create her dream. It was the last thing Olivia would wish for herself, but she hoped Peyton got what she so desired.

**Peyton: Plans for tonight?**

**Ollie: Not sure, but I think it might involve pizza now.**

**Peyton: LOL. Thad says hi. OK, I am off to bed, big day tomorrow, heading to Pompeii. Love you, night.**

**Ollie: Say hey back. Have fun. Love you too. Xox**

Ollie sat there for a few moments longer, sipping her tea and staring at the screen and missing her friend. *She's married now, things change, but you know she will always be there so stop being silly.* Thad had been very quick to understand the depth of friendship Ollie and Peyton shared and had not once tried to come between them, she didn't see that changing just because they were now married.

"I need pizza," she announced to no one. Ollie grabbed her phone and sent a message. While she waited for a response she took her finished tea and packed up her morning tea tray and headed into her apartment to get her washing done and change her sheets. Her normal Saturday morning routine.

Her phone beeped to announce a message as she emerged from having scrubbed the shower. A slow grin grew as she looked at the response her message had elicited.

"THIS WAS A GREAT idea." Remy looked out over the vista of the Melbourne skyline from their vantage point. "I forgot the feel Melbourne has at night."

"It has a 'feel'?" Ollie was surprised. She had spent her entire life here and didn't realize that it had a unique vibe.

"Oh, yeah. There is always something happening. People moving around to big events, bustling in and out of theatres, stadiums, the casino complex, the laneways with all the funky clubs. It's an almost electric feel—a sense of anticipation and a blending of cultures. Chinatown, Lygon street, live pub bands mixed in with techno spilling out from the doors of the latest hotspot." His handsome features were alight with excitement and she couldn't help but feel his joy.

They sat on a rooftop bar, cold drinks in hand, tucked away in a corner. Pretty hanging lanterns were strung up and a duo was playing all the Aussie classics that you just don't hear overseas but set the crowd to singing at the top of their lungs at home. Ollie looked out at the sparkling Yarra River and the crowds of people walking along South Bank and had to agree there was an undercurrent of expectancy, the prospect of having the greatest night.

"Here you go," the waiter put a pizza down in the middle of the table.

"Thank you," said Remy.

Ollie inhaled the delicious smells and sighed. "I have been fantasizing about this all day."

"About our date or the pizza?"

"Oh, definitely the pizza." She winked at him. "I spoke to Peyton via Messenger this morning and she mentioned pizza; I haven't been able to stop thinking about it ever since."

Remy laughed his loud, raucous guffaw and several people turned to stare. Ollie grinned, glad it was him drawing attention with his laugh rather than her for once.

"How are they?"

"In love, happy, making wishes at the Trevi Fountain. All the things you would expect on a honeymoon in Rome."

"You ever been to Rome?" he asked.

"Nope, I haven't been out of the country. I have worked in every state in Australia though."

"You travel for work?" he guessed.

Ollie nodded and drew her attention away from his gorgeous hazel eyes and picked up a slice of pizza. "I work for a movie distribution company so when we have blockbuster releases I travel to make sure everything is set up correctly." She took a bite of her pizza, the cheese stretched so far that in the end, she had to break it off with her fingers. It was just the way she had hoped it would be.

They ate in silence, listening to the band and the crowd singing, and watched the flames shoot into the air from the huge columns that lined the front of the Crown Casino complex. The night was warm, but they both carried a jacket—it was Melbourne after all and its unpredictable weather was well documented.

Olivia smiled as Remy began to hum to the song being played. "Another thing you missed?"

"I missed many things, but I am home now. Care to dance?"

The dance area was crowded but they managed to find room and danced for the next several songs. Remy wasn't a great dancer but Ollie appreciated his efforts as many men refused to get up and move. If only they understood how appealing it was to a woman. Eventually, Remy put his hands up and stated that he was thirsty. On the way back to the table he ordered them drinks.

Ollie flopped down onto her seat and smiled at the gorgeous man in front of her. All the dancing had given her other physical ideas and she was contemplating how forward she could be in her want to take him home. She knew most women would wait for the man to make the first move, but she was not most women and she had already taken him home once.

He broke into her lascivious thoughts. "Do you know you haven't asked me a single personal question?"

"I didn't know I was supposed to."

"Isn't that what people do? Talk to each other?" Remy looked at her with a quizzical look.

Ollie was confused. What was he implying? "Ah, we do talk."

"Yes, we talk about light stuff. We joke and flirt and party, but we never talk about anything serious."

"I have no idea what you mean." Ollie was becoming uncomfortable. "I know heaps about you. I've met your family, I hang out with your brother. I know that you went to America to study and never came back, which continues to make your mother sad, but everyone is so proud of you and they talk about your achievements to everyone. You are the third child within five siblings. I even know your middle name. What more do I need to know?"

"What about my plans and dreams?" Remy prompted.

"Ah. I thought you understood that I wasn't interested in a commitment. I am a little confused as I didn't think you would be either."

He frowned at her and took a sip of his beer. "But I still want to get to know you and you me. How can that happen if we don't share things?"

"Okay, tell me something I should know about you."

"You should know that I want a family."

"Well, yes most people do," she interjected. Ollie didn't see the point of knowing that. As far she could tell she was the only one who felt that having a family held no appeal. She wanted a good time with no commitments. As soon as people got serious they started making demands and everything lost its appeal and grew stale.

"That was defensive. Did I say something wrong?" He went to take her hand, but she moved it off the table and into her lap, the other one was occupied with holding her glass.

"No, nothing wrong. It's just not how I view things."

"Can I ask how you view things?" he spoke softly as if afraid she might become more annoyed.

"My home life wasn't the best growing up and my only semi-long term relationship turned into a yawn fest after a few months and I just don't want that. I want lust, fun, and no tears." Her answer was flippant and mostly true.

"So, a party girl at heart?" His smile was warm and held no judgment.

Ollie shrugged, there was no answer to that statement. She reached across the table and squeezed his hand, hoping he understood that this was as close to intimacy that she would allow.

"Hey," Remy sat up straighter and stared at her. "How do you know my middle name? I don't tell anyone that information."

Ollie laughed or rather snorted at him. "I can understand why you don't give out that information."

Remy joined his hideous laughter to hers and it drew attention but she didn't care. "I have no idea what my parents were thinking."

## Chapter 4

The bathroom sparkled and Ollie stood back and admired her cleaning skills. She sang to the music that played throughout her modest apartment as she completed her Saturday morning rituals. Ollie was in a wonderful mood, her week had been great. The first week of summer had been spent playing netball, partying with friends, and consulting with her bosses in Australia and America as they prepared for Boxing Day Blockbuster releases in cinemas across the country. She had been to Sydney and Brisbane the week before that and had not caught up with Remy since their pizza hook-up.

Ollie checked her watch, she still had two hours before her lunch date. Enough time to take a leisurely soak in the tub and get her frizzy, dark-brown hair under control.

The warm, fragranced water did its magic and refreshed her spirit and soul, which allowed her mind to wander. Ambient music played in the background, having replaced the Keith Urban album she had been streaming earlier. Her father's birthday was next week and she considered what to buy him, several unkind thoughts about a backbone came to mind before Ollie shunted the whole idea aside. Her relationship with her father was just as difficult as the one she had with her mother at times. Ollie could not understand why he hadn't left and taken her with him when her mother's drinking became a problem. Instead, like many marriages, it was kept secret and hidden until it couldn't be anymore, but because he was a man he wasn't encouraged to leave as a woman would be, or at least that is how Ollie felt about it.

Olivia attempted to shift her thoughts to happier things. She knew she would go to dinner and pretend she was fine with everything and hope she could leave before her mother got too far in her cups and begun questioning her on all her life decisions and why she wasn't dating anyone seriously. How do you tell a parent that because fun and laughter were so rare at home that was all she required to make her happy? And the thought of having a marriage like her parents' marriage made her ill and keen to remain a spinster forever? *Maybe I should just skip dinner*, the idea popped into her head.

After several false starts, Ollie was able to tell her brain to stop worrying about it and focus on something else, but this was only achieved when she distracted herself by picking up her tablet and finding something else to look at. Remy's face. Ollie found herself scrolling through his photos as Facebook had suggested him as a friend. *It's not a big deal,* she told herself as she found herself going back further than a year in his posts. Though there were not many posts, mostly him being tagged in holiday photos around America by his friends. There was one girl who appeared in many photos but had disappeared about six months ago. *It's not your business,* she reminded herself. *He is allowed female friends, you don't own him or want him as more than the occasional hook-up, so mind your own business.*

The bathwater grew cool as Ollie sat there and contemplated sending him a friend request. If she sent it would she be sending him the wrong signals? Would she want him seeing all her posts, as her settings were set to friends only? Why was she so worried about the whole thing? Ollie shivered as it finally registered how long she had been sitting there, and even though the day was warming up to be an early Melbourne summer scorcher, she had grown cold in the tepid water.

The Facebook friend request remained unsent as she placed the tablet on the bathroom shelf and hauled herself out of the tub and grabbed a huge, gray fluffy towel that almost covered her entire small frame. Ollie looked in the mirror and wailed with annoyance as she looked at her hair in all its frizzy glory. She had been sitting in the bath for too long and now wouldn't have time to straighten it. *And that is why you don't go all soft over a man, no matter how cute he is... they are a time suck.*

It didn't take her long to get dry, dressed, and apply a small amount of make-up. Ollie wore a thin-strapped, wide-leg jumpsuit with a black and white vertical stripe in varying widths. It was belted at the waist with the same striped material, and she had completed the look with white high-heeled sandals. Everything looked great, but the hair was still a mess. With a resigned sigh, she grabbed her brush and an elastic and began to drag it back from her face and up into a ponytail. Her long, horrid hair now sat in a high ponytail but now that it had been brushed was even frizzier than before. Muttering to herself about her blasted hair, she plaited it with practiced ease and then wound it around the base of the ponytail to make a large bun. On such a hot day it would be good to keep her hair up, she tried to convince herself.

Her watch alarm went off and after one last squirt of hair spray, she was good to go. Ollie grabbed her bag and phone and clicked the lock as she left. The drive to the cafe by the bay took her no more than twenty minutes and she was grateful to find a car park quickly. As she walked to the cafe she took several deep breaths, marveling at the scent of the sea air and reveled in the perfect summer day. Ollie was grateful to live so close to the city as well as the beach. Maybe after lunch, she would take off her shoes and walk along the white sanded beach?

Ollie was the first to arrive and told the waiter who greeted her the reservation information. She was guided to a table that sat next to a large open window where the sounds of the passersby, seagulls, and the beachgoers wafted in. She ordered a latte, not knowing how long she would have to wait on her own. Ollie wouldn't mind waiting in this location, it was peaceful and she was in no hurry to be anywhere.

OLLIE'S PEACEFUL SILENCE WAS shattered by the clicking of heels and a loud squeal of delight as her best friend, Peyton, entered the cafe. With a grin, Ollie greeted her and was soon engulfed in a bone-crunching hug from her tall, elegant friend. "Oh, I have missed you," Ollie spoke as she kissed Peyton's cheek.

"I missed you more," countered Peyton.

"I doubt it. I am sure you were too busy with Thad,"—she wiggled her eyebrows suggestively at her—"to think of me."

They settled into their seats and Peyton ordered a Sprite. "You look wonderful. Rome and married life seem to suit you." Ollie looked at her friend. She had a glow to her that came from within, Peyton had had it on her wedding day and it hadn't disappeared yet. *Maybe being in love wasn't as bad as first thought if it can do that to you.* Ollie quickly pulled herself up on that notion. Peyton wore a short, white sundress with small daisies on it and short cuffed sleeves. Sunglasses were the only thing that held her wealth of wavy, dark-blonde hair away from her square face.

"You look gorgeous. I love the outfit." Peyton smiled warmly at Ollie. "Shall we order before we dive into our catch up?"

"Great idea." Both of them perused the menu and ended up ordering the same thing. A lamb Greek salad, with extra olives.

As the waiter took their order and menus, Peyton pulled out a small velvet box from her bag and pushed it in front of Olivia. "I wanted to say thank you for always being there. I know things will be different now that I am married, but I wanted to give you this as a reminder of our friendship and as a thank you for all the support over the years and especially dealing with my mother during the lead up to the wedding."

Ollie looked at the box and then back at her friend. "You didn't need to get me anything. I treasure our friendship just as much as you do, and you have to put up with my mum too." A lump had formed in her throat, but there were no tears. It took a lot for Ollie to cry as she had repressed it for so long.

"Go on, open it," urged Peyton.

The box snapped open with a jerk and revealed an exquisite Pandora charm. It was in the shape of a love heart and had the word *family* scrawled across the front of it. "It's perfect."

Peyton reached across the table and squeezed Ollie's hand. "We have the family we are born into and neither of us can control that, but I believe we also have the family we choose and I choose you. You are my heart sister, the one person who gets me and I needed you to know that it doesn't matter how our lives change, you will always be my family and be a part of it."

The lump in Ollie's throat grew in size until it was almost impossible to swallow, yet the tears didn't come. "Thank you. It is the most precious gift anyone has ever given me." She hugged Peyton and whispered into her ear, "I choose you too."

Unlike the dry-eyed Ollie, Peyton had a few tears as she helped her friend put the new trinket onto the bracelet she always wore. The waitress arrived with their food and then they raised their drinks in a toast to family, the one you choose.

"Sooooo," Peyton drew out the word and Ollie instantly knew where the conversation was headed. "Rumor has it you went home with a charming young man from my wedding."

Ollie was correct in her assumption. She continued to eat her lamb salad as technically Peyton had not asked a question.

"Well?"

"Well, what?" Ollie grinned just to irritate her friend.

Peyton narrowed her green eyes. "Don't be coy with me. Did you go home with Remy?"

Ollie's own brown eyes narrowed in imitation of her friend's. "You are truly telling me you don't know?"

Peyton laughed—her laugh was pretty, like a gentle waterfall. "It turns out Remy is being as hush-hush as you are about it. He has been asked by just about everyone and he simply explains that he made sure you got home safe."

That surprised Ollie. She had not told him to keep their dalliance a secret. *Maybe it has something to do with the girl in all those Facebook photos. Oh, shut up,* she told her inner voice. Ollie ate her lunch and considered what she wanted to tell Peyton now that she knew Remy had not told anyone. In the end, she decided to treat him like she would treat any other of her male 'friends' when it came to what she disclosed to Peyton. "We got together your wedding night."

"And?"

"And we hung out the next day, where I made it crystal clear that I was not looking for anything. He appeared quite happy with that arrangement so we met a week later where we spent the night together and most of the next day. It was fun."

"Oh, wow." Peyton winked. "So, he was worth hanging out with again I take it?"

Ollie laughed loud enough to draw the attention of several people in the cafe. Peyton could be such a prude. "Yes, he satisfied a certain itch that I was happy to see him again. I was thinking of texting him today. He must be almost ready to go home soon and I wanted to catch up with him maybe one more time before he goes."

A frown crossed Peyton's face as her fork stopped halfway to her mouth. She put the utensil back down and looked seriously at Ollie, all the joking put aside. "Olivia, Remy has been in hospital the last two days."

# Chapter 5

The hospital lobby was busy as Ollie walked across to the lift. She had to negotiate with several squabbling children and a hospital bed before she could enter and select her floor. Peyton had given her Remy's floor and room number as they were leaving the cafe. Ollie couldn't explain why, but it was important for her to see for herself that he was okay. She rode the lift up in silence. Watching the lights of each floor light up until they came to a halt and the door dinged as it opened. Ollie exited the lift so others could get in but now she had arrived she wasn't convinced that this was a good idea. Maybe turning up without a text or phone call first was rude? Maybe he would get the wrong impression? *Why are you overthinking everything these days? He is unwell and you are here as a friend.* With those final words to herself, Ollie went in search of his room.

It didn't take her long to find his room and she was grateful to discover it was a single room so no one could hear them if the conversation became awkward. As Olivia stood at the door and took in the sight of balloons, flowers, and a teddy bear, only then did she belatedly remember she should have at least brought a card. Maybe she could sneak down to the kiosk before he saw her and grab something? "Hey, you," Remy's voice called to her and it was too late, she had been seen.

Plastering a smile on her face and still uncertain as to why she had come to visit, Ollie walked into the room. "Hey, you." The powerful emotions that welled inside her as she saw Remy in his white hospital gown and hooked up to a beeping machine made her want to spin on her heel and make a quick escape. Her heart pounded harder and while she fought the desire to run away she also fought the urge to run at him and smother him in hugs and kisses and check every part of him to make certain he was fine.

All of this debate went on in her head in a manner of seconds as she sedately walked to the side of his bed, not letting on the internal struggle she was dealing with. Ollie bent down and kissed him on the cheek. "How are you feeling?"

"I am fine. Everyone is overreacting. I had a mild episode." Remy dismissed his family's and doctor's concerns with a short gesture of his hand. "But I can be sicker if it gets me a proper kiss."

Without speaking, Ollie leaned back in and kissed him gently, lingering for a second too long on his full lips. "Better?" Ollie pulled up a chair and looked at him. He was pale and his beautiful hazel eyes didn't hold their usual sparkle. "Peyton didn't say you were fine and everyone was overreacting."

"How did Peyton put it?"

"You went into a diabetic coma and that if you hadn't been found in time you could have died." Ollie glared at him, she wasn't even sure why. "Are you telling me Peyton is lying?" she challenged.

Remy laid his head back in the pillows and let out a sigh. "No, she isn't lying."

"Why didn't you tell me you had diabetes?"

Remy gave a short, sharp laugh. "Are you kidding me? You were the one who clearly told me that we were not to share personal information."

Ollie couldn't argue with that, so instead, she continued to glare at him.

"You look gorgeous today. Where have you been?"

"Lunch with Peyton. I came from there to see you on my way home," she lied. She had driven half an hour out of her way to get here, but he need never know that.

"Did you have a good lunch? What did you eat?"

"Stop with the charming and changing subjects." Ollie didn't understand why but his flippant behavior bothered her.

"You find me charming?"

"Yes," she said bluntly. "Now, what happened?"

"Why? What does is it matter?"

Ollie bit back a smart retort and took a breath, why was he pushing her buttons today and why did she care? She was beginning to regret coming. "It is customary when you visit someone in hospital that they regale you with the tale of their misfortune so one can ooh and ahh over it and claim how horrible it must have been."

"If I tell you, you have to promise not to lecture me." Remy gave her a soft smile and her annoyance abated slightly.

"Mmmm... that implies you are responsible for your own misfortune."

"It does, doesn't it?"

"I have changed my mind. I do not need to know how stupid you are."

"Woah, that is unfair."

Ollie smirked. "Life is unfair."

Remy laughed his raucous laugh and she joined in with her heinous snort. What a pair they made. "May I inquire as to how I came up in conversation with Peyton?"

Ollie managed not to blush. "Peyton was asking for clarification regarding after the wedding as it appears you are a gentleman who doesn't kiss and tell." She took his hand for a moment and squeezed it. "Thank you for that." She returned her hand to her lap. "I was explaining that we had been out a few times and that I was thinking of texting you as it had been two weeks and I was impressed you had respected my wishes. That's when she told me you were in hospital."

"You were planning on messaging me again?" He sounded surprised.

"Why do you say it like that?" She tried not to sound defensive.

"Ah, because it had been two weeks and you had made it abundantly clear I was just a fling."

"But a fun fling, and why can't we carry that on?"

"I will admit I am having a certain amount of difficulty keeping you at arm's length."

The room was silent as Olivia digested that. Remy rushed on to clarify, "I just meant that I enjoy hanging out with you and I was having trouble not texting you to ask you out again. I didn't want to frighten you off."

"You should have texted. I know we don't have heaps of time so it would have been great to get together again."

Remy gave her a funny look and opened his mouth to speak.

"Knock, knock," they were interrupted by a cheerful voice.

Ollie turned to see Mariella, Remy's Nona standing by the door. She stood to offer her chair and moved to the other side of the bed and perched on the wide window sill. Ollie was surprised to be embraced in a warm hug after Mariella had greeted her grandson. "How wonderful to find you here, Olivia."

REMY SMILED FONDLY AT his Nona as she tucked his blanket in a little tighter. "Thanks." She ruffled his short hair and beamed at him like he was six and had won the sports carnival.

Mariella looked as marvelous as she had at the wedding and Ollie could only wish she looked that put together when she got to Nona's age. She wore a dress in a teal satin fabric with a geometric repeating shape in gold and silver. The neck was round and it had short sleeves and a full pleated skirt, Mariella had finished it with beige mid-heeled pumps. They sat and made small talk for a while and Ollie guessed that Remy had already received his lecture from Mariella as she did not question him once about what had happened. She was more concerned about when he would be discharged.

"The doctors will be coming in soon to take this out,"—he gestured to the IV that ran into his hand—"and then they just want to monitor my sugar levels for a while. Everyone is guessing tomorrow morning if all goes well."

Ollie cleared her throat before they could continue their conversation. "I am going to head off and give you two time together. Can I get you a cup of something before I go?" Ollie asked Mariella. "I saw a small kitchenette that I am assuming is for making cups of tea and coffee." Ollie turned to Remy. "Are you allowed to have anything?"

"No, they are monitoring everything at the moment, but thanks."

"I would love a cup of coffee but will accompany you so I can find it on my own if I need another one while I visit."

The perfectly groomed elder lady took hold of Ollie's arm and Olivia noted that she was the same height as Nona. It was nice not to be towered over for once. It didn't take Ollie long to make Mariella her cup of coffee and she offered to carry it back to the room for her. As they made their way back Mariella cleared her throat. "Please forgive an old lady for interfering but I couldn't help but overhear what you said to Remy just before I knocked on the door."

Olivia frowned. "I don't recall what I said," she admitted.

"You said that you knew Remy didn't have a lot of time. To what were you referring?"

"Oh that. I just know his time here is limited before he heads back to the States."

"Olivia, what makes you think that?" Mariella pursed her lips. "He is home for good. He has told his family he is staying, which everyone is thrilled about. He couldn't go any further in his career unless he became a citizen and he has no want to do that. He has been looking for work here."

Ollie stopped and looked at Nona. "I think I just assumed it. It certainly explains the weird looks he gives me when I say something about him leaving."

She began to move again but was stopped by Mariella's hand on her arm. "I am genuinely happy to find you here."

Ollie became suspicious. "And yet not truly surprised."

"No, not surprised."

"You know."

She raised a perfectly groomed eyebrow at Ollie. "I know what?"

Ollie chuckled. "Okay, keep your secrets."

They both began to move again and returned to find the doctor and a nurse removing the IV from Remy's arm. Ollie placed the coffee on the tray that held a few puzzle books, Remy's phone, and a pen and tried to stay out of the way. It was over quickly and a bit of gauze and tape were the only reminder he had of the IV.

It was time to go. "It was lovely to see you again, Mariella." She kissed the wonderful, sassy woman on the cheek. Ollie looked to Remy and hesitated, not sure what she should do. In the end, she gave him a quick peck on the forehead and grabbed her things. "Take care of yourself and please let me know if I can do anything."

As she made her way out of the room, she heard Mariella speak loudly to Remy, "A very pretty girl that one and genuine, would you agree?"

"Yes, Nona, she is very pretty and smart too. Can you keep your voice down, please?"

Ollie grinned to herself as she turned a corner and walked out of earshot and sight. Her grin slowly slid from her face as the realization of what she had just been told sunk in. Remy would not be going back to America, he would be living here. The lift doors slid open and she pressed the button without conscious thought. Ollie was so distracted that when the lift doors opened she walked out only to discover she was still in the hospital, only on another floor instead of the ground floor. To hide her mistake she waited for the lift doors to close and move downward before she pressed the down button. This time she was more aware of her surroundings when she emerged from the elevator and made her way to her car.

*What are you panicking about?* Her inner voice intruded as she started her car. *You just need to readjust your thinking and be very clear that while you like him you have no intention of changing for him and as soon as he makes a demand he is gone. Just like any other guy.* Ollie tried to ignore the fact he wasn't like any other guy, he was Thad's brother and she would now have to deal with him at many family events. Maybe it would be best to just stop everything now? While the idea had merit she didn't find it appealing and she didn't want to examine why.

"Maybe I shall just ignore it and it will all go away," she announced to the interior of her car. "Yes, great plan." And with that, Ollie turned up the music and attempted to pretend she had it all under control.

## Chapter 6

"Happy Birthday, Dad." Ollie hugged her father as he greeted her at the front door. She held out a large pot with a tiny tomato plant in it.

"Olivia, thank you. Let's see if I can keep it alive till my next birthday," he joked.

"Oh, don't do that, then I will have to think of something else to get you for your birthday each year rather than just replacing that."

"Cheeky girl," he smiled at her as he stepped aside to let her in.

Her father fancied himself as a gardener, but he killed every plant he attempted to grow. Ollie had a suspicion that he had built the glasshouse in their back yard and spent so much time in it to get away from his alcoholic wife and whether the plants grew or not was irrelevant.

Ollie followed him through the house and into the kitchen to find her mother stirring gravy with one hand while sipping her red wine with the other. She kissed her mother on each cheek as was their custom. "Can I help with anything?"

"You can see that the table needs to be set," her mother said with a nod to the empty kitchen table.

*Great, the snarky has already commenced.* "Yes, Mother." *Just be quiet and get it done,* Ollie told herself. *The sooner you eat the sooner you can leave.* Ollie set the table for the three of them as her father carved the roast and her mother continued to stir the gravy while sipping her wine. As usual, the television was on in the background, it was like they used it to fill the silence in the house as they barely spoke to each other.

Without being told, Ollie got out plates and took the roasted vegetables out of the oven and began to serve up the meal with her father heaping the succulent roast beef slices onto their plates. Her mother continued to stir and sip. Finally, dinner was served and Ollie got herself a glass of water—not offering to pour either of them a drink.

It was her own personal protest and the only thing she felt she could control when she came to visit.

"How was Peyton's wedding?" her father asked. This warranted a sniff from her mother.

"It was all that she hoped for. A bit too large for my tastes, but that's what you get when you marry into a huge family."

"How many guests did she have?" her father continued the conversation.

"Around four hundred."

"Ridiculous," her mother snorted.

"Peyton looked beautiful and loved her honeymoon, they went to Italy." Ollie spoke as if her mother had made no comment.

"I must say, Olivia, I was a little miffed not to have received an invitation." Her mother got up to refill her wine glass, her food barely touched.

Olivia looked to her father, who kept his eyes on his plate and didn't acknowledge the statement. In the end, Ollie decided her best course was to do the same thing. After all, her mother hadn't asked a question. They ate in silence with the television filling the void for several minutes.

After a few small bites, Ollie's mother put her knife and fork down, indicating she was finished with her meal. This usually meant that she had started drinking earlier in the day, and like many heavy drinkers lost their appetite when they started drinking. "We haven't seen you in over a month, Olivia, where have you been?"

"I had the lead up to the wedding and then I have traveled for work."

"I thought perhaps you may have finally found someone that will put up with your idiosyncrasies. You do have a lot, after all."

"I am too young to settle down. I am having fun going out."

"You will be left on the shelf with that attitude. All the good ones will be taken by the time you are ready."

Remy's face appeared in her mind and she was reminded of his gentleness and generosity. *Not all the good ones are taken.*

Ollie finished her meal and quickly collected the plates. She told her father to sit down as it was his birthday she could do the dishes. Her mother stayed at her position at the head of the table and drank her wine and continued to make snide comments about Ollie.

"You are looking a little bloated. Not very becoming."

"What are those pants you are wearing? You are too short for that style."

"Why don't you cut that terrible hair off and have a pixie cut like you did when you were little?"

With every question, Ollie felt her shoulders sag a hint more. It was exhausting listening to this running commentary of how bad your life was and how it was all due to the way she looked and behaved. By the time the table was cleared and the dishwasher packed, her mother was ready for another refill and her father was yet to say anything.

"Dad, did you hear from the boys for your birthday?" Ollie hoped a change of topic would stop her mother's criticism.

"Josh dropped in on his way home from work. He couldn't stay as the kids needed to be picked up from school and get them to tennis lessons and April was still at work."

"That April is a cold woman, I have never understood what Josh sees in her," was the comment given.

Ollie and her father ignored it. April was terrified of her mother-in-law so appeared cold when she was at family events. "And Robbie?" Ollie prompted. Robbie was the most like their mother and had begun drinking heavily in his teens and had never stopped. He was single, like Ollie, but for different reasons. Robbie couldn't keep a job or a woman and it had only been recently discovered that he had a gambling problem. What woman would want him?

"I got a text from Robbie about midday apologizing that he wouldn't be able to make it tonight."

"I am amazed he even remembered it was your birthday," was her mother's contribution. She drained the dregs of her glass. "Three children and none of them care enough about us. Watch Olivia rush out of here now that we have eaten. Ungrateful, the lot of you. Gave up the best years of my life raising you unruly shits. And this is the payment I get, no one comes to see me."

That was indeed the indication it was time for Ollie to leave. The words no longer had the power they once had or that is what she pretended. Her father stood there and said nothing as her mother continued to rant about life's injustices and Ollie gathered her bag and bit her tongue as any response would be considered wrong and earn her further rebuke.

Ollie said her goodbyes as quickly as she could and got in her car, driving off as if she were being chased. She drove around several streets until she got to the local park and pulled into the empty dark car park. Too worked up to drive home.

Ollie sat in her car and deliberately clenched and unclenched her fists, breathing in as she clenched and out as she released. It didn't take too long to get her emotions in check and push the hurt her mother's words caused back down where it belonged. The worse part was that she would be expected to do it all again in two weeks when it was her mother's birthday.

## Chapter 7

Her phone buzzed for the fifth time and Ollie had an internal battle not to pick it up. It had been a week since her visit to the hospital and there had been no contact between Remy and her since then. When his name had popped up on the first message she had turned the screen face down and went back to her Saturday morning ritual and poured herself another cup of tea from her fancy teapot.

Ollie had spent the week attempting to figure out what she wanted to do with the information Mariella had shared and why Remy had not been clearer about his intention to stay. Could it be that he was frightened that this would be her response? Was she behaving exactly like he thought she would? That didn't sit well, but she had almost convinced herself that was irrelevant. Olivia had a life plan and that didn't include falling in love. She wanted fun. No commitment, no one letting her down, and no one relying on her. Knowing he had a serious illness was not what she had wanted to hear either. And yet... Ollie was drawn to him. His laugh, his sincerity, his body, his witty talk, all made him difficult to resist.

"Maybe one last hurrah before I give him up?" she spoke to the cool, empty air on her balcony. Ollie put down her teacup and picked up her phone. There were three messages from Remy, one from Peyton and one from Thad.

**Remy: Hey, you. Sooo, you offered to help me with my recovery... still interested?**

**Remy: I was thinking we could get together tonight if you have nothing on? If not tonight then maybe tomorrow?**

**Peyton: O, what's happening? If you are free tonight thought you might want to come around for a BBQ?**

**Thad: Hi Ollie, looking forward to catching up soon. Peyton says she invited you over for dinner—if you come you are welcome to bring Remy—as you are already 'friends' this can't be classed as a setup, right?**

**Remy: Aren't you talking to me? I miss your laugh.**

With those final words, Ollie chuckled and sent Remy a message.

**Ollie: You are a liar. Miss my laugh... bwahahaha.**

Ollie sat and pondered what she wanted to do about the dinner invite. She had not made plans as the week had been busy and she was tired and still recovering from the dinner with her parents. The offer of someone cooking her a BBQ sounded wonderful, but did she want to invite Remy? Would it give everyone the wrong idea? Ollie sipped her tea as she thought about the whole mess and at last, came up with a plan that got her what she wanted without it looking like it had anything to do with her.

**Ollie: P, BBQ sounds perfect. What time and what can I bring?**

**Ollie: Hi Thad, just told Peyton that a BBQ sounds great. As for your brother, if you want to invite him I won't object as we are 'friends.'**

**Ollie: Hey, you, I am busy tonight, though I would have been happy to hang out. You can't expect a girl not to have plans on a Saturday night. If things work out the way I hope tonight I will be busy tomorrow too. Maybe another time.**

Ollie smiled and gave herself a mental pat on the back for her cleverness and then set about tidying up as she waited for her phone to start receiving messages. It didn't take long.

**Peyton: Can you grab a loaf of bread, please? Only thing I forgot when I went to the shops. Around six is great. Xox**

"Perfect," Ollie stated aloud as she cleaned up the breakfast dishes and brought them inside. "That gives me enough time to get to my appointment and still get my hair washed and under control for tonight." Ollie had her monthly waxing appointment and body massage booked in at her favorite local salon.

**Thad: Heads up—Remy will be joining us. Looking forward to catching up, haven't seen you since the wedding.**

It was true, Ollie hadn't seen Thad since the wedding and now that she thought about it, she had missed him and his sunny disposition more than she thought she would. Thad had won a place in her heart when few other people could. Ollie didn't allow many in for the risk to her was too high, but Thad had managed it by being consistent and honest and always kind. *Remy has those qualities too,* a tiny voice inside piped up. *He also makes you laugh and relax.* Her phone beeped, putting an end to her internal chattering.

**Remy: Turns out we will be hanging out tonight. I have to go out this afternoon for a while and will need to go by your place to get to Thad's, would you like a lift?**

Ollie smiled with satisfaction, though she tried to ignore why this made her so happy. It was an odd situation for her to be in and most of the time she didn't want to think about itshe just wanted to enjoy it. Thinking about her feelings made her mind wander to her parents and then she grew depressed or angry depending on her mood. Life was easier when you put the big emotions away and enjoyed the simple pleasures. This was probably why she was yet to process how she felt about Remy keeping the truth from her. Did she care enough to get upset about it? Did she want to even begin to think about why he had done it? It seemed too difficult, so she put it away for another day.

**Ollie: A lift would be amazing. I'll be ready at five, so any time after that is great.**

**Remy: Sounds good, see you then.**

It wasn't until Ollie received the final text did she begin to regret what she had just agreed to. It was all just sinking in. She was about to have dinner with a guy she was sleeping with, her best friend, and her new husband, who was the brother to the bed partner. Was it a little too much happy family for her? Had she just made a truly bad decision?

"So, is this what you had in mind when you told me yesterday that you were going to be busy today?" Remy's hand trailed along Ollie's bare shoulder. Her bedroom was warm as the afternoon sun poured through the flimsy white fabric that passed as a curtain. Her ceiling fan spun slowly, barely moving the air. Ollie was torn between getting up to switch it to a faster setting and staying exactly where she was, languishing next to the naked body of Remy.

Her Sunday had been wonderful and just what she had hoped for when she had set her plan into action the day prior. After a relaxed, enjoyable night with Peyton and Thad, Remy had offered to give Ollie a lift home rather than her get a taxi. Of course, she had accepted and when they had arrived back at her place had invited him in for a night cap, and even though the night had been strenuous she had made sure he got enough rest before they headed out Sunday morning.

Olivia and Remy had begun with breakfast in town, down one of the famous alleyways that housed tiny cafes that served the world's best coffee. The morning had then been spent in the Bourke St. Mall and surrounding areas, shopping for Christmas presents and watching the buskers earn their few coins. They had then caught a City Circle tram and explored several of the gardens before settling on a place where they had had Chinese for lunch and after more city exploring had found a cute cafe and had gelato for dessert.

Melbourne had provided some perfect summer weather and Ollie was hoping to get to the beach tomorrow afternoon. She was contemplating asking Remy but didn't want to give him the wrong impression by spending too much time with him too many days in a row. It was also a rule she had created as she didn't like women who threw aside their female friends when they got a partner. Maybe she would invite him only if her friends couldn't make it... but maybe that was worse; only asking him because there was no one else to go with. *You know that is not true.* She was quick to tell herself. *You don't want to give him the wrong idea so are making up excuses—he is the one you want to take to the beach,* she argued with herself. *Oh, just be quiet.*

Ollie had been mindful and had noticed Remy had begun to look a little worn after lunch and had suggested they head back to her place, which was closer. They had spent the afternoon watching Netflix and hanging out. She definitely didn't want to be the one to have to tell Mariella her grandson was back in hospital because on his first day out Ollie had not cared for him.

Watching Netflix had quickly turned into a make-out session on the couch which rapidly moved to the bedroom. Ollie had trouble keeping her hands off the heavy eye-browed, straight-nosed man, with his hot compact body and hilarious laugh.

"Who hurt you?" he asked quietly. His fingers continued to trace patterns on her naked back and she felt drowsy.

"Why do you think someone hurt me?" Ollie turned her head to face him.

"Do you know you have the prettiest brown eyes?"

She smiled at him. "You don't have to charm me; I am already in the bed."

He returned her smile with a sad one. "I am serious. Who hurt you?"

"No boyfriend hurt me if that is what you are alluding to," Ollie didn't want to have this conversation. She got tired of this question. Why couldn't people understand that a monogamous relationship, where you are tied to one person was not something she wanted? She had tried it and it had been tedious, demanding on her time, and not something she cared to repeat. She ignored the voice that reminded her she may have picked someone who wasn't compatible on purpose.

Remy's light touch on her back gave her goose flesh in the best kind of way and her thoughts headed back into the steamy direction. "How are you feeling? I haven't exhausted you?"

"Don't change subjects, Ollie."

"I am not changing subjects. I thought the subject of my lack of wanting a committed relationship had ended. I have not lied to you nor changed my mind, so I am not sure why we continue to discuss it." She knew her voice held a hint of exasperation and she didn't care. What did it matter to him? Ollie decided to give him a serve of his own medicine. "Why don't you take care of yourself?"

She almost smirked as an uncomfortable look crossed his handsome face. His hazel eyes wrinkled as he narrowed them. "Nice try."

"No, I am serious." Ollie turned her body toward him, rather than just her head. "You know you could get really ill and lose body parts but you continue to eat crap and party rather than take proper care of yourself."

Remy moved in to kiss her and Ollie held her hand against his chest in an effort to stop him. Remy laughed and shook his head. "You are using my illness to hide from my questions."

Ollie snorted which made Remy laugh harder. "I am doing no such thing."

"Okay, let's play a game. You appear to like games." He arched an eyebrow at her suggestively.

"What's the game?" She got the feeling she wasn't going to like the answer.

"You answer my questions and I will answer yours." He took advantage of her momentary lapse of pressure on his chest with her hand and kissed her.

"Can't we just play that game instead?" Ollie asked as she brought her hands up to his face and pulled him closer to her.

"You know I won't be distracted forever?"

"Shhhhh and kiss me," she whispered.

THE CALAMARI SALAD THEY had ordered in was amazing and Ollie was content as they sat on her balcony watching the sun dip below the tree line. She took a sip of her lemon, lime, and bitters and audibly sighed.

"You enjoying that?" Remy grinned.

"Yes, I have never ordered from there before, but will be doing so from now on."

"I was thinking I might stay the night—how do you feel about that?"

Ollie's mood changed and she became wary. "I have gym in the morning."

"Skip it. You look hot, one less session won't matter." He winked at her.

"I like to start the week off with a workout."

Remy pouted and Ollie would have thought it cute ten minutes ago, but now it got her back up as she realized he was like every other man she had dated. They get to a certain point, and then they want her to accommodate them and start changing her life to suit their needs. "You're just like my mother—always demanding she be put first when it is never reciprocated." The words came out before she had time to consider what she was exposing.

"Huh? How can it be reciprocated when you kick me out or never ask anything about me? For God's sake, you wouldn't even ask me to the BBQ, you had to get Thad to do it."

"How do you know I got Thad to do it?" she countered.

Remy was silent and Ollie fumed.

"Okay, so you want to go all 'poor me?' How about you tell me why you didn't correct me when I thought you were leaving? You made me look like a fool. Or have you been lying and only interested in a fling too, so are trying to make me feel bad and then I end it with you and you come out looking like it was all my doing? Ollie and her reputation." Her voice dripped with sarcasm. "I am sure everyone has 'warned' you about me."

He remained silent and her frustration grew. "And then to lie about your health. How did you hide that? Aren't you supposed to check your sugar levels before you eat? Were you just guessing while we were out? You put me in a difficult position by not telling me that and by not taking care of yourself." She was getting worked up and Remy went to move toward her. Ollie rapidly stepped back. "Don't you dare. You made a fool of me for no reason. I know I was clear about not wanting anything more, but maybe you should have been clear about your things. You led me to believe you were different than who you are while I have been honest with who I am. What were you hoping to achieve? A relationship built on deception?" She stopped and took a breath and realized just how upset she was.

"What does it matter? You wanted a good time, not a guy with baggage," he bit back.

"So, you are going to put this back on me? You are not who I thought you were at all."

Remy looked alarmed. "No," he swallowed hard, "don't say that. I thought I was doing the right thing. You wanted it light and I thought if I kept it that way you would continue to see me and that something might change with what you wanted." His voice caught as if it was stuck. "I never meant to lie to you. I fell for you and you are right, everyone warned me not to." His voice faded away.

She could see him struggling to find the right words and she didn't care. Her temper flared and his excuses just made her angrier. "How kind of everyone to let you know what I am like." That one hurt. She would deal with Thad and Peyton later, but for now, she wanted to keep the argument about what it was supposed to be about—Remy's omissions. It was something her mother would do, twist things until they were discussing something else that had nothing to do with the original topic and suddenly everything was your fault.

Remy blinked as if he was only now catching up to the conversation. "No, no I didn't mean it like that. All I heard were good things about you, but that I was crazy if I was planning on trying to get you to fall for me."

Her eyes narrowed, there was something else in there that he wasn't telling her. "And?"

"Thad and I talked after you left the hospital. He arrived just as Nona was leaving and she told him you had come to visit. It turns out Nona is trying to play matchmaker and told Thad we make a great couple. Thad tried to explain to her you had a rough upbringing and the thought of being tied to one person terrifies you."

Ollie clenched and unclenched her hands in an attempt to reign in her retort. "Seriously? That's what he said?" The words stung, but if she wasn't so caught up in her anger she would have to accept them as truth, regardless of how uncomfortable it made her feel.

Remy nodded, a guilty look on his face. "Please don't be angry with him. He loves you like another sister and I think he wants to protect you as well as me."

"He's been trying to protect me from the moment we met," she admitted, some of her anger leaving. "It doesn't change the fact that you lied to me." She held up her hand to stall his response. "Remy, you wanted something from me and you lied to get it. You can't manipulate your way out of it." She hadn't realized how much the disclosure of his illness and travel plans had affected her until this moment.

His shoulders slumped and he hung his head. "You are right. I could have told you the truth. It's not like you physically gagged me," he mumbled the admission and got to his feet. "I should have just been honest." Remy looked up at her and she was startled to see unshed tears in his eyes. "I am truly sorry for hurting you."

*He lied to you*, it reminded her heart. *But he cares for you*, her heart countered. *So? Men have cared for you before and you always let them go.* Her heart beat a little harder, *Yes, but this time you care back,* it whispered. Ollie's internal dialogue continued but she said nothing to stop Remy from gathering his things and leaving. As the door closed behind him, she closed her eyes and counted to ten before tightening her robe cord and heading to the kitchen, all while pretending nothing was wrong—she was good at that.

## Chapter 8

The whistle blew and Ollie cursed silently, they had lost by four and it stung. She had been looking forward to this Thursday night netball game all week and it was great to get some aggression out of her system after a frustrating week with not being able to resolve her emotions and the argument she had had with Remy. A game of netball and a few drinks with the girls was always a great way to set her in the right frame of mind for the weekend.

Once they had shaken hands with the opposition and collected their water bottles and belongings, they gathered in the car park as they usually did to discuss where they would go now. Ollie became quickly disappointed when one by one her teammates informed them that they needed to get home because their husbands were alone looking after the kids, or they had school lunches to make, business shirts to iron, or washing to finish. Where were the young, carefree women she had hung around with for the last five years? They were gone, replaced by Stepford Wives, all rushing home to do their husband's bidding. It drove her insane when someone told her that their husband was at home 'babysitting' his own child... um, that is called *parenting.* She had been known to point it out often enough that everyone was more careful with what they said to her. In her own way, Ollie hoped one of those women understood what she meant by it and registered how wrong it was to think that way.

"Okay, well, we are off to get a drink. I'm thinking a lovely fresh cider as it's still sticky heat," announced Peyton as she waved goodbye to the girls and dragged Ollie away before Ollie said something to upset someone, as she was known to do on occasion.

Ollie had to agree, cider would be perfect. The early summer night in Melbourne had not lost its heat from the day. Fortunately, the courts were close to a local bar, and in no time they were seated in the beer garden, listening to a guitarist and sipping on icy-cold ciders.

After several minutes of silence and both of them pretending to listen to the musician, Peyton broke the quiet. "You want to talk about it?"

"Talk about what?" Ollie hoped her round brown eyes looked innocent.

"Really? You think I can't see that you are hurting?"

Ollie took another sip. "I am fine," she lied.

"Why haven't you asked me to go with you tomorrow night?"

"What?" Ollie frowned. "What's on tomorrow night?"

Peyton gave her a look of pity and instantly Ollie remembered what her friend had been referring to. "Your mother's birthday."

"Ah, yes, that." Ollie shrugged as if she didn't care. "I was thinking of not going."

"Really?"

"Well, I don't see why my brothers can get away with just dropping in, but I am expected to stay and do the whole dinner thing. Dad's birthday was horrid enough, Mum's will be hideous." Ollie didn't add her father's birthday dinner had taken her to a dark place for a few days before she was able to mentally shake the sting of her parents' toxic home. "I don't think I want to put myself through it anymore."

"Good for you," Peyton said slowly.

"You don't sound convinced."

"Well, I've never heard you say that before." They sat in silence for a moment before Peyton added, "If you change your mind and need support I am willing to go with you."

Ollie grimaced at Peyton. "Thank you."

"Want to get something to eat?"

"No, thanks. I am not hungry."

Peyton's eyebrows shot up so quickly they ended up behind her fringe. "Okay, what is going on with you?"

"Huh?"

"You aren't seeing your mum and now you aren't hungry." Peyton said nothing further, just sat there and stared at her.

Ollie began to feel uncomfortable under the scrutiny. The tension was broken by Peyton beginning to chuckle. The chuckle turned into a full-throated laugh.

"What?" Ollie demanded.

"I just figured it out."

Ollie scowled.

"You and Remy are acting like..." she battled to find the right word. "Well, I don't know what like, but it is amusing after all these years to see you finally upset about a man."

"You are doing a lot of assuming."

"Am I wrong?"

"Well, I don't know what Remy is doing, but no you are not wrong." Ollie's face twisted as if she had swallowed something bitter. "Though I do have something to say to you and Thad about interfering and 'warning' him about me."

Peyton shifted in her chair and studied her cider. "I was a little torn. You are my heart sister, and Remy is my brother-in-law. I needed him to understand that if he pursued you it was on him and I would not hear anything against you if it ended not to his liking." Peyton looked sad. "Am I to understand that it didn't end to his liking?"

"It didn't end to anyone's liking."

Ollie looked at her friend and the concern etched on Peyton's face made her decide to come clean. "It was a disaster. I accused him of lying and he told me that no matter what he did I would find fault to get rid of him." It hurt to say it.

"Did he lie?"

"Yes, by omission. He didn't tell me he had a lifelong illness and he led me to believe he would be returning to America soon. He did apologize profusely, but I was so angry I asked him to leave."

"You have every right to be angry. That was unfair of him to blind-side you." The empathy in Peyton's voice made Ollie feel better.

"There is just one small problem with the whole thing."

"Okay?"

"Well, as you know, this would be a perfect excuse for me to never speak to him again."

"True." A smile spread across Peyton's face.

Ollie screwed up her face and exhaled. "Peyton, I don't know what I want to do. I like him, more than anyone I have ever been with or around and it terrifies me. I want to push him away out of fear, but I want to see him every moment too. I am so confused."

Peyton leaned across the table and gently touched Ollie's forearm. "I am here no matter what you decide, but you alone have to be the one to make your decision."

"Great! You are no help," Ollie said crossly.

"Fine, here's another thing to consider." Peyton stopped for a moment and watched Ollie, her eyes softened as she spoke the next words. "Maybe it is time to stop running from your feelings."

Ollie met that statement with a scowl.

# Chapter 9

The words Peyton had spoken continued to echo in Ollie's head the following morning as she got ready for work. It was hard for Ollie to be honest with herself about her feelings as she had become so adept at hiding from them. Her first instinct was to delete Remy's number and vow to never speak to him again... that would be the simplest solution. Yet, her underlying want was to ring him, apologize profusely—even though she knew he should take half the blame—and then admit she wanted to have a relationship with him. But all of that made her feel physically ill. That would be opening herself up to be criticized and ridiculed and if he wanted to he could hurt her beyond imagining. *For how could he care for me if my parents couldn't?* a tiny voice whispered. A voice that held all of her fears that she kept locked inside for they made her vulnerable.

The day dragged on as her internal dialogue continued as Ollie argued back and forth with herself. By the time she drove home, Ollie had to come to terms with the knowledge that the facts were clear. She either kept hiding from herself, as Peyton had pointed out, or she pulled on her big girl pants and took a chance on the first lover she had come to trust. The irony wasn't lost on Ollie that the only other man she trusted was Remy's brother.

Ollie sat in her car, parked in her driveway, as she held her phone and tossed up the notion of ringing or texting Remy. Texting won as that way if he declined or was rude she wouldn't have to hear it in his voice; she wouldn't be exposed and he hear her pain. She stared at the blank screen of her phone and couldn't decide what she should say. Should she act casual, like nothing had happened? Ollie put her head back on the headrest and groaned. "Why does this have to be so hard?" she muttered.

After agonizing over the message for a further quarter of an hour, Ollie finally thought she had found the right mix of casual but caring she wanted to convey. Before she could revise her text again she hit send and gathered her things to go inside.

**Ollie: Hey, Remy, I am hoping you are available to catch up as I would like to clear the air after what happened on Sunday.**

By the time Ollie had got into her apartment, taken her shoes off, and poured herself a cold glass of water Remy had responded.

**Remy: I am surprised to hear from you. Clearing the air sounds good. Are you free tonight?**

Ollie looked at the message and tried to fathom whether he was happy to hear from her. Maybe he wanted to clear the air so it wasn't awkward if they ran into each other?

**Ollie: Tonight works for me. Where do you want to meet?**

She decided to be as concise as he regarding the texts. *Can you ever not gameplay?* she wondered.

**Remy: How does Uber Eats at your place sound? I don't think we need to do this in public—do you? Or you can come here?**

Ollie liked Thad and Remy's mum and dad, but Remy was living at home since his return from America and while he looked for work. She didn't feel it would be appropriate to go over there and not sit and chat with his parents.

**Ollie: Here is good. We could walk around the corner to the local hamburger place if you like and then bring it back? They do great onion rings.**

**Remy: Okay. Time?**

She tried to ignore the short, sharp response.

**Ollie: Anytime. I am home now.**

**Remy: I'll be over in an hour.**

The final text came through and Ollie's heart sank a little as the coldness of the message settled in. Maybe this was all a huge mistake and she had misread how much he cared for her?

As Ollie tidied up her place and put away the few items she had left out from getting ready that morning, she wondered how she was going to feel when he arrived. This was all new territory for her and she wasn't sure this was truly what she wanted. The safety of her built up walls was looking mighty appealing at this point.

She changed her clothes three times before finally settling on a cute red shirt with white polka dots that tied at the waist and white denim mid-thigh shorts. Ollie completed the look with a pair of red sandals that laced up around her ankles.

The hour dragged slowly by and Ollie found that the last half of it was almost painful in its crawling progression. She attempted to watch the news but with all the political wrangling that was happening around the world, it just made her more anxious. In the end, she flicked off the TV and put on her favorite playlist, and went about clearing out her fridge.

As she was putting the trash in the bin, Remy arrived and her heart raced and her breathing picked up. He wore a fitted black t-shirt that showed his trim torso, and tight blue jeans that made her fight to not make a comment about his cute toosh. His full lips spread into a hesitant smile as he spotted her by the bin. This made her heart move up higher into her throat and she took a few deep breaths to get herself together. God, this man had such an impact on her physically. But she would also happily sit and listen to him talk about his favorite things or his job as he was fascinating and hilarious.

"Hi," she said softly.

"Hi." His smile widened.

Remy followed her into the apartment and made himself comfortable on the couch while Ollie went to wash her hands. "Do you want a drink?" she asked as she headed for the fridge.

"No, thanks."

"Oh, okay." Ollie turned around and came into the lounge room and took a chair opposite Remy. She didn't think it would be wise to sit next to him as she was struggling not to touch him as it was. "How have you been?" she asked.

"Fine. How have you been?" he replied.

Ollie felt her heart slowing as reality set in and silence filled the void between them. This was not the beginning she had been hoping for.

SAY SOMETHING, THE VOICE in her head yelled at her. *You asked him here. He is waiting for you.*

Ollie cleared her throat and Remy watched her. His brown eyes serious, but she thought they looked slightly glazed. "You sure I can't get you a drink?"

"A water would be good. I have been thirsty today."

Ollie launched herself off the chair now that she had a task to keep her occupied for a moment. "Job hunting yet?" she attempted small talk.

"I haven't started. I still need to get myself back into shape after having all this time off since I got home."

"Fair enough. Did you want to grab dinner before we talk?"

"If it's okay with you I would rather talk first."

Ollie bit her bottom lip as she handed Remy the glass. "No problem." Once again she settled into her chair and the silence grew. "I'm not very good at this."

"I would never have known. You appear so comfortable," Remy smirked.

This made Ollie snigger and it released the tension in the room. He was good at easing her anxiety. "I wanted to talk to you about our disagreement and make sure you understand that whatever happened between us will not be a problem when I run into you at family gatherings. I can separate the two. I have had a lot of practice at keeping up appearances." She didn't know why she put in that last bit. He didn't need to know that.

Remy frowned at her as if what she had said was not what he was expecting to hear. "Well, that is good to know," his voice was cautious. "Though, I am sure you could have said that in a text or phone call."

"True," she admitted. Ollie looked around the room in the hope a hole had opened up and she could disappear through it. This was excruciating. It was time to be a grown-up. She closed her eyes and spoke her truth. "I am sorry for the other day, my emotions took me by surprise, and my defense mechanisms kicked in."

Ollie opened her eyes to find Remy standing. It stung to realize that she had finally fallen for someone and they weren't invested in her. She thought he was leaving, but he moved around the coffee table and came to kneel before her instead. He held out his hands and she placed hers on top of his. He spoke before she could. "At first, I just didn't tell you that I was sick because I didn't think it would matter. We had a great night at the wedding and after and it was only once I spent the following day with you that I came to realize just why Thad always talks about you. Ollie, you are incredible."

She flushed at the compliment.

"I don't look at myself as being sick most of the time. I have an illness that I have to manage like millions of other people in the world. It doesn't make me special or unique. My family has always made a much bigger deal out of it than I have." Remy reached out with one hand and touched her cheek, tracing his fingers along her jawline. "I liked you looking at me without seeing the worry in your face. I wanted you to continue to look at me that way." His voice was sad.

His touch was soothing and electrifying all at once. "I can understand that," Ollie acknowledged. She leaned into his hand as it cupped her face. "It probably wouldn't have been such a big deal if the first time I found about it was not when you had been admitted to hospital."

"Fair enough." He moved in and kissed her softly on her cheek. "I am sorry," he whispered.

Ollie sighed as the kiss stirred her emotions. "What about the other thing?"

Remy let go of her hands and sat back on his heels. "I don't know why but I thought you knew I was home for good, but then you said a few things and it finally registered that you thought I was going back to America." He looked to the floor. "In not my finest hour, I quickly came to understand that if you knew the truth you might get rid of me so I didn't tell you."

*Well, that was unexpected,* she sat back in the chair. *I don't think I have ever had a man be that honest with me.*

"Thank you for being open with me," she said.

"It is what you deserve."

Ollie couldn't stop it, the words came out before she could think it through. "I am so sorry for the way I behaved. You were right about me, but you were also wrong." She stopped and looked at him, this time not closing her eyes to hide from his reaction. "Peyton and Thad were right to warn you, I have always just been after a fun time and never a commitment and I can see they didn't want you getting hurt. And after the great night at their place, I could see we could be together, like truly together and I got scared." She took a steadying breath. "And then we fought and I realized I wasn't okay with you lying to me when normally it wouldn't have bothered me and it would have made the perfect excuse to get rid of you, but this time it hurt. I lashed out because this time I cared."

Remy sat on his haunches, smiling shyly at her admission, but Ollie noted he had a slight sheen to his forehead.

"Are you feeling okay?"

"I'm fine, just having an off day." He retook her hands, "I would like to hear more about how much you wanted to not like me but..." he let it trail away.

Ollie laughed and picked up his sentence, "it would appear that I do like you. I would think that would be obvious as I have contacted you to get together quite a few times."

Remy came back up onto his knees and put his hands on her thighs. "You may think you are being obvious, but I think you have concealed your feelings for so long that it is going to take some more work to get you to show them."

As Ollie went to explain that she would try. his eyes rolled up into his head and Remy passed out, knocking his head on the coffee table on the way down.

OLLIE COULD NO LONGER ignore the emotions she felt as she stared at the sleeping form of Remy in his hospital bed. There was no use in hiding it any longer. It appeared love had finally found her. She had ridden with him in the ambulance telling them she was his girlfriend, which through all the panic she noted didn't sound nearly as frightening as she thought it might. While they had tended Remy, Ollie had made the call to Thad to tell him what had happened, where they were taking his brother, and that she would stay with him until a family member got there.

He had been quickly admitted and had woken enough to answer a few questions about how he was feeling and what he was eating. He confessed he had not eaten a great deal in the last few days and had not been monitoring his sugar levels as he was preoccupied with other things. Ollie knew he was referring to their disagreement and while she felt bad she also felt angry. She would not be the brunt of someone else's health issues.

Now they were alone and she took his hand, it fit so perfectly in hers and she took a few moments to relish how it felt. "You need to stop punishing yourself by not looking after yourself. Every time you make a decision that affects your health, it affects all the people who love and support you. You need to listen to those who love you. You need to listen to me," she pleaded softly to his sleeping form.

He opened one eye and smiled at her. "I need to listen to you?"

"Yes. All your family and friends love you and only want to see you well. Why do you do this when things don't go right? Do you not think you are worthy?"

"What about you hiding from the world and your emotions?"

"This isn't about me. We already talked about me. Stop deflecting. You know I want you to be well."

"Yes, but why?" He pushed her. His eyes pleading for her to be honest.

Ollie returned his stare, hoping her eyes didn't reveal the thudding of her heart as she chose her next words. "Because I love you and the only way I will be with you is on equal footing, which means I will not be your keeper." She scowled at him for emphasis.

"Well, that was the most romantic thing anyone has ever said to me." His charming laugh filled the room. He struggled to sit up while she still clutched his hand. He pulled her up out of the seat and made room for her on the hospital bed. As she snuggled into his side, her head resting on his chest, he kissed the top of her head. "Will you stay with me forever if I promise to take care of myself like an adult?"

"Forever is a long time. Why would I do that?" She needed to hear him be honest about his emotions to feel less insecure about her own.

"Because I love you too. I want to be the best me for us."

"You are making it sound appealing," she admitted. *More appealing than I ever knew possible,* the thought appeared in the back of her mind. "I need you to hear me. I know I have been avoiding your questions and I thought I had given you the whole truth, but this all took me by surprise. Your illness woke things in me I thought I had long buried and I didn't know how to react." She straightened up and looked at him. "You know my mum drinks too much and my father's complete lack of ability to stand up to her and leave or protect me from her drunken ravings makes it hard for me to trust or want a relationship as I don't know what a healthy one is. The closest I ever got to one has been watching Peyton and Thad. My one relationship was, I guess a way for me to hide and show everyone I was 'normal,' but he was the wrong guy and it made my feelings about commitment worsen and justified."

Remy said nothing as she spoke, his wide hazel eyes just gazed at her full of love and acceptance. It gave her the courage to continue rather than shy away as she normally would. "I can't or rather won't take care of you as that is what I had to do for my mother. I would come home from school to find her passed out on the lounge room floor in a puddle of her urine. I would have to clean up the mess and clean her up and if she roused too much from her drunken stupor she would yell at me as if it were my fault." Tears built and threatened to spill over as she clenched and unclenched her fists in an effort to keep her emotions under control.

"Oh, Olivia, I am so very sorry." His words were kind and her undoing. "No one should have to endure that. No wonder love is confusing for you. It is supposed to be considerate and kind and unconditional from a parent, all you got was demanding and spiteful."

Ollie allowed herself for the first time in many years to bring down the walls enough to cry. She never cried as she never knew if she could stop again. It was easier to swallow the pain and let it sit in her gut rather than it getting loose and having the potential to destroy her in its grief. For someone whose laugh was loud and her life lived large, Ollie cried silently. Her shoulders shook and tears streamed down her face but no sound escaped. She had learned to cry quietly when she was little to avoid the wrath of her mother who could change personalities rapidly when she felt attacked. And for unknown reasons, Ollie's tears were somehow perceived as an attack.

Remy pulled her in tighter and stroked her hair, repeatedly telling her that he loved her. He promised to take care of himself and he would no longer dismiss his illness as he could now see how something this big affected those who loved him. "There is one thing I want to do for you."

"What?" She barely got the word out.

"I want to take care of you. I want to worship you and love you and adore you and most of all I want to show you are worthy of love."

Ollie lifted her head, not ashamed to show him her tear-stained face. For the first time in her life she was not frightened of the reaction she would receive.

## Epilogue

Ollie looked down at her hand entwined with her husband's and squeezed it tightly. She hated plane landings. Remy's thumb ran over the sparkle of her large diamond engagement ring with its matching wedding band and smiled at her, distracting her from the discomfort she felt. "Welcome to Rome."

"Thanks," she answered dryly.

"Do you have any idea where you want to visit first?"

"Yes, the Trevi Fountain. I have a wish to make. Peyton went there and her wish came true within six months, so it has a proven record as far as I am concerned."

"What are you going to wish for?" He raised an eyebrow.

"It's the first wish I have made in fifteen years and I won't be sharing it because I want it to come true." She smiled and winked, knowing how silly she sounded and not caring.

He chuckled, "fair enough."

"Where would you like to go first?" She kept up the conversation as she heard the landing gear go down.

"Anywhere. I am not fussed." He moved closer to her and whispered in her ear. "Don't tell me you have forgotten what you do in Rome..." he let it hang there.

Ollie giggled softly as she remembered their first conversation at Peyton and Thad's wedding two years ago. "Well, no one ever talks about it, but when in Rome..." Her eyes glittered.

Remy moved in closer still and kissed her just as the plane wheels hit the tarmac. It was perfect timing as Ollie was completely enamored by the tender kiss that she didn't worry about the sounds the plane made when the brakes were applied. As they pulled apart, Ollie gave him a wry smile. "Great diversion you have there."

"Mmm, I thought it was clever."

The plane taxied down the runway and the seatbelt sign went off, signaling to all the impatient people that they could begin to gather their belongings. Ollie and Remy remained seated, hands intertwined, enjoying their moment.

"Ladies and gentlemen, you may now switch your devices back on," the steward announced to the plane.

"You had better turn it on," Ollie said. "Everyone will be checking in." It had taken Ollie by surprise how welcoming Remy's entire family was once their secret dating had been uncovered. Ollie had always felt accepted by the family when she had gone anywhere as Thad's guest, but this was the next level. Her own family had been happy for her and Remy, but it was a difficult, fractured relationship that Remy had walked into. He never said anything about her parents, he just accepted them for who they were and supported her in any way she needed.

Ollie waited as Remy took out his phone and turned it on, watching it search for a company to connect to. After a few moments, it found what it was looking for and the phone vibrated in his hand several times. "We have messages," he announced.

Ollie liked the way the 'we' sounded—it was even more perfect now they were married. "Should we wait until we are at the hotel to read them?"

Remy groaned. "Really? I don't know if I can wait that long. Besides, I had other plans about what we would do when we got to the hotel." He wiggled his bushy eyebrows at her.

"Is that so? I was thinking a nap would be good."

"A nap would be good, but after a bath and consummating the marital vows again."

Ollie snorted, which gained her a few stares, which of course made Remy laugh, which increased the stares by a few more. "Seriously, I think we have consummated our vows enough to make it clear we are happily married," she whispered.

Remy took her chin and pulled her to him so their faces were close together and it felt like everyone on the plane had vanished. "You need to hear me, my bride. It will never be enough. I love you." He kissed her on the tip of her nose before releasing her chin.

Now Ollie couldn't wait to get to the hotel room and have that suggested bath. "We had better check those messages so we are not interrupted later."

The Trevi Fountain was still crowded, even though there had been a steady drizzle since the moment they had got off the plane that morning. Ollie fought the jet lag as she waited patiently for the tourists to take their photo, toss their coin, and get out of the way. She decided that having that short nap in the early afternoon had not been the best idea they had ever had. After making her wish she might suggest an early dinner before going to bed to get up and start their honeymoon fresh tomorrow. She fought another face splitting yawn and grinned as Remy did the same.

Finally, the tourists thinned out and Ollie could get in front of the stunning monument to have Remy take a photo of her to text to Peyton. *Making my own wish*, she captioned the picture and texted it to her heart sister. Ollie took a few photos of Remy in front of the fountain and a lovely couple offered to take a few photos of them together.

"Here you go," Remy held out a coin.

Ollie took the coin. "Are you making a wish too?"

He held up his coin. "You bet I am," he winked at her.

Ollie pretended to look shocked. "I hope it is nothing lewd. We don't want to offend the fountain gods," she warned.

Remy took her hand and kissed her palm. "I promise. Nothing that will get us in trouble with any of the gods." He held up his coin. "Ready?"

Ollie held up her coin. "Ready."

"And go."

Ollie closed her eyes and threw the coin into the clear water of the Trevi Fountain. I wish for this happiness to never end, and because I haven't had a wish in so long I am also sending it out there that I would one day hope to have a daughter that I can name Mariella. She released her thoughts and opened her eyes to find Remy gazing at her. As she saw the love in his gorgeous eyes she knew she would never need to wish for her happiness again.

# CHLOE

Reflections of Love Novella Collection

Book Four

# TAYA RUNE

# Chloe

### Chapter 1

CHLOE CHECKED THE REFLECTION on the mobile screen and not happy with what she saw, turned to fuss over the placement of the purple throw pillow on her bed for the third time; it just wouldn't sit right in the shot. She placed the book she was currently promoting in front of it and gingerly crawled backward off the bed, hoping to not dislodge the now perfected arrangement. With a huge sigh of relief, nothing moved. She took several shots with her camera at different angles before putting the camera down and picking up her phone and moving onto the bed. This time she was not as cautious as she scooped up the book and settled onto the pillow.

The sun on her back was warm and comforting and Chloe knew that if she sat there long enough it would make her sleepy. Holding her phone at an angle, Chloe studied her reflection on the screen as she held up the book, A Discovery of Witches by Deborah Harkness, and smiled in her typical closed mouth way; the world did not need to see her crooked front teeth. She took a few moments to drape some of her long, streaked purple and pink hair over her shoulder and made sure she still had enough lip gloss on. Her fake tan looked good in the sunlight and her freckles were barely visible. Satisfied with her appearance, Chloe checked that the background of the photo showed nothing but a clean, artistically-styled bedroom. She took several selfies at varying angles — her holding the book with the cover showing, her reading the book, and a time-lapse video of her flipping through the pages.

Tossing the book aside, Chloe leaned over the side of the bed and grabbed her laptop from the pile of clothes it rested on. It didn't take her long to upload all the photos from the camera and phone; then she quickly chose one and posted it to her Instagram with the hashtag #TVshoworbook? She would work on creating reels and story content for both Instagram and TikTok later, once she had studied what was trending that day.

Chloe was twenty-five and a mid-range Social Influencer, and while she hated the label, she used it to her advantage when promoting her Instagram and TikTok posts. Her career dream was to be a screenwriter, but she was well aware that having an extensive social media following for anything was advantageous to the money men Hollywood type producers of the world, so for the time being she played the game by being a reviewer of all things "in." She studied screenwriting online part-time, and made money through her content creation courses she had started running once a month and endorsements she got from a few companies. After watching her newest post gain likes and responding to a few comments, she put the phone down and was assaulted by her true reality.

The corner of her bedroom that was the background for her content was pristine. It was flooded with warm early morning sunshine from the nearby window. The walls held a few funky canvases in gray and purple tones and the bed cover was a plain mauve, with a soft gray mohair rug strewn artfully across the bed, and many different sized pillows in geometric patterns filled the corner. The remainder of her room was a mess. Plastic tubs filled with early childhood memories overflowed with paper, clothes, and old teddy bears. Make-up, books, and the many different products that had been sent to her to review filled all the available space. Clothes that never managed to get put away were piled on a chair near her door, and the wardrobe doors couldn't be closed as it was overstuffed with clothing that was rarely touched.

As always, Chloe felt defeated and disgusted when she looked at the mess, and as usual, she pushed those feelings down before taking a bracing breath and leaving her bedroom. Doing her best to ignore the piles of newspapers, tools, fishing paraphernalia, boxes of clothes, old photos, and piles of odds and ends that filled the wide hallway down one side and all of the rooms she walked past, Chloe made her way to the kitchen.

Surprisingly, the kitchen had always remained relatively hoarder junk-free. It was still cluttered by anyone else's standards, but by her father's standards, it was almost a minimalist look. The kitchen cabinets were filled with boxes of appliances that had never been used, but at least the doors closed. The surfaces were covered with cookie jars that held more utensils than a Michelin star restaurant, and there were no less than five chopping boards leaning against the wall behind the toaster. There were two kettles, just in case one broke, and a large stack of folded drying towels that much like the clothes in her room, were never put away.

Chloe opened the fridge door and stared blankly at the contents until the fridge began to beep at her. Without taking anything, she closed the door and took a seat at the old wooden table. Feeling despondent, she leaned forward and placed her forehead against the cold, smooth surface, attempting to ignore the sick feeling she felt in her stomach. The only sound throughout the too silent house was the constant pinging of her phone.

She missed her father's heavy footsteps.

It had been a month since she placed her father in a nursing home, as his Dementia had become too advanced for Chloe to handle. He was all the family she had and Chloe was finding it difficult to adjust. Her parents had been told that they couldn't have children so they were delighted, when in their early forties, Chloe was conceived. Sadly,

Chloe's mum had died a few years later from cancer. It had been just Chloe and her dad, John, for the last twenty-five years.

She got up and poured a glass of water before plonking back down. Looking around at the ordered piles of stuff, she sighed wearily and whispered to the photo of her father stuck on the fridge, "I miss you." The silence made her sad, so she filled it with chatter before it became overbearing. "I've made a huge mess of things and I don't know how to fix it. I just know I can't keep putting it off."

John's lined face smiled at her, offering no words of wisdom, just never-ending support.

## Chapter 2

THE WATER LAPPED GENTLY around the pontoon's edge as Chloe settled onto the low camping chair and adjusted the thin straps on her pink floral top. She then took a few minutes to set up her fishing rod, the book from her earlier post, arranged her sandals against the leg of the chair, and placed her white-framed sunglasses on the top of her cute tackle box, decorated with sparkly dragonfly stickers. Chloe knelt back and looked at what she had created with the calm lake sparkling in the background. She took many photos of the book propped up against the varied items before settling into her chair with the book in her lap, and taking a couple more selfies of her trademark closed-mouthed smile before posting #simplelife on her Instagram account.

She added "get teeth fixed" to her ever-growing mental list of things she needed to take care of. She hated how her two front teeth slightly crossed but her father had refused to have them fixed as it reminded him of her mother's beautiful, crooked smile. Chloe would love to smile fully in her photos and show straight teeth. Once she had paid off her course fees, she would explore the option of invisible braces.

Taking a block of cheese from the tackle box, Chloe threaded it on the hook as she had been taught, and cast her line. She placed the butt of the pole into the little holder that her dad had attached to the leg of her chair, and settled a little deeper into the seat, the fishing pole loosely held in one hand.

Chloe closed her blue eyes and absently twirled strands of her long, purple and pink-streaked blonde hair and listened to the laughing and squealing of the young children playing on the man-made beach on the opposite side of the small lake. Instinctively, she placed her hand on her lower stomach and the thoughts she had been suppressing for days bubbled to the surface. This time she didn't have the strength to squash them. She let them come, fill her mind, and wonder what the future held.

The pontoon rocked a little more heavily and a shadow fell across Chloe as someone joined her on the small, wooden, floating area. She picked up her book to show the interloper that she was not interested in chatting.

"Hi," said a familiar voice.

Chloe looked up, startled to find her boyfriend of eighteen months standing there.

"I saw your post on Insta and thought you might like some company. I know being here must be hard for you." His freckled, hawk-like nose wrinkled in concern.

Her heart beat a little faster; it didn't matter how often she saw Pierce, her body always responded to him. He had shaggy blond hair and wore very casual clothing that suited someone who should be surfing off the coast of Australia, not running a successful IT company. He was of average height with an average body and slightly heavy around the middle. Chloe often joked that they were perfectly matched as she was also of average height with an average body and a slightly heavy middle. He just laughed that they were working on their Mum and Dad bods a little early. She adored his sense of humor.

She nodded her acknowledgment of how difficult it was being here, not trusting herself to speak as she recalled the sudden confusion and panic that had engulfed her father when he was partway through reeling in a fish and his body had lost its natural responses to fishing. It had been heart-wrenching to watch. She couldn't imagine the terror that filled her father's mind when these events occurred. That had been the moment she realized that things were never going to be the same, and she needed to make some serious choices about his care in the future. The frightened look on his face as she understood that he, for a split second, had no idea who she was and why they were there had stayed with her for months.

Chloe watched as Pierce sat cross-legged on the pontoon next to her, gazed around for a few seconds, taking in his surroundings, then pulled out his phone. Her anger rose rapidly but subsided just as quickly. She could hardly complain that he was on his phone when her life was lived on hers. *But it's not your real life,* her inner voice whispered. *It's your hashtag life filled with very little truth.* She shut that thought down and reached out to squeeze Pierce's forearm in a silent gesture of thanks for being here, but not intruding on her quiet time.

They sat there for half an hour, the silence comfortable to begin with, but as the time passed, Chloe's mind whirled into overdrive. She had too many secrets and the effort to keep them was making her physically sick, and causing her anxiety to spike. Chloe was keeping secrets from her social media life; though they had no right to know what was going on, they did have a right to not be shown half-truths that served her purpose but created lies. She had kept Pierce a secret from her father and now it was too late; his moments of lucidity growing less and less by the day. Chloe felt nauseous, her mouth dry at the idea of what she needed to tell Pierce. The secrets had grown to a point that she fretted they might simply burst forth and reveal everything to Pierce. *But did he not have the right to know who she truly was?* her conscious reminded her. It was now or never. She loved the man sitting next to her and he needed to see her true self, not the carefully crafted one she showed the world.

"Pierce..." she began and stopped. Chloe cleared her throat and tried again. The sick feeling growing and her chest tightening. "Pierce?"

"Mmmm?" He didn't look up from his phone.

Short and sharp, she told herself to do it quickly, like ripping off a band-aid. "I'm pregnant."

He stood abruptly, shock clear on his face at her announcement. The pontoon swayed heavily and his phone slipped out of his hand and into the lake. "What!" he exclaimed.

"Your phone!" Chloe shouted as the phone landed with a splash and disappeared into the brown murky water.

"Stuff the phone. Repeat what you just said."

"Your phone." Chloe couldn't resist. She also stood and rocked the pontoon.

Pierce laughed. "Very funny. The bit before that."

"Ah, the 'I'm pregnant' bit?" She tried to keep her voice light.

"Yes, that bit."

They stood there staring at each other.

"Well?" Chloe prompted after several moments.

"I want to say that's wonderful, but by the look on your face I'm not sure if you think it is," explained Pierce, a slight frown creased his forehead.

Chloe didn't know how to answer that. She was thrilled at being pregnant by Pierce, but anxious he might leave her if he knew the whole truth. Fighting her fear, she swallowed hard and pushed on. "It is wonderful." Her voice was soft. "I know we haven't planned it, we haven't even spoken about it, but having a baby with you will be amazing."

Pierce pulled her into his arms. "How did you think I would react?" He sounded puzzled.

Chloe rested her cheek on his shoulder, feeling his warmth and comfort. "It feels silly now to say it, but I wasn't sure." She wrapped her arms around his middle and squeezed him. Her nerves and nausea having subsided slightly.

"How pregnant are you?"

"Ten weeks. I only did the math yesterday and then went and bought a few tests. They all came back with the same result."

"And you kept it secret even when I spoke to you last night?"

"I am good at keeping secrets," she muttered. before continuing on a little louder. "I wanted to tell you to your face, not over the phone."

Pierce pulled her hair away from her face and moved to kiss her. The kiss was gentle and full of love and acceptance. "You're going to be a mum," he whispered.

She squeezed him again and smiled. "You're going to be a dad."

He patted his rounded stomach. "I told you I have been practicing." He grinned. "There is so much to talk about, now that I have stopped to think about it." His gray eyes were wide and startled, and Chloe was certain she had looked the same when the third stick she peed on had given her the same positive result.

Her joy at seeing his excitement didn't last long as the huge secret she had been concealing their entire relationship still hung over her. Chloe felt sick at the next words she had to say, but there was no way she could keep up the pretense of a neat and ordered life any longer. She only hoped that once Pierce knew the truth, he would still want to be with her. Chloe bit her lip before uttering the words that would change everything. "There's more. Are you free this afternoon?"

He pulled back from her hug and stared at her. "I'm free now." He searched her face for any clue to what she might be alluding to before he pulled her back into his embrace. "Wow, a baby."

"I know," she whispered into his shoulder. Chloe wanted to be excited—she should be rejoicing—but everything had become messed up. And now her anxiety overrode it all.

THE CAR SAT IDLING in the driveway, the music played softly on the radio, yet Chloe took no notice of it as she sat there breathing deeply and trying to stop her thoughts from racing. Pierce was going to arrive at any moment and she was going to have to reveal her shame, the thing that held her back in so many aspects of her life. It had always been her father's shame and she had lived with it, but now he was gone from the house and she had made no attempt to throw anything out. Chloe had had to accept that she, at some point, had also become complicit in his hoarding traits. Would Pierce understand or be disgusted?

Chloe turned off the car and got out. She left the fishing gear and chair in the boot because if she were honest, there was nowhere else to keep it. The house and garage were full. As Pierce pulled up to the curb, she took a moment to see the house from his perspective and silently shuddered.

John had always maintained the outside of the house to a standard where no one would guess the level of stuff stored within its walls. He had taken pride in the home he and his wife had created for Chloe, but as his illness set in, he was less able to do those things, and Chloe hadn't recognized how far she had let the exterior deteriorate until this moment. Her anxiety levels rose inch by inch as she saw what everyone who passed the house truly saw, and the shame burned deep. The overgrown garden beds were filled with nothing but gnomes, fairies, and weeds. Nothing had been cut back in over a year and several of the bushes that were supposed to look like low shrubs under the window had grown so large that they stopped all sunlight from reaching inside the room beyond. The grass was patchy, long in some areas, short in others, and bare dirt in sections. Weeds choked the few flowers that attempted to live between the enormous amounts of garden ornaments her father had bought for her mother and continued to after she died. The large willow tree in the center of the front yard looked like Chloe felt; burdened, sad, and heavy. Usually, the willow brought her happiness; its full, overhanging branches always made her smile, yet today she saw the weeping willow and could feel the heaviness of its limbs and fought to hold back tears.

Chloe walked to meet Pierce at the step that led to the front door. Her mind still trying to find ways to avoid what was to come, her heart thudding against her chest and her hands sweaty with fear. Pierce looked at the garden and back at her, his expression unreadable. On the few occasions he had picked Chloe up from the house, he had commented that he would be happy to help tidy the front as he knew how sick her father was. For several reasons, Chloe had declined the generous offer and now she was about to reveal them. The mountain of lies she had told to maintain her secrets were about to be revealed. What had seemed like the perfect solution at the beginning of their relationship, in the clear view of hindsight, was significant and not easily forgivable.

"Are you going to finally let me in?" Pierce asked the question and Chloe realized how symbolic it was. For him, it was a matter of her letting him into her home. For her, it was an entirely different situation. He was about to be let in on her secret. The secret that had kept her from making friends throughout her entire life.

Chloe hesitated. This was such a huge step. She had been avoiding this moment for eighteen long months. She swallowed hard as an explanation stuck in her throat.

He took her hand. "Your dad is in care now, there is no reason for me not to come over. You don't need to worry about upsetting him anymore." His eyes were so sincere; his voice gentle and understanding.

It made Chloe feel wretched for her lies. "It was never about that," she admitted, looking down at her feet, too scared to look at his handsome face.

Pierce frowned. "You've been lying for a year and a half?"

Chloe felt sick; this was not a good beginning. "Yes..."

Before she could finish, Pierce spoke over the top of her. "Well, aren't you just full of surprises today?" he asked sarcastically, dropping her hand. "I am not even sure what I want to know more. What you have lied about or why you have lied to me for our entire relationship?"

The words stung; Pierce had always had a sharp tongue. Most of the time it was used with good humor and she found it entertaining, on the rare occasion they argued he could cut her to the core with it. Her first reaction was to defend herself, but her rational side knew he was right. She had made a mess of everything because she was too embarrassed with her reality. She loved this man and it was time to set things right if she wanted to keep him, she just hoped she wasn't too late.

Tears began to fall, but he didn't try to comfort her. He was clearly angry and she didn't blame him. Chloe sniffed and wiped her eyes but she was having trouble controlling herself. "I'm sorry," she said through the tears.

"For what?" His voice remained cold. The happiness he had shown at having a baby with her was completely gone.

Her hand shook as she brought her keys up to unlock the front door, but she stopped. One section of her brain screamed at her to let him in, the other part told her that she was crazy to think he would understand and love her once he knew her truth. *Stay hidden behind your phone screen,* the voice whispered.

"Chloe? Are you going to tell me what is going on? Because I am coming up with all sorts of things."

She lowered her head and shook it. It was too hard; she couldn't do this today. She had told him about the pregnancy; that was enough for one day. *And you even lied about that,* the voice whispered, *telling him you only found out last night. You have known about it for two weeks; you were just too scared to tell him because your house of lies would topple too.*

She heard Pierce let out a breath. "I am leaving now. Give me a call when you are ready to tell me what is going on with you."

He stood there a moment longer, but Chloe didn't look up. "Fine," he muttered under his breath before he walked away. Still, Chloe didn't raise her head until she heard the car door slam and him drive away.

Slowly, she let herself into the house and made her way to the bedroom, where she lay down, curled up on her side, and let the tears of self-recrimination fall.

## Chapter 3

NO MATTER HOW MUCH concealer she applied, Chloe could not cover the bags under her eyes. She had had a sleepless night, filled with fits of self-pity and remorse, and in the end, had given up trying to sleep altogether. Chloe gave up trying to fix the dark circles and tried to pretend that the bathtub overflowing with newspapers didn't bother her as she returned to the kitchen table to attempt to do a little more studying.

Her screenwriting course was focusing on different ways to pace a story through the varying conventional acts that writers typically used. Chloe had to pick a movie and watch it, ascertaining if it fit into a three-act, five-act, or seven-act structure, or maybe it could be two of the three or all three different types. She had been looking forward to this assignment as she could also use it to watch one of her favorite movies and record her reaction as part of her YouTube channel content.

Chloe jotted down the basics of each act structure on separate pieces of paper so she could take notes as she watched. She sipped on her ginger tea and wished for her nausea to pass and for Pierce to call. It was hard to remain focused on her school work when she was miserable.

Gathering all her notes, Chloe moved into her bedroom and set up her ring light, trying to only think about her next step rather than the mess she had made with her life. She straightened the bed and arranged the pillows into a nest that she could sit in the center of and record herself, as well as take notes on a little folding table she set up to the side of her wide shot. Next, she applied her lip gloss, ran a brush through her hair, and made certain that the off-the-shoulder light sweater she wore only revealed as much as she wanted it to. Chloe decided to put on a pair of sparkling dangling earrings in the hope that it would make her appear brighter on camera as well as lift her mood.

Once everything was in place, Chloe climbed into the middle of her nest of pillows and settled a few more around her until she was completely comfortable. And there she sat, blindly staring into space, her heart aching.

She missed her dad. She missed his love and support and ready smile. Being just the two of them for so long had made them incredibly close, and watching him slip into oblivion, his memories disappearing, was soul-destroying. *How did people cope with it?* she wondered. Memories of them fishing, playing at the park, flying kites at the beach, him teaching her to ride her bike, and telling her she was beautiful when she was worried that she would never have a boyfriend as a teenager swirled in her mind. He was a wonderful role model as a man and father, and she knew she was blessed to have him. Now she was pregnant and her baby was never going to have the honor of knowing its grandfather; it made her melancholy. Tears formed again and she blinked rapidly.

Chloe counted to ten slowly, taking a deep breath in between each count, in an attempt to calm herself. "Gah, why am I so quick to cry?" she asked her room.

*Because you are pregnant,* her mind whispered back at her. *Your hormones are working overtime as you grow a baby.* Thinking of the baby made her instantly think of Pierce and the tears threatened to overwhelm her again. She was a mess.

She needed to stay busy. Chloe was an expert at avoiding her emotions and her reality, and she employed every tactic she could to distract herself at this moment. She knew she had to face Pierce but the right words escaped her, and exposing her lie was clearly harder than she thought it was going to be.

*Watch the movie and think about it later. Get your assignment done. Keep your mind occupied and you won't keep crying over your dumpster fire of a life.*

Chloe flicked the switch that turned her ring light on and plastered a closed smile across her face. She pressed record on her camera and launched into her well-versed YouTube greeting.

The next few hours she watched *How to Train Your Dragon* and analyzed its plot points and what type of act it fit into. She became absorbed in the process of her work and enjoyed explaining to the camera what the writer's goal was and how they had cleverly built up to the sad and profound moments in the movie. It was early afternoon by the time she had completed the recording and notes for her assignment. She still hadn't figured out how she was going to make everything right with Pierce, so she put it aside and continued to try not to dwell on the fact he had not contacted her.

Chloe made herself a ham and cheese sandwich and sat at the kitchen table editing her video; pretending that everything was fine within her world. She looked easy-going and happy on the screen as she analyzed the movie—it seemed that deception and showing only the good bits was what she excelled at.

Feeling sickened by that thought, she closed the lid of the laptop and wondered how she was going to fill her afternoon. "Why don't you just try cleaning a small section?" she said to herself as if it were the easiest thing in the world.

Slowly, Chloe walked through the house, taking note of the piles of junk mixed in with her father's belongings and her mother's heirlooms and it all seemed hopeless. It was easy to say just start small, but she didn't even know where to begin. She found herself standing in the kitchen once again. All she had managed to do was a lap of the house and find an empty box to pack things in, but nothing had made it into the box.

Deciding that she couldn't clean or tidy anything in the white sweater she had on, Chloe took off her sparkly earrings, tied up her purple-streaked hair, and pulled on a pair of old jeans and a faded gray t-shirt. As she tied up her worn sneakers, she decided that maybe she should start outwards and work in. The front garden was not insurmountable, so perhaps she could start with the gnomes and fairies? Grabbing her favorite green striped sun hat off the teddy bear that usually wore it, she threaded her ponytail through the back hole and pulled it low, to make certain it covered her nose and cheeks from the Perth sun. She had enough freckles.

Picking up the box, she braced herself to go outside and start something. "Just start," she said softly. "Face one thing." Chloe nodded to herself as she opened the front door, only to discover Pierce standing there, holding his own box.

## Chapter 4

PIERCE AND CHLOE STOOD there, holding their respective boxes and stared at each other for several moments. Her mind raced with all the things she wanted to say, but they were caught behind a wall of fear and guilt that was of her own creation. "I didn't know if you were going to come back," she finally said.

Pierce grimaced, his confusion clear. "I am not sure what is going on with you." He frowned unhappily. "I am hurt that you are keeping secrets. But I love you and want you to know that I am not going anywhere until I know the truth. So, take your time and tell me when you are ready." He said it in a rush as if he had practiced it and wanted to get it out.

"I am sorry I hurt you." She bit her lip and willed herself not to cry—damn pregnancy hormones.

Pierce held up the box he carried, almost like a peace offering. "I thought you might want some help with the garden. Maybe we can pack up your favorite gnomes and fairies, and once the baby comes I can build a magical yard for them to play in as they grow?"

A sob escaped her as Chloe dissolved into tears. Pierce was a beautiful man and the thought of losing him was too much. He tossed the box aside and gathered her in his arms and made shushing sounds as she cried against his shoulder. How had she found someone so kind and forgiving when he didn't even know what she was hiding? Her uneasy feeling grew and her anxiety kicked into overdrive as the reality of her situation sunk in. The truth was the only thing that was going to heal the issue. He would be wonderful, but she didn't want him staying because they were having a child together; she wanted him with her because he wanted to be with her. And that meant showing him all of her.

Chloe's tears eventually ran out and she lifted her head to look up at him; his expression was one of concern. He ran his hand through his shaggy blond hair before bringing it down to gently wipe her tears. "Please tell me what is going on." He kissed her sweetly.

"I need to show you something." She reached behind her and opened the door before she could reconsider and shrink from the truth again.

Her face burned as she led him through the hall and into the main lounge room. She watched as Pierce's eyes darted around, attempting to take in the mountains of chaos.

"What? How?" He looked overwhelmed.

Chloe understood the feeling. "It started when Mum died and it just got worse. Dad wouldn't throw out anything that reminded him of their time together. I'm sure it's one of the reasons Dad never remarried, as who would want to live in this? I remember in my early teens him dating several women, but they would disappear after a few weeks." Chloe was rambling; she knew it and couldn't help it. She led him into the slightly cleaner kitchen. "Would you like a drink of something?"

Chloe took out a ginger ale from the fridge, hoping it would help settle her stomach. Wishing the nausea she was experiencing was morning sickness returned and not the fear she knew she was radiating.

"Just a water will be fine," he answered as he took a seat at the cleared space at the kitchen table. His gray eyes were still wide with shock as they roamed the area.

Chloe handed him a glass of cold water and took a seat next to him and slowly sipped her drink. She continued her effort to explain the hoarding. "When I was much younger, I tried to reason with him, but he would always put me off. Always promising that he would do something about it in the new year. But what had started as just not being able to throw out Mum's things became him not being able to throw out any of my things either." She spoke in a monotone, trying not to let her emotions color the story. "When I started high school,

I even tried to tidy things by myself, as I wanted to have friends over, but he became so agitated that I never tried again for fear of upsetting him." Chloe remembered those days and how isolating her high school years had become as she had withdrawn from her friendship group and became labeled as strange. The only people she socialized with now were online, where she could be whoever she wanted and represent herself in a way that pleased her. But it was fake. Pierce was the only person she had allowed into her life, and that had been woven with misdirection and half-truths to avoid this very moment.

Tears burned the back of her throat as her emotions warred between humiliation at her living conditions and being mortified that she now found herself in the same situation as her father. Her hashtag life was so much easier and prettier.

"Your dad has been gone for a month, have you not attempted to begin the clean-up?" Pierce sounded bewildered.

The threatened tears escaped. "I tried, but I feel guilty for getting rid of Dad's stuff. It all represents a happier time when he was whole." Her voice broke. "Sorry, I seem to be crying all of the time. It appears I have no control over my tears as much as I have no control over my wanting to keep everything."

Pierce held her as she cried. "I told Mum what had happened; she is part of the reason I am here. She told me that pregnant women can be very emotional and that what you think is a huge secret might not have been as bad as what I thought it could be." He wiped her tears for the second time. "Let me help you." His eyes searched hers. "I see no reason why you won't be able to slowly declutter; I don't believe this is who you are."

"Really?" How had he come to that conclusion?

"Your bedroom is clean. All of your posts show an immaculate room. Which shows you can keep something clean and free of stuff if it is important and you won't have anyone fighting you on what goes and stays."

She had never considered that. She did find keeping her recording space tidy quite easy.

Pierce looked around and let out a slow breath. "I think it is a matter of starting in one spot rather than tackling everything at once. Will you let me help you start on the hallway tomorrow?"

"You don't hate me for lying?" She was amazed at his ability to forgive.

"Of course, I don't hate you. I will admit this was definitely not what I was expecting your lie to be about. Is it odd that I am relieved?" He looked around at the mess. "I want to be a family with you, but we can't bring a baby into this." His gorgeous gray eyes looked intently into her own blue ones. "You are the mother of my child and I want to be with you forever."

He was saying all the things she needed to hear. Maybe with all of his love and support she could get through this and they could share this house as a family.

# Chapter 5

THE DAY SEEMED BRIGHTER and Chloe pulled out one of her father's favorite albums and put it on as she waited for the kettle to boil and Pierce to arrive. Sounds of Bruce Springsteen filled the overstuffed house and for once Chloe didn't see the mess and chaos; she just felt the love of her surroundings. The kettle whistled to let her know it was done and she quickly made her herbal tea, singing loudly as she did. A loud knock on the front door interrupted her crooning.

For the first time in her entire existence, she did not hesitate to open the door. It was a moment she wished she could stop and cherish but knew that it would probably make her cry. It seemed that even when she was thrilled with something, that too could trigger her tears. *This is going to be a fun nine months if I can't control myself*, she mused.

The sight of Pierce standing there, baseball cap on backward, jogging shorts showing off his gorgeous legs, and an old black t-shirt with the Crash Bandicoot character on it made her heart beat faster—in a good way. Chloe was giddy with relief to have her secret out. She reached up, wound her arms around her boyfriend's neck, and kissed him deeply, hoping to show him just how much she loved him.

He pulled back and grinned at her. "Do that again and I will insist on seeing your bedroom and we can clean up another time."

"Tempting." She laughed before letting him go and stepping aside to allow him through.

"Great music," he noted as he waited for her to close the door.

"Dad's favorite. I remember him playing it when he mowed the lawns and we pretended to tidy the house on a Saturday morning."

"Have you decided on a room?" he asked as they walked into the kitchen.

"No." She picked up her tea. "Do you want anything?"

"Coffee would be great, thanks." Pierce sat back in his chair and crossed his arms over his chest. "I need to discuss something serious with you before we start to tackle the house."

Chloe's heart stopped for a fraction of a second, and she stilled. *Do not jump to conclusions,* she told herself. "Okay." She put the mug of coffee in front of him and sat down. "What do you want to talk about?"

"Have you ever thought about us living together?"

Chloe almost laughed at the question. If men only understood how often women daydreamed about living together with the guy they are dating. "Of course, I have, but there was Dad to consider and I just didn't know how to explain all of this to you." She swept her hand around, indicating the piles of papers, tea towels, boxed goods, and so on.

"Oh good. I have been thinking about it for a while too, but didn't want to push you, as dealing with your father was taking its toll."

"About that..." Chloe realized that she still hadn't come clean with the whole deception. "Dad wasn't as bad as I said at the beginning. He probably would have loved to have met you, but that meant bringing you into the house, and at first, I was embarrassed and I lied to keep you from wanting to come in. Telling you that Dad would have been stressed and upset to have you here was my way of keeping you from pushing the issue. And as time went on and we fell in love I didn't know how to fix it without being ashamed of how we lived."

"I wish you had trusted me in the first place, but strangely I can see your reasoning behind the whole thing." He squeezed her hand. "You have nothing to be ashamed of. We can fix this together."

"I hope so." She wanted to believe him.

"When you thought about us living together, where did we live?" he asked.

Chloe was surprised at the question. "Well, here. But now you bring it up, that seems odd."

"No, no, I am okay with that." He looked around ruefully. "Well, not in its current state, but here would be great."

"You wouldn't mind living here? But you already have a great place. Or we could buy one together?"

"My place would become too small. It's only two bedrooms and we need at least four the best I can figure it. Our bedroom, an office for me, an office for you, and a nursery. We can either sell mine and buy something bigger or we can live here and rent out mine as an investment. It makes sense to do that, but only if you want to."

"I want to." She beamed at him. Truly happy for the first time since she had discovered she was pregnant and that she would need to come clean and reveal her secrets.

"Great. So let's get started in making this house our own."

The smile slid from her face as the daunting task once again felt like it was closing in on her. "I don't know where to begin," Chloe admitted.

"That's easy," Pierce declared.

Chloe lifted her eyebrows. "It is?"

"We start with the most important room of the house."

"Which is?" she asked.

He looked at her as if he was surprised, she hadn't thought of it. "Our bedroom."

"I like the sound of that."

"You do?"

"Yes, especially the 'our' part."

Pierce chuckled. "I figure we do the rooms we will need first. Once our bedroom is done then onto my office and then I can move in, if that is okay by you?"

Relief flooded Chloe and her nausea eased; she stood and pulled him into a hug. "That sounds perfect to me, but I am not sure if you noticed that the bathrooms are full too?"

"Really?" He looked shocked.

"Pierce, aside from where you are standing, and my bed and filming area, there is stuff everywhere. The shower in the ensuite has so much stuff in it that I am almost frightened to open the door and you can't use the bath in the main bathroom." Chloe took his hand and led him to her parent's room. She hadn't opened the door since her father had been moved into the nursing home. The room smelled damp and musty and she wrinkled her nose, but couldn't do anything to fix it as the window was inaccessible with boxes stacked in front of it. The only surface not overflowing with items was the actual bed.

"I think we are going to need a plan."

Chloe nodded, completely overwhelmed and had no idea where to start.

"Maybe we should get a few boxes and put them on the bed?" suggested Pierce. "We label them *keep*, *donate*, and *throw out*."

"Yes. That seems reasonable and something I can do."

"Great. I'll get the boxes from the porch. Do you have a marker and tape?"

Chloe laughed. "Um, I have everything. It is always just a matter of figuring out where it has been put."

Pierce laughed with her. "Give me a yell if you get lost in this and I will try and find you."

The joke stung, but she also appreciated that he was trying to find the funny side of the situation. She hoped one day to be able to find the humor in it too.

It didn't take long for Pierce to get the boxes and bring them back into the bedroom, and after a few minutes of going through the kitchen drawers, Chloe found a tub full of markers shoved in the back of the bottom drawer, and wide tape for the cartons in the cupboard in the hallway. Though it had taken some effort to move the boxes in front of the cupboard door, and now they sat in the middle of the hallway. Which to Chloe was always the most depressing part of trying to clean up because she felt like she was chasing her tail and simply moving things to make space for other things.

Chloe carried the tape and marker to Pierce who took them off her and kissed her cheek. "You ready?" he asked.

"I think so." She tried to ignore the tightening of her chest and that all of a sudden she felt hot. She knew the feeling well; it was the beginning of a panic attack and she refused to allow it to stop what they had started.

"This isn't working. I am just making you frustrated." Pierce took off his cap and ran his hand through his hair. "I might leave you in here to sort this out and I will start on the front yard."

Chloe reigned in her temper and nodded. "Good idea."

"Yell if you need me."

Pierce left and Chloe sat down on the corner of the bed, careful not to dislodge anything and have it topple down on her. She looked at the dirty doll in her hand and considered Pierce's word again, trying to not let emotion color her opinion. *'You really going to give that to our child to play with?'* The question had been direct and had instantly made her defensive. Was she going to give this threadbare, dirty toy with its missing eye to their child just because it belonged to her and her father had kept it? *How many teddy bears do you have in a tub in your room that you could give them instead?* her inner voice asked.

Chloe looked at the three boxes on the bed and felt guilty.

The keep box was already brimming with items, while the donate and throw-out box had a handful of things in each. It had seemed that every time Pierce held up an item for her to decide what to do with it, her first response was to say keep. And with every time she uttered 'keep,' a look of resignation crossed his handsome face, but he remained silent until he moved to put the doll in the throw-out pile without consulting her and she had grabbed it like he was tossing her mother's engagement ring away.

Chloe had flushed at the look of horror that had crossed his face when she had explained it was her childhood toy and her father had kept it. That was when he had suggested he go work in the front yard for a while.

The doll was beyond repair, and when she thought about it she couldn't even remember playing with it. Yet, it was almost like there was an invisible force making her keep things just in case. In case of what, she did not understand, but that didn't seem to matter.

After sitting there for what felt like forever, but was closer to fifteen minutes, Chloe gave up trying to do anything, put the doll down, and went in search of Pierce. She was finding the experience overwhelming and just wanted to escape the room.

The sun was wonderful and she stopped on the porch and stretched her hands over her head, enjoying the warmth on her face. Chloe stood still and focused on bringing herself back under control. Her breathing was steady, her chest not quite as tight, and her palms not as sweaty as her anxiety settled.

She stepped off the front step and looked around to find Pierce in the corner, amongst the weeds with two boxes beside him. As she approached, she noted that there were several boxes already packed with garden ornaments and they sat in two distinct areas. Chloe frowned. "Hey," she said as she came up behind him.

Pierce looked up. "Hey."

"You seem to be packing quicker than me," she observed, trying to make it sound like a good thing when she was becoming nervous about what he had done now she had seen the boxes. "What is with the two piles?"

Pierce stood and looked over to where she pointed. "Just like inside, but there is no donate pile. Just keep and throw out."

"What do you mean to throw out?" Her voice rose an octave.

He raised a blond eyebrow. "I kept everything that needs a little love and paint. Anything that is broken I put in the throw out boxes."

"You just made that decision?" Her voice was louder to match the higher tone.

"I was going to check with you, I wouldn't have thrown anything without your permission. It just made sense to separate them like that."

"To you, maybe." She could hear herself; she knew she was being unreasonable, that he was only trying to help. And yet it was like she had no control over her impulses.

"Maybe that's enough for one day." Pierce tried to grab her hand.

"No, we can't give up." Chloe jerked her hand away. She was alarmed; if she gave up already, she may never start again.

"No one is giving up. I can feel my temper rising and I am trying to understand and help. I don't want to say the wrong thing and upset you and the baby, and that is what I seem to be doing."

Chloe had no answer to that. Until today, she hadn't realized just how much like her father she had become.

"I did some reading last night on hoarding and how it can be generational. I was trying to help; the boxes were a suggestion of a website. Maybe you need to do your own research and find something that you think might work for you?" His voice was kind. "Trauma can trigger it and I know losing your mum is what started it for your father, but maybe something wonderful like the baby can give you the want to reset everything?" Pierce shrugged. "I don't know, I'm rambling now. I'm going to go. I need to do some work this afternoon anyway." He kissed her and tucked a few strands of her purple hair behind her ear. "I'll talk to you tomorrow?"

"Yes, okay." Her voice was small. "I am sorry," Chloe apologized.

"Don't be. You have done nothing wrong." He kissed her again, and moved to her ear. "Just remember, the sooner you get the bedroom and where my office will be clean, the sooner I can move in."

He breathed softly on her ear, sending a shiver down her spine. "That is a damn fine incentive." Chloe smiled, relaxing slightly.

"Love you." He returned her smile.

"Love you more." She gave their standard answer.

"Impossible." Pierce kissed her again. "Don't bother moving the boxes; it's not going to rain for a few days and I will do it when I come back."

Chloe watched him climb into his car and pull away from the curb. She sighed dramatically as she turned back to the house. *What now?* she asked herself.

## Chapter 6

THERE WAS NOTHING TO do but turn and face her existence. With a melodramatic sigh, Chloe looked at the boxes filled with garden gnomes and fairies that filled her front yard, the pile of weeds Pierce had pulled while rescuing the ornaments, and wondered why she couldn't just trust him to throw out the broken ones. With a sense of defeat, she dragged her feet as she walked into the house, shutting her front door, and closing out the world.

Tears pricked her eyes, but she refused to feel sorry for herself. Chloe needed comfort and security and she had now, for the second time, driven away the man who offered her that without demanding more than he was willing to give himself. Again, once the silence descended, she missed her father, but now it was tinged with a hint of anger that he had left her to deal with his mess.

She stood looking at the piles of newspapers, the stacks of clothing, the boxes of never-used fishing gear, records that had not been played the last two decades, and books that had been purchased but never read and didn't fit on the overstuffed bookshelves. She looked at all the items that filled her hallway and she had a moment of clarity.

"If having all of these things is supposed to make me feel happy, why do I feel nothing but paralyzing, life halting dread?" she spoke to herself. "Because this is not who you are, this is who your father is, and you don't want to disappoint him so you carry on what he started." As Chloe continued to talk to herself, she walked into her room and looked at the clear space that was her work area. "Pierce is right; you never need to clean that space. It is valuable to you, so you instinctively keep it clean because you need a clear head to work."

Chloe flopped down on her back and stared up at the ceiling, taking in what her moment of lucidity truly meant. *If you want this bad enough, you can do it and maintain it. You just need to start,* she told herself. *But I don't know how.* Doubt crept in.

After lying there for a few moments longer, Chloe rolled over and pulled her laptop towards her. She would take Pierce's advice and look up ways to help her start. What she found when she Googled *hoarders* was extreme and terrifying. To think if she did not get this under control then she could end up in a similar situation to what was being shown was confronting. Instinctively, she put her hand over her tummy. *If not for you, do it for your baby. It is unsafe to have all of this around and you don't want them growing up with the same issues.*

Chloe grabbed the notebook that she always kept on her bedside table to jot down helpful tips she thought she might be able to use as she wrestled control back over her situation. She needed a plan, accountability, a realistic time frame to have it completed, and to remember why this was important. As she took notes, she grabbed her phone to snap a few shots to put up on her Insta account and to label the post 'planning,' when it occurred to her that by calling it that, while true, it was only half-truth. Making a snap decision, Chloe rewrote the title and posted the pic before she had time to second guess herself.

Putting her phone down, she quickly set up her camera, turned on her ring light, and sent out an alert on YouTube that she would be doing a pop-up stream starting in ten minutes. It was time to be her. Not the put-together, well thought out, perfectly assembled Chloe, but the hot mess, clothes don't match, no make-up woman who was trying to live her best life, and that meant being honest... with everyone.

While Chloe waited for the final few minutes till her unplanned live stream began, she pulled up websites of rubbish collection and donation collection companies around her area. Quickly, she jotted a few down and took notes of what they would and wouldn't collect. It was astonishing how much happier she felt just by doing those few small things.

The fancy timer she had created began to count down twenty seconds before she went live and she settled herself more comfortably on the bed, took several deep reassuring breaths, and watched as her followers began to join the stream.

"Hi, I'm Chloe and I have a secret." Chloe stared into the camera lens not blinking. She held her head high as she faced her fears. There would be no more hiding. She needed to free herself, unburden herself from the shame she had carried for so long it had become like a close reliable friend to fall back on and hide behind when things got difficult. She knew her cheeks were flushed as the heat rose as her anxiety set in, but she kept going. This was her time, her realization that she would never move forward without owning everything, and that meant being who she was without the filters.

"I have kept this secret since I was a child and after revealing it to my boyfriend two days ago and discovering that he didn't love me any less, I think it would be helpful to reveal it to everyone else. Maybe some of you are like me."

She watched as more of her followers joined the unscheduled YouTube stream, and fought to keep her nerves steady. "We all hear about social media only representing a small portion of a person and not the true reality or personality of who they are, and this is true for me. You watch me talk about books and movies in my pretty room; on Instagram you see my posts of places I go, and everything is artfully arranged. While none of that life is a lie, it is not my complete truth." Chloe moved to the camera and picked it up, slowly rotating it. "This is my truth." Her room, filled with absurd levels of belongings was revealed to her subscribers and in reality, to anyone with an internet connection as this could be kept and viewed forever. Her voice quivered as she continued. "I need your support, love, and acceptance.

Anyone with negativity, not willing to face their own truth, or who is only here for my film content, I get it. This isn't for you, and I bid you farewell if you choose to unsubscribe."

Chloe took one final moment to steady herself before she opened her bedroom door and stepped out into the house she never had a friend visit. "This is my reality and I hate it." She walked down the hallway and into the lounge room where there was nowhere to sit as every seat was covered in piles of newspapers, knick-knacks, coupons, plastic bags full of wool, and clothing that didn't belong to anyone. Chloe turned the camera back onto herself, her heart racing at what she had done. "My review content will be the same, none of it will change, but I will be adding new content as I face this life struggle and get it under control. I want you to join me, as I am sure many of you have your struggles, and I think rather than hiding them we should face them together." She smiled at the camera, her crooked teeth forgotten. "Tomorrow I will begin the clean-up and I will document it. Expect an update and short stream so you can see my progress."

Before Chloe began to ramble, she decided that it was time to sign off. Rather than her customary cute tag she chose to say something that meant more and seemed right. "Always remember, together we are stronger."

## Chapter 7

CHLOE STOOD THERE, HER camera turned off and hanging limply from her hand. She had done it and survived. The ramifications of what she had exposed began to settle in her mind and she bit her lip with trepidation. *It's too late for self-doubt. It's out there now,* she told herself.

Her nausea rose and her chest tightened; she felt a hot flush creep up her face as her anxiety built. Music began playing from her bedroom, which was the perfect circuit breaker for her spiraling thoughts. Green Day filled the house and Chloe smiled with relief; Pierce was calling her. She knew she wouldn't make it in time to answer so didn't rush, not wanting to trip on anything and risk the baby or causing an avalanche of epic proportions. She would call him back when she got there. She found her phone on her bed and picked it up as the music stopped. She had just missed it. Chloe didn't wait to see if he left a message, she called him back immediately.

"Hi," she said shyly, as he answered the phone.

"I am so proud of you," he spoke quickly. "It took so much courage to do that."

Tears came, but this time they were tears of relief.

"Would you like to meet at the park? I think you need to get out of the house and we need to talk," he asked.

Her heart thudded to a halt for a few moments. What did he mean they needed to talk? "Sure, getting out of here would be welcome. Meet you there in half an hour?" She tried to sound casual.

"Perfect. I will meet you in the car park."

Pierce hung up and Chloe fought the desire to over-analyze the situation. *You are pregnant, over-emotional, just revealed yourself to everyone, and feeling a little exposed. Take a breath, you are fine and he is not leaving you,* she reassured herself.

Rather than dwell on it further, Chloe chose a lightweight jacket to wear, picked up her keys, and got in the car. It took her about ten minutes to get to the park and find a spot. She was fifteen minutes early, but she didn't mind; it was better than being at home surrounded by memories that she was coming to fully understand weren't actually hers. Now she had to free herself of the guilt she felt.

Rather than wait in the car, Chloe got out and walked to the playground where she could sit and watch the children play. She must have lost track of time because the next thing she knew, Pierce was calling her name and waving at her from a distance. Chloe stood and waved back, making her way toward him.

He hugged her hello and gave her a quick kiss. "I was wondering if you want an ice-cream cone while we walk?"

"Oh, yes please." He took her hand as they made their way over to the ice-cream truck.

"What would you like?" he asked as they stood to the side looking at the vast menu displayed on the side of the van.

"Single waffle cone with vanilla soft serve, dipped in chocolate and sprinkles," she said without hesitation. It had been the same order since she was a little girl getting ice cream at the park with her father.

Pierce raised his eyebrows. "I am feeling very indecisive now."

Chloe laughed. "Well, that is unusual. It's nice to know you haven't got everything under control, even if it is just a food order."

Pierce frowned at her before stepping up to place his and her orders. This gave Chloe a moment to try to figure out why he had frowned at her jest. When it dawned on her that she sounded ungrateful and that she had been implying that by him offering to help her and giving her ideas on how to deal with her situation had been controlling. Bugger, that is not what she meant at all. Everything had become so complicated; both were walking on eggshells and trying not to upset the other all because she had been lying to him. It was completely her fault and she needed to fix it; she just didn't know how.

"Thank you." Chloe smiled at Pierce as he handed over her ice cream cone.

"You are welcome. You want to go for a walk?" he asked.

There were many tracks around the small lake and they chose one by simply walking down it. "Pierce, again I am so sorry for deceiving you. It was never my intention to hurt you. I was embarrassed at first and then it got more difficult, and the secret became harder to reveal. You could have easily walked away, but you stayed, and I want you to know that I love you and hope you are staying because you love me and not for the baby." She stopped in the middle of the walking track as her words sunk in. Her blue eyes grew wide as she considered that he wasn't doing all of this because he forgave her and loved her, but because he was a good man who was trying to do the right thing for the mother of his unborn child. Until that moment, that thought had not occurred to her.

The ice cream dripped down her hand as she continued to stand there, scared of what his next words would be. Chloe only became aware that she was blocking the path when a bicycle bell rang to let her know someone wanted to get by. Quickly, she moved to the side and they slowly began to walk again. They ate their treats in silence as they walked along the path. Pierce seemed to be lost in thought, while Chloe anxiously waited for reassurance that he was not with her for the baby's sake. In the end, Chloe couldn't wait any longer so she asked the question, "Pierce, why did you forgive me so easily?"

"It wasn't easy," he admitted. He took her hand and pulled her over to an empty park bench where they sat down; she was happy when he didn't let go of her hand. He reached out and tucked the few errant strands that always seemed to be in her face behind her ear, as he always did, and ran his thumb along her cheek before sitting back in the seat. "I can forgive you because, in reality, we all have secrets. Things we are ashamed of, things we don't think people will understand, things that society has told us are not normal." She watched him look up at the pale blue sky and wondered whether he had a secret like that and hoped that one day he would feel safe sharing with her. He continued to watch a flock of birds circle high above as he spoke quietly. "And there are also secrets we carry that are really someone else's secret, and I think sometimes those are the most difficult because do you ever get to decide if there is a right time to share that secret?"

## Chapter 8

IT TOOK LONGER THAN Chloe thought it was going to. The frustration, relapses, and copious amounts of tears were expected. What was completely unexpected was the level of acceptance, warmth, and people reaching out to her via her social media to offer their support and reveal their secrets. Some did it privately, while others had chosen to reveal it in her comments because they felt it was more honest. A few fellow Youtubers had asked if they could jump on board the idea and do their reveal, of course, crediting her with the idea in the first place. She thought this was wonderful and was proud that people thought her honesty and message were powerful.

Chloe sat on the porch in the fading Perth sunlight and twirled her hair around two fingers, willing herself not to go any further. She had marched out from the kitchen and managed to stop herself when she got to the front door. "You don't need it," she told herself.

*But you might.*

"NO," she said it loudly.

Chloe had been having this same conversation with herself for the past day. Pierce had taken out a stack of books that were not in her favorite genres to read, but it didn't matter. They were books; they belonged on her bookshelf.

"But you won't read them," she told herself.

*But you might one day.*

That seemed to be her brain's favorite sentence.

She had now been sitting on her porch, battling with herself to not go and grab those books for ten minutes.

Her phone buzzed in her hand and she looked down to see that she had received a message from someone with a vaguely familiar name. Clicking on the message, she was surprised to find that it was a girl she had been friendly with at high school, but had always kept at arms-length.

Jennifer had been hilarious in class and a bit of a trouble maker, and Chloe had always envied her easy-going nature. They had sat together in history class for two years until Jennifer had left to become a hairdresser.

**J: Hi, I am not sure if you remember me, but we sat together in history class. I wanted to reach out and tell you that I have been following your posts on Insta for a while, but only started watching your YouTube channel recently.**

Chloe wondered what Jennifer thought of her big revelation. She could see the three dots that showed Jennifer was typing. But instead of waiting, Chloe answered. She was ready to start making friends and maybe Jennifer would be her first. Rather than typically overthinking it, she quickly typed back.

**C: OMG. Of course, I remember you. How are you?**

**J: I am doing well. I just wanted you to know that I wouldn't have cared about your house. My house was always a mess. With so many siblings there was always a stack of stuff lying around.**

**C: I am slowly coming to understand that people who liked me would have accepted me with the mess I lived in, but as a teenager it was just too hard to take that risk. Sad thing is, I just don't know how to connect with people any more that isn't behind a screen.**

Chloe stared at the last sentence and almost deleted it, but stayed brave and hit reply instead.

**J: I am living in Adelaide and running my own salon, but the next time I come home to visit my family I want to catch up with you, if that is okay?**

**C: I would love that.**

**J: I also wanted to let you know that you inspired me to stop hiding from a difficult situation. I have finally told my parents that I am bi-sexual and am seeing a woman. They actually took it better than I thought they would.**

**C: That is wonderful that you have found someone. I hope they are happy for you.**

**J: I think they are. I have to run, but I am glad we got this chance to chat rather than me just leave you a message.**

**C: Me too.**

Chloe took a moment and then wrote something she wouldn't have four weeks ago because she would have been scared of rejection. Jennifer had reached out and Chloe wanted to respond in kind.

**C: Anytime you want to chat I am here. I would love to know more about what you are up to and how you ended up in Adelaide.**

**J: That sounds great. I want to know more about this wonderful man in your life. And please reach out if you need support with your decluttering... I would love to help you, like you helped me. Xox**

**C: Now you have said it, I definitely will. Take Care. Xox**

EVENTUALLY, THROUGH SHEER DETERMINATION on both their behalf's, Pierce and Chloe had found a system that worked for her and they had managed to clear out the entire hallway, front yard, and main bedroom. Pierce had cleaned out a small section of the overflowing garage and Chloe had remained inside, attempting not to think about it and trusting him to make good decisions about what to keep of her father's tools. She had stayed busy by slowly boxing up her mother's clothing. Each piece she held for a moment as if saying goodbye before folding it carefully and putting it in the boxes marked *donate*. The only item of clothing she had kept was her mother's vintage wedding gown. Chloe had a few ideas about what she might like to do with it.

After all the clothes had been boxed up, Chloe then left them at the front door, where Pierce would carry them out to the garage. Once in the garage, they had agreed that nothing would be done for a week, giving Chloe the chance to bring anything back into the house that she couldn't stop thinking about. After the seven days were up, Pierce would load the car up and drop the boxes at a donation point.

Once her mother's clothes had been put in the garage and a few days had passed, Chloe had started on her father's clothes. This had been a little more difficult as these were her memories she was now dealing with, but the clothes that truly reminded her of her father were with him at the nursing home where he resided. After a false start and tears in the morning, she had refocused and grown determined to not falter and began to box up his clothes. In the end, she had kept a tie she had given him a few years prior and his good watch and a pair of cuff links that had been passed down from his father. Some of his clothes had still carried his scent and those made her remember him and the happier times they shared, but she was now understanding that even though his clothes were going, just like his memories, hers would remain and she would be able to pass them onto her child like he had to her about her mother.

She would tell her child about his kind but gruff voice, his love of fishing, and his ability to fix anything that broke. How he had chased the monsters away at night and how Chloe would employ the same strategy for her children. She smiled as she thought about all the wonderful times they had had together and was grateful for them.

Every day after that, Chloe had chosen one thing to tackle, rather than a whole room. She chose a tub, drawer, stack, or pile and didn't stop until it was completely sorted. This took weeks, but it kept the overwhelming desire to keep everything to a minimum, and also knowing they were going to the garage rather than getting thrown out made her feel more comfortable with her choices. On the days it got too much and she knew Pierce was about at breaking point, she would contact Jennifer, and her new found friend would help calm her and remind her what her end goal was.

Chloe documented everything for her Youtube channel. And while there were always those few negative people who didn't understand the struggles she faced, the majority were incredible in their desire to help her through this with a shared experience. She even created a spreadsheet where others could put their goals and continuing achievements, so she could celebrate with them when they were attained.

Chloe pushed the packed box with her foot down the empty, wide corridor toward the front door. It was an exhilarating feeling to be free of the piles of paraphernalia. A few boxes stood near the front door ready to be taken out. For the first time last night, Chloe had swept and washed the entire hallway floor. The hardwood showed clearly where everything had been stacked but she didn't care as she celebrated the victory of the completely cleared hallway. As she neared the door, she heard a car door close and grinned to herself. When she got to the door, she flung it open to find Pierce stepping up onto the porch.

"Hello, beautiful," he greeted her cheerfully. "How are my girls today?"

Chloe rolled her eyes but no longer corrected him. Pierce had decided they were having a girl and had taken to calling her and their unborn child 'his girls.' Tomorrow was the scheduled ultrasound and they had decided to find out the gender. Chloe just wanted the baby to be healthy, gender was irrelevant to her, but agreeing on a baby name might take some time, so narrowing it down to one sex would be helpful.

"Your girls are great. We started on a new room today."

"Wonderful. My office?" He looked eager.

"Actually, no." She bit her lip. "I started the nursery. I hope you don't mind?"

"Don't you want me to move in? Are you trying to tell me something?" he joked.

Chloe caught an undertone of concern. "Don't be silly, of course, I do. With the ultrasound tomorrow I was feeling inspired when I walked by the room, and I just thought I would start at the doorway and work my way in." She stepped aside to show him the four boxes she had brought down to the front door so far today. "It turns out the room was full of broken toys, piles of what I assume were Mum's women's magazines, more linen than anyone will ever need for a single bed that I haven't had for ten years, and stacked up packets of clothing patterns for knitting. Though the knitting patterns make me think that somewhere in the house there will be a ton of knitting needles and yarn."

Chloe reached out and tugged on his hand, drawing him into the house. She led him to the room that they had chosen to be the nursery as it was the furthest from the one allocated to be his office and closest to the master bedroom. "See," she said proudly, spreading her arm wide as if she were a game show model.

Pierce whistled with appreciation. "You have made quite a dent. I am impressed."

"It gets better." She jumped up and down with excitement at how free she felt. Chloe pointed to a huge pile of papers, magazines, and knitting patterns. "It can all go."

"Sure thing. I'll take it out to the garage now."

"No, you misunderstand, it can go. Throw it out. I do not need any of it and it is useless to anyone else." She beamed up at him. "Truly, I feel good about this. Just take it and load it into your car."

Pierce put his hands on her shoulders to stop her from hopping foot to foot. He leaned in and kissed her. "I will make a deal with you. I will load it into my car and keep it there for one full day. If you tell me tomorrow afternoon that it can go, I will get rid of it."

Chloe thought about it and even though she wanted it gone now, she understood his hesitancy. There had been a few moments over the last month where she had gone backward and forwards in her assertion that he could toss something, only to stop him at the last moment. "That sounds fair. But keep in mind, the sooner I get this room done, the sooner we can work on your office," she reminded him.

He gave her a slow wink. "Trust me, I haven't forgotten." He kissed her again. "I want to say something, but not upset you." He paused.

"Okay."

"You are doing so well, but seriously it is costing a fortune and we are running out of bin space to get rid of everything slowly. Now that you are doing better and feeling more in control, perhaps you could think about hiring a skip one weekend and we can do a huge clear out. Of course, we can store most things in the garage until that point."

At the thought of tossing everything into a skip in one go, Chloe's stomach clenched and her chest tightened, but she knew the idea had merit. "Let me think about it. I think I just have to get used to the idea."

## Chapter 9

THE GEL WAS COLD as the sonographer tech squirted it on Chloe's belly in preparation for her ultrasound. Pierce stood to the left of the bed, holding her hand and watching intently as the monitor was switched on and the prepping continued. Chloe watched him instead of the goings-on. She was nervous, though she had no reason to be. She guessed that every woman who did this felt the same way. Vague anxiety and hope that their baby was healthy. So instead of focusing on the nurse, she watched the man she loved.

His gray eyes were merry as he took in what was going on. Chloe noted that his shaggy blond hair almost reached his collar, as he often forgot to get a haircut. He had made a little more effort with his clothing and wore jeans with no holes and a navy polo shirt. She wondered whether their child would end up with her boring light brown hair or their father's blonder locks. One thing she knew was if it had crooked teeth they would be fixed if the child wanted it. Chloe mused that she must be odd to be thinking about crooked teeth at this time.

They had come so far in such a short amount of time. She had never been so in love as she was now. Pierce had proven himself to be the man she thought he was and she found it comforting; especially while her hormones were out of control and she was still adjusting to her life without her father. She wondered for a moment if that was the reason she had chosen to clean out the nursery instead of Pierce's intended office. Was her subconscious telling her that it wasn't the right time?

"Ready?" the female tech asked as she pulled a round swivel stool out from under the bed and sat down.

'Yes." Chloe smiled nervously.

For the next ten minutes, Pierce and Chloe *oohed* and *aahed* as the tech walked them through their baby's details. Chloe's relief lifted as each check was marked off as normal and she lay there mesmerized by the fast-beating heart. Pierce squeezed her hand at one point while they watched the chambers of the tiny fetus's heart pump blood, and Chloe swallowed hard around the lump in her throat.

"Do you want to know the sex?" the tech asked.

"Yes, please."

"You are having a boy."

Chloe was thrilled. A boy was perfect, though she knew if the woman had said she was having a girl, Chloe would have thought that was perfect too. She looked up at Pierce who gave her a thumbs-up signal as the tech had already started explaining what else she was looking for.

After another ten minutes or so, the procedure was complete, and after printing out a photo the tech left the room so Chloe could get dressed.

"We created this." Pierce stared in awe at the black and white photo they had been given.

"We did," Chloe agreed happily, only half listening as she focused on wiping the sticky clear gel from her lower stomach.

"So, I was wrong. We are having a boy." He beamed at her as she swung her legs over the side of the bed.

Pierce handed over her t-shirt and she pulled it on over her head. He couldn't stop smiling and it was contagious; she found herself answering his smile with one of her own. This moment was perfect and she wanted to make certain she remembered it. Chloe had been thinking about this moment for several weeks, all the anticipation and worry had dissipated and been replaced by sheer bliss. It was a moment to be commemorated as the perfectness of moments like these didn't happen often.

"Pierce? Are you happy?" she asked softly.

"Yes, you are amazing, growing a person inside you while dealing with all your baggage has been tough, but you have been an inspiration to so many." Pierce gave her her tailored grey jacket.

"I am not talking about others, I am asking about you. Are you happy?" she asked more forcefully.

"Yes, completely. I don't think I could be happier." He handed over her sneakers, which she took but placed them on the bed beside her rather than put them on.

Finally, he stopped and looked at her. "Why? Are you not happy?"

"I would be complete if you consented to marry me." The formal words burst out of Chloe before she could stop them. She had been considering asking him for several days, though there had never seemed like a right time, and suddenly there had been something pure and sweet about this moment that told her it was now or never.

"Did you just ask me to marry you?" He laughed.

Not quite the response she was after. "Yes."

"Oh, Chloe, you are my girl and there is nothing that would stop me from marrying you. But we might need something to make it official." On the cold lino floor of the doctor's office, Pierce knelt on one knee and pulled a black velvet box out of his jacket pocket, causing Chloe to gasp. "It seems we both had the same idea." Pierce opened the box and the most perfect solitaire diamond ring glinted at her. "Marry me, Chloe, and make me officially the luckiest man alive."

"Yes—" A thought dawned on Chloe and stopped her from accepting the proposal mid-sentence. "There is one more thing I need to fix."

"Okay?" Pierce waited for her to finish.

"You need to meet my dad."

## Chapter 10

THE RAIN SOFTLY TAPPED on the restaurant window and dribbled down to puddle on the wide brick sill. Chloe watched it absently as she considered the last few days and all they had achieved. After the sonogram and the marriage proposal Monday afternoon, Chloe had felt something change within her. A calm had settled. An understanding that once she was free of the chains of the past by letting go of belongings that were neither hers nor important, she was inviting in more meaningful moments and was looking forward to a life she had only ever dreamed of.

Her father was a wonderful man and an incredible dad, but he had done damage to her by allowing her to live in such conditions. By not seeing that she was making no friends and hiding with shame. He had chosen to live that life, she had not. Yet, when the skip had arrived early yesterday morning and Chloe had taken stock of all the junk she had piled in the garage to throw out, all she could see was how sad his life had become, caught in the spiraling moments of the past and never moving forward. Some things had still been difficult to throw out, but most of it was so old and worn or rotted that it was useless, which made it easier for her to part with.

Pierce walked back from paying the bill for brunch at the counter and sat down. "Ready when you are." He interrupted her thoughts.

Her eyes moved away from the pooling rain and settled onto the face of her wonderful fiancé. "Thank you," she said simply, hoping to convey all she felt behind those two words.

"Anything for you." He smiled and reached across to take her hand. "Shall we go and see your dad?"

"Yes, it is time."

Chloe waited under the awning of the cute cafe, watching the sea pound against the white sand. It had been drizzling steadily all morning, stopping most from heading out on this cool Saturday, and anyone out had their head down or were sheltered by an umbrella hurrying to their destination. Not Chloe. She was waiting for Pierce to get the car so was able to enjoy the incredible, and sometimes strange art installations that spotted the empty sand near the Cottesloe Surf Life Saving Club as they sparkled in the late morning rain. They were beautiful in their silent stance against the elements. Chloe had always enjoyed the Sculpture by the Sea exhibition they had run, but usually, the beach was filled with people. To experience it like this was unique and she took in the moment. And in that instant, she understood that that was how she needed to view the rest of her life. These individual moments were to be treasured, but you didn't need anything from them other than the feeling they brought you.

A car horn honked and she was pulled out of her reverie to see Pierce pull up. Careful of the wet path, she headed into the drizzle and climbed into the car. He had put the heater on and the warmth after the chill from the early autumn rain was welcome.

As she settled in her seat for the short drive to the Aged Care facility, Pierce cleared his throat. "I need to ask you something, but I want you to hear me out before you panic, okay?"

As always, her chest tightened and her anxiety appeared. She was never good with new things.

"I need help to move the furniture out of the house. The rest I have been able to do by myself, but I am going to need help with the beds, couches, and kitchen table."

Chloe sat there for a few minutes, her mind racing. "What is the plan?" she finally asked.

Pierce kept looking at the road, but his voice was gentle. "I figure we have two options. One, I ask my two closest mates to come over and help, or two, we hire those people that come and take away anything you want. Whatever you would be more comfortable with is fine by me."

Chloe considered his words. Would she want his friends to see her place, even though it was probably about half completed, or would she prefer strangers to be the first people who didn't love her to be in her home? She had met Pierce's friends on many occasions, and they were kind, generous, and funny, but did she want them—Chloe stopped. This was what her Youtube revelation had been about. Stopping the judgment, being honest, stepping out of your comfort zone. She took a deep breath. "Having Rory and Darren come over to help would be great." Once the words were out she felt better. "Maybe we can order pizza as a thank you?"

"I love that idea. The skip is getting picked up tomorrow morning, and the rain is supposed to clear in an hour or two. Would it be alright if I asked them to help today? Anything you are not sure about we will just move to the garage for now. But if we want to paint the house and do the floors we need the furniture gone." He turned the car into a vacant spot.

She pursed her lips for a moment. He was being so sensitive to her feelings, but she could feel the urgency in the undertone of his voice. "This afternoon will be fine. I will work on the main bathroom with my earpods in to distract me."

Pierce got out of the car and pulled out his phone, but before he used it he stared at her for a moment. "I just want to tell you you are amazing. I am so proud of you and how hard you are working to change so our son has the best chance at a happy life."

Chloe blushed. "Me? No, it is you who is amazing. Not once have you made me feel wretched for keeping secrets."

Pierce stared at her for a few moments with a strange look on his face. "I have told you before, we all have secrets, some are just not as huge as others and some aren't ours to share." He held out his hand and they walked toward the entrance.

"This is my last secret, and then I am free," Chloe said.

He kissed her hand but said nothing more. Pierce quickly typed and sent a text one-handed before turning the mobile on silent and putting it in his jeans pocket.

Pierce squeezed her hand as he used the other one to pull open the door to the nursing home. He watched silently as she entered the code to get into the next section of the building and deftly intercepted an old lady with a walker as she made for the now opened door. Her heart sang for the man she would forever be connected to. He was gentle and kind to everyone.

Chloe's anxiety grew as they went through the second door and signed in. Pierce had never met her father as she had told him that her dad was easily confused and got upset around strangers and sometimes became aggressive. This had given her the excuse for Pierce to never come over. Part of it had been true; her father would often get confused which resulted in frustration and sadness, but never aggression or anger. Chloe felt guilty for painting her father in that light. There had been too many half-truths to hide her secrets.

"Hello, Chloe, he is having a good day today," Sandra, the nurse in charge greeted them.

Chloe smiled. "Thank you. Let's hope it stays that way while I am here."

She took Pierce's proffered arm and guided him down the hall to her father's door. Softly, she pushed it open to find John sitting up in a chair and looking out onto a rain-drenched garden.

"Hey, Dad." She steeled herself for the look of confusion that was becoming more his norm. It broke her heart every time she entered the room and he didn't recognize her.

"Chloe." He smiled warmly as his blue eyes lit up, so much like her own. "And you finally brought Pierce."

Chloe stopped mid stride. "What did you say?" Chloe was confused. She mustn't have heard her father correctly.

John and Pierce exchanged glances. Pierce sat gingerly on the end of the hospital bed, leaving Chloe the chair for visitors. "When you started dating Pierce I got the feeling that he was different, but you never brought your boyfriends home so I tracked him down and went to meet him. I knew I was getting worse so needed to know you were going to be well taken care of," her father explained.

Chloe was astounded. She rushed to hug her dad while he was still lucid; he had not been like this for several weeks and she understood all too well how quickly he could disappear back into the fog of dementia. "You did that to make sure I would be okay?" She was amazed.

"I hope you don't mind, but I just knew that it was important. I never understood why you didn't bring him over and then when I got home from meeting him and I opened the front door it dawned on me that it was the house you were keeping him from, not me."

Chloe felt his frail, thin arms tighten around her. "I am sorry I did that to you," he whispered.

Tears rolled down her cheeks. "You don't need to be sorry. You are the best father a girl could ever want."

She looked over at her fiancé. "So this is your secret?" she guessed, as she wiped the tears away.

"I hope you aren't angry?" Pierce spoke quietly. "John asked me not to tell you that he went behind your back."

"It would seem you were right; sometimes our secrets are not ours to reveal," she said. "And how can I be angry when you have forgiven me all my secrets?"

"Who has secrets?" asked her father, looking at them both.

Chloe's smile widened to a glorious grin as she realized that even with all its difficulties, real life could be beautiful sometimes. She put her hand on her rounded stomach and looked back at her father, grateful for this moment. "I have a secret you are going to love, Dad."

## Epilogue

HER SMILE WAS WIDE as she stood with Pierce and their children. It had been a year since the straightening of her teeth had been completed, and Chloe had never been happier to smile. Johnathon with his shaggy blond hair, so much like his father's, stood pressed against her left leg. Chloe's hand rested on his head, her other hand rested on the top of her heavily pregnant belly. To her right stood Pierce, he carried their second child, Vin, on his hip, her head resting on his shoulder, her gray eyes closed as she slept through her brother's fifth birthday party.

It didn't matter how many parties, gatherings, Christmases they had with friends and Pierce's family at the house, Chloe was still in awe of how different her life was since freeing herself of her secrets and the junk that held them in place. She now had plastic tubs with secure lids that lived in the garage, each labeled with a family member's name and that was where any keepsakes were kept. One tub per family member and so far the system had worked well. Once a year she would sit down with the tubs and go through the lot, throwing out anything she realized held no intrinsic value or no beautiful memory. Her life was about living and being present and the most significant moments were photographed or videoed, but never to the detriment of living in the now.

"All done," announced Jennifer, who had made the trip from interstate to be at her Godson's birthday party. There were days when Chloe still thanked the universe for the beautiful friend that Jennifer had become. "I think I got some great shots, but can you check?"

Pierce went over to Jennifer and watched as she scrolled through the photos on her phone to make sure they were happy with the result. Chloe trusted them both to make that decision, so instead bent awkwardly to speak quietly in Johnathon's ear. "Go play with your friends, I will be out in a few minutes with your cake." She kissed the top of his head, cherishing the smell of him before straightening up and letting out a grunt at the effort. She had forgotten how much her lower back had ached at thirty-six weeks with Vin.

Chloe watched Johnathon run to the magical garden that Pierce had created in the back corner of their yard. At the moment, it was besieged by ten or so children, all invited from his school class. They swung from the rope that had been tied to a large tree that kept most of the garden in shade through the summer months. The garden had a toadstool table with fake stumps of wood for chairs and you had to cross a small wooden bridge to get to the inner garden where all the gnomes and fairies that had been rescued from the front yard all those years ago had been resettled. Fairy lights had been wound around the tree trunk and dragonflies hung from the branches. A large sandpit sat to one side of the garden and on occasion, it was rumored to be full of quicksand or sharks depending on what game Chloe had created for the children to play. Pirates were the current favorite of Johnathon's and Chloe had asked Pierce to rig up a "plank" that they could lower from the fence over the sandpit.

The sound of children playing in her once completely quiet house never ceased to make her feel anything but complete. And as always at these events, Chloe stopped to take a moment to remember her father and wish he was here with her. He had only been alive long enough to meet his first grandchild, and she would cherish those memories forever. She had come so far in five years and yet one thing had remained the same. Her love of Pierce and how supportive he was of her and any decision she made. Her hoarding instinct had never truly disappeared, but now she knew her triggers and was far better equipped to cope and not react by keeping everything. Chloe had also taken the step of speaking to someone professionally and it had helped immensely, and she was now, with Pierce's blessing, writing a screenplay about their courtship, her secrets, and how setting them free had changed her life completely.

"Would you like a hand with the cake?" Pierce asked, drawing her out of her thoughts.

Chloe smiled at her husband. "That would be great."

She waited while he handed Vin over to Jennifer, who sat on the back decking area overlooking the yard. Pierce took a moment to adjust the dragonfly wings Chloe had made for their daughter, and smoothed down the white satin skirt that had been made from the material of Chloe's mother's vintage wedding dress. Chloe still had plenty of tulle and the satin fabric so could easily make their third child a dress, if they so desired.

Pierce straightened after placing a kiss on his daughter's head. "I finally get to see what you have been secretly working on?"

Chloe laughed and took his proffered hand, and they headed to the kitchen, leaving Jennifer, and her partner, Abbey, in charge of the sleeping toddler and playing children. Chloe squeezed his hand and winked at him. It turned out that living your life rather than what you thought your life should look like thanks to social media was a better choice. "Some secrets can be good secrets you know."

# Taya's Steamy Books

<u>Steamy Contemporary</u>

Champagne Resolutions

War of Hearts


<u>Steamy Fantasy</u>

The Charming Thief

Outcast

Lethal


Check out her website for all her current works.


tayarune.com

# About Taya

Taya Rune is a writer of romance, a sucker for happy endings and has a knack for asking people uncomfortable questions.

She is a two times USA Today Bestselling Author and a member of the Romance Writer's of Australia. Taya has had her work published in many different anthologies and publications.

Taya resides in Melbourne with her husband, sons, and dogs. She loves the unpredictable weather, the varied cultures, food, and great stage shows. She can't wait for the world to open up again - there is always something new to see and experience.

# Acknowledgments

I would like to take a few moments
to say thank you.
To my husband, thank you for being
my partner in crime. I love the way you still make me laugh.
To my children, thank you for
teaching me to let go of the small stuff. I am proud of you.
To my family, thank you for the
love and support you have shown me throughout the years.
To my friends, the ones that have
my back and are forever in my corner – I cherish you.
To my editor, Rochelle J. Simas – IDK art.
Thank you for the kind words that
always accompany the return of my fabulously edited manuscripts.
To my PA – Emmie Jean Johnson.
Thanx for doing so much of the behind
the scenes heavy lifting for me. I am forever grateful for you.
To my ARC, Street and Beta Teams.
You rock!

# Follow her on your favorite platform:

Website:

https://www.tayarune.com

Facebook:

https://www.facebook.com/taya.rune.75

Facebook Group:

https://www.facebook.com/groups/tayasromanticrealm

Instagram:

https://www.instagram.com/tayarune/

Twitter:

https://twitter.com/TayaRune

Bookbub:

https://www.bookbub.com/authors/taya-rune

Goodreads:

https://www.goodreads.com/author/show/21156065.Taya_Rune

TikTok:

https://www.tiktok.com/@tayarune

Pinterest:

https://www.pinterest.com.au/TayaRune